GUILTY

A JOHN GREYSON INVESTIGATION

JAMES T. MALONE

Dedication

As always, I want to thank my family and friends for their support and encouragement; I couldn't do this without you. Love you to the moon and back.

ALSO BY JAMES T. MALONE

The Blackstone: A Murder Mystery

Murder on the Bluff – A Jack Murphy Murder Mystery

THE CRIME

It had been raining and cold for days as if the sun had burned itself out. There was a silver lining, however. Few souls ventured out to battle the elements and that was a positive for him. February was like that in Memphis, a coin toss at best. He watched fascinated as a sudden gust of wind sent the tops of nearby oak trees dancing. It was a struggle as old as time itself, nature trying to kill. A cigarette would be nice he thought, as his hand brushed against the hard pack of Marlboros in his jacket pocket, but no, not now. The timing was wrong; he'd waited too long for this night. Headlights from a car turning into the driveway brought him back to the moment. She was here; he heard her talking to someone just seconds after the car's engine died.

"No, I just got home," she said with a small laugh. "I enjoyed the evening, too. Yes, tomorrow night around eight. Okay, okay, I've got to go. I'll talk to you later, and thanks for checking on me."

Just a little longer he thought as he clutched the garrote he'd made especially for tonight's performance. It was just two pieces of hickory and piano wire, but it would do the job. A drunk in Birmingham had been his beta test, and he'd made refinements since then. No, there'd be no surprises tonight, he was sure of it.

He watched hidden from feet away as she fit her key into the lock and stepped inside. That's when it suddenly became real. He slammed her into the mudroom wall, quickly slipped the wire over her head, and jerked it tight. He felt her struggle, but there was no scream. Now it was just a matter of weight and leverage. His heart was pounding as she fought to slide her fingers underneath the thin metallic thread cutting into the soft flesh. Once he had her down a knee in the middle of the back, the skirmish was over, but she didn't give up. He could appreciate that. He wanted her to fight for every breath, to struggle to live, and realize in the end there was nothing she could do to save herself. After it was over, he moved quickly. He picked up the body and placed it in the trunk of her Mercedes. Firing up a Marlboro, he inhaled deeply and slowly released the smoke a satisfied smile reflected from the car's rear-view mirror. It had been a surreal night he thought as he backed down the drive. It felt like a good beginning.

"Fucking A," he shouted laughing aloud. "Game on!"

***

The graveside service had been scheduled for ten o'clock, and Jamie Hurtado had been called in to chop up and cart off a tree that had blown over in last night's storm. Nightmarish winds and two inches of rain had doomed the old, gnarled oak. To be honest, it was a miracle it had lasted this long. His boss laughed when Jamie had asked for help.

"Why should I pay two people for a one-man job?" he'd scoffed. "Get your ass to work and call me when you're finished."

That's how things usually played out at Mt. Moriah, thought Jamie. Do what you're told, don't make waves, and be prepared for the abuse anyway. It didn't take much to get on the boss's bad side, and he held a grudge like no one Jamie had ever met before. That's why they couldn't keep employees. It was beginning to spit rain when he parked his twenty-year-old Ford pick-up in the parking lot behind the funeral home and got out. Another ugly day in the River City; he needed to hurry if he wanted to finish the job before the service began. Grabbing a raincoat, Jamie loaded the Cushman with two chain saws, more than enough gas to do the job, and was halfway to Miller's Garden when he saw what looked like a mound of fresh dirt. But that didn't make any sense. It was in a section of the cemetery that had closed before he'd been hired.

"What the hell is that?" he whispered softly. "That wasn't there yesterday."

As he looked, it started to rain harder. Rivulets of water ran down-hill toward the Cushman as he trudged toward what he assumed was a mound of dirt. Twenty feet from his destination his heart stopped, and Jamie grabbed his cell phone. When the 911 operator answered, he was in a panic.

"I want to report a body," he gasped.

THE FIRST VICTIM

Greyson couldn't remember the last call he'd gotten from Doc Richards, the county medical examiner, but this one he'd never forget.

"I'm sorry to bother you on your day off, John, but I thought you'd want to know. Judge Levitt's body was discovered this morning at Mt. Moriah Cemetery. I'm on my way there now."

"Are you sure it's Julia? Who's on the scene?"

"Marcy Thomas, and she called me personally. It's Judge Levitt."

"Goddammit!" exclaimed Greyson. "I told her she needed a security detail. I'll be there in twenty minutes. Thanks for the heads-up, Doc."

Greyson had met Julia Levitt when her name was Julia Allen, before she'd married a prominent psychiatrist almost twenty years her senior. A sit-in at the university, which was more of a nuisance than a protest, had ended with her being handcuffed and placed into the back of his police cruiser. He smiled remembering that initial encounter. She'd been defiant her thick curly mane of black hair falling in her face as they'd had to pick her up and carry her out of the dean's office at the school of law.

"What were you thinking?" he'd asked as he drove the young woman to the station. "I told you I'd take you downtown if you didn't leave the premises."

She'd echoed Eleanor Roosevelt – something about women learning to play the game like a fucking man. The quote needed context, but Greyson had to admit she wasn't wrong. He could hear her now not giving an inch and expecting none in return. God, Julia had been a force he thought sadly. And she had been his friend, even after that first ugly introduction. He'd followed her career as she'd graduated from law school, became a star in the prosecutor's office, and almost ten years ago had been named to the bench. Her marriage to Gene Levitt came out of the blue. She didn't talk about it, and he didn't pry, but it seemed more of a business arrangement than something romantic. With their busy schedules and differing interests, they came home to the same house but lived worlds apart he thought. It seemed to Greyson like an odd arrangement, but what did he know.

Arriving at the cemetery, Greyson was directed to a service road and followed it until he saw yellow crime scene tape and the medical examiner's van. Getting out of his car, he trudged through the mud dreading what he was to come. Marcy Thomas met him halfway.

"John, you need to stop, don't go there…please. I don't want you to see Julia like this. This is not where you need to be."

Greyson gave a sad smile and looked away. Eventually he said, "I have to, Marcy. I owe it to Julia and our friendship to find the bastard who did this."

"How many times have you told me emotions have no place in an investigation?" cautioned the woman detective. "Let me work this."

"How about we work it together?" said Greyson. "Come on, we have a lot to do."

***

Doc Richards moved aside as Greyson approached. He watched as the homicide detective slowly circled the body, his path's circumference tightening with each step. Periodically, he would stop, write something in a battered leather notepad his wife had given him years ago, look around and then move on. It had stopped raining, and now the sun tried to peek through low hanging clouds that refused to give way. Richards said nothing as Greyson bent down and examined his friend's body. He watched him take more notes, and then look toward the access road.

"How did the killer get the body here, Doc? He didn't come that way," he said nodding toward the service entry.

"How do you know the service road wasn't used and the killer is a 'he'?" asked Richards. "A strong woman could have overpowered the judge. She wasn't very big."

"The service road gate was locked when the first officers arrived on scene," replied Greyson. "Someone from the funeral home had to unlock it. Also, the only tracks leading to the body came from your van, Doc. As for the killer being a man, Julia was small but no pushover. She was in shape, and taught Krav Maga classes at the synagogue. I've seen her fight. No, I believe a man killed Julia, and from the wound he had to take her from behind. When you do the autopsy, look for a bruise where the killer placed his knee to hold her down."

"There's a street camera on the main road," commented Marcy looking at her notes. "I'll have it checked out."

"Who's at Julia's house?" asked Greyson.

"Emily Morgan, she's covering for Alonzo. He's in a training class at Quantico," came the reply from the woman detective.

"Okay, that's good. Emily knows the ropes; she'll look under every rock. Doc, you can move the body but let me know when you have the results from her autopsy." Turning to Marcy, Greyson ordered, "Get someone on Julia's credit card receipts and phone records. I want to know every charge and call she's made for the past thirty days."

"Already on it, John."

"Good, let's go," said Greyson impatiently. "Overtime is approved on this one. We don't stop until we catch this sonofabitch. Is that understood?"

***

They took separate cars to the judge's house in Midtown, which was located a stone's throw from Overton Park and the zoo. It was in a mixed neighborhood of old and new money, of small children and grandmothers driving land yachts. A patrol car blocked the driveway as they pulled to the curb, its lights flashing a warning to stay away.

Donning booties and gloves they were waved through after their IDs had been checked. They found Emily Morgan talking to a crime scene technician in the mudroom.

"What do you have for us?" asked Greyson glancing into a house he'd been in many times before.

"It looks like Judge Levitt was attacked here, John. I have two officers canvasing a four-block radius talking to the judge's neighbors. Maybe, someone noticed something during the storm last night."

"Canvas from Poplar Avenue to North Parkway and McLean to the park," ordered Greyson. "If more men are needed get them."

"I talked to the judge's court clerk," Emily said. "She said her boss was meeting someone after work."

"Do we know who?" asked Greyson.

"No, but she thought it was a man from the voice she heard on speakerphone during recess. And she said Judge Levitt was dressed to party, which was unusual."

"Has CSI found anything here?"

"A small amount of dried blood, which more than likely came from our victim," said Emily. "Two sets of fingerprints were collected in other parts of the house. When I arrived this morning, the outside door adjacent to the driveway was open. It looks like where the attack occurred. Judge Levitt was probably rushed, her head slammed into the wall where we discovered the blood, and she was murdered here."

"Anything else, Emily?" asked Greyson.

"Yes, Judge Levitt's car is missing. She drove a black 2020 Mercedes GLC 300. I issued an APB, but there're a lot of black 2020 Mercedes in Shelby County. It'll take time to locate it."

"Marcy, have someone check the street camera near the cemetery to see if Julia's Mercedes was used to move her body. We need to find that car before someone ditches it."

"Most of the houses near the park have home security systems," stated Emily. "I'm assuming you want them checked."

"I do," ordered Greyson. "We might get lucky."

After Marcy and Emily had left, Greyson began to sift through his friend's personal possessions. This was a part of his job that he hated the most; it was like killing the victim for the second time. Digging into their innermost secrets, the ones he or she wanted shrouded from others, but murder changed things and never for the best. He opened a desk drawer in his friend's home office and looked inside.

"God, Julia would hate this," murmured Greyson in a low voice. "I'm so sorry, Sweetie."

***

He stayed at the house going through closets, opening dressers, looking through desks and drawers until late in the afternoon. Julia's electronics and a stand-alone safe were taken downtown to be analyzed later. There were a few surprises. Greyson found a small quantity of cannabis in a purse, which he disposed of, there was a nightstand filled with an assortment of sex toys and lubes, and in a bedroom next to the master he discovered a walk-in closet filled with seductive lingerie and dresses. All this was out of character for the woman Greyson knew. Before he left upstairs, he spotted a velvet- covered box pushed out of sight on a shelf in the master bathroom. Inside were nearly a dozen notes from past lovers, some signed but most not. He took those with him. On the drive home, he got his second call of the day from the medical examiner.

"John, just calling with an update on Judge Levitt. Cause of death was asphyxia, and you were right. There was a bruise in the middle of Julia's back between the scapulae. I'd estimate time of death as sometime between eight and midnight. Julia wasn't raped. There were no signs of sexual penetration or DNA present in the autopsy."

Greyson then told Richards what he'd found in Julia's house - the sex toys, lubes, and bawdy lingerie.

"She was a young woman and single," the medical examiner said matter-of-factly. "When did her husband die?"

"Dr. Levitt committed suicide about two years ago; he hanged himself on Christmas Eve. Julia found him in his office at the university."

"My god, how horrible," commented the medical examiner. "Were there problems in the marriage?"

"Julia wouldn't talk about it, that wasn't her, but Dr. Levitt was considerably older, and they spent a lot of time apart. I discovered after his death that he'd battled depression for decades and had recently quit taking his meds."

"From my experience that's not uncommon for psychiatrists, especially if they're tempted to treat themselves," commented Richards. "Okay, I've got to go, John. I'll give you a call after I get Julia's toxicology report. It should be interesting from what you've told me."

"Doc, I don't need to remind you but no leaks to the media. They'll be all over Julia's murder, and she doesn't need her personal life exposed to the world."

"I'm going to let that comment go, detective" responded Richards calmly, "but don't push your luck. I was doing this job when you were in high school. We'll talk later," he said before ending the call.

"That's great" Greyson muttered to himself. "I just insulted a man who's been doing this job for almost as long as I've been alive. What the hell was I thinking?"

***

Blue was at the door when he got home. His dog was ready for their evening jaunt through and around Central Gardens. They had a loosely constructed routine that changed as often as it stayed the same. Most of the time they wandered aimlessly until they found something new or ran into someone who was willing to stop and talk. Greyson did his best thinking during these strolls, and tonight he needed all the help he could get. They usually ended up in front of Barksdale's Restaurant but not tonight. Tonight, they found themselves standing in front of Julia Levitt's house. It was only a few miles from where they'd started, and with a wind from the south, it was a nice evening to be outside. The earlier storms had reluctantly moved out of the area, and the forecast for tomorrow called for a high of seventy-four degrees with bright sunny skies. That was Memphis. If you didn't like the weather, wait twenty-four hours. Greyson unhooked Blue's leash and stepped under the yellow crime scene tape that had been stretched across his friend's driveway.

In his mind, he could see the attack. See the killer as he waited hidden among the overgrown shrubs. See him carry the body to her Mercedes and drive away. The question was why? Why had someone killed Julia? He didn't take her money or jewelry, and according to Doc Richards, the judge hadn't been raped. A voice from behind surprised him.

"Is that your dog?" asked a young woman wearing tights and a reflective running shell. He noticed she carried a can of mace in her left hand.

"That's Blue," replied Greyson as he reached inside his jacket for his badge. "I'm a police detective and I'm investigating Judge Levitt's murder. Do you live around here?"

The young woman stepped a little closer to look at his identification, but he noticed she kept a safe distance and didn't put away the mace.

"I do, and it's horrible what happened to Julia. Do you know who did this?"

"Not yet, but I will. Have you seen anyone suspicious in the neighborhood recently?"

"No, but the park is at the end of the street," she said pointing. "Someone is always walking a dog or jogging down our street to get to the park. That's where I was tonight, running the trails."

"It's late to be out by yourself," cautioned Greyson, "especially now. Sometimes a killer returns to the scene of the crime."

"I usually run with a group and carry mace, but no one wanted to get out tonight, you know, after what happened. I couldn't stay inside. Julia was my friend, and I don't know how to process this. It's all so horrible."

"She was my friend, too," echoed the detective, "and I know what you mean. My name is John Greyson and that's my trusty companion," he said pointing at Blue.

"I'm Ginny Barnett, and I live in the brick house on the corner, the one with the big magnolia in the front yard. My ex wanted it cut down, said it was a deal-breaker. The magnolia is still there," she said laughing. "Obviously, we had more problems than just a tree. Mainly, he thought it was okay to sleep around, and I disagreed. Julia helped me send him packing and keep my inheritance. In retrospect, I now see that he married me for my money, but he was slick. I'll have to give him that."

"Do you think your former husband could be involved in Julia's murder?" asked the homicide detective.

"I don't know," replied Ginny looking away for a moment. "He has a temper, but it's a stretch to think he could kill someone."

"Do you mind giving me his name?"

"Not at all," replied the young woman, her eyes lighting up at the prospect of the cops visiting her ex. "His name is David Barnett, and he owns a motorcycle shop on Elvis Presley, near where the Southland Mall used to be."

"Thank you, Ginny," said Greyson writing down her ex's name. "Why don't you go home, and Blue and I will make sure you get in safely, and please be careful. I have a feeling this guy isn't finished."

***

It was almost eleven when he and his four-legged best friend finally found their way home. Blue grabbed his comfort blanket and disappeared. He was done for the night. Greyson poured himself a stiff drink and went to his office intent on setting up his murder board. He taped Julia's picture in the top center. It was one of his favorites and had been taken a few years ago at the Shell, Julia's big grin framed in a mass of black, curly hair. She'd hated her curls and waves, but he thought they were her best feature…that and her big personality. Being on the small side, standing barely five feet tall, his friend wasn't an immediately commanding presence, but there was something about her you couldn't forget. God, what a waste he thought feeling angry and sad at the same time. Writing on his board, Greyson started his to-do list:

Interview David Barnett
Check threats
See who benefitted from Julia's death
Talk to co-workers and friends. Find out what was going on in her life.
Look for similar crimes in Memphis and the surrounding areas.

Analyze the notes found in the velvet box
Check security cameras in the neighborhood
Run Julia's credit card receipts and phone records

It was close to midnight when he dialed a number he knew from memory.

"Damn it, John! Do you know what time it is? This better be good."

"I need your help, Horace," replied Greyson. "Julia Levitt has been murdered."

"Give me a few days to rearrange my schedule. I'll call you when I leave."

THE INVESTIGATION BEGINS

Their meeting room used to be just storage. It was on the first floor of the Public Service Building at the end of a narrow, poorly lit, dead-end hallway. Combined the effect made visitors feel more than a little claustrophobic. Greyson preferred to think of the room as a pressure cooker. It was perfect for the results he wanted. He'd stopped by Java Cabana and picked up breakfast croissants, bagels, and coffee strong enough to pour itself. Besides himself two street cops had been temporarily assigned to work the case, along with detectives Marcy Thomas, and Emily Morgan. His murder board anchored the center of the room fronting two battered tables that had been dragged together and encircled by a mishmash of chairs from who-knew-where.

"Okay, grab your food and take a seat," declared Greyson. "I have a few announcements to make before we start. First, Julia Levitt was my friend. That's why Marcy Thomas will lead this team, and I will assist. Secondly, many of you may remember Horace Mann. I have the director's approval to bring him in as a paid consultant. He's not a police officer, but I'd advise you to listen to what he says and recommends. Horace is a decorated public servant with more than twenty years of working homicides in this city. He will be here in a few days. I have discussed the case with Marcy, and I'll hand over the meeting to her. Any questions?"

When no one raised their hand, Marcy replaced Greyson at the front of the room.

"This is a high-profile case, so I want nothing released to the public without it going through me or John first, and we'll meet here each morning at seven sharp unless you hear otherwise. Don't be late. Officers Hernandez and Veal, I want you to talk to every homeowner in the judge's neighborhood. Ask if they are willing to integrate their outdoor cameras with our Connect Memphis program. Also, ask if they observed anything unusual in the neighborhood prior to Judge Levitt's murder. If no one is home, go back a second time. Emily, interview the judge's coworkers and friends. Look for threats and find out what was going on in her personal and professional life. John and I are going to interview the former spouse of one of Judge Levitt's neighbors. If there are no questions, let's get to it."

***

Barnett's Wildside Cycles was located on Elvis Presley Boulevard in an old car dealership. The area had seen better days, but there were a few signs of revitalization. The city had recently upgraded the main throughfare's streetlights, and a repaving program was in progress. The biggest sign of renewal, however, was a major grocery store chain that had opened a new store on the block. There were still too many boarded-up businesses and men huddled in the shadows drinking from brown paper bags, but the general impression was mostly positive.

Turning to her partner, Marcy asked, "How do you want to handle this, John?"

"You start and push hard. I want to see how Barnett reacts to a woman in charge. I'll play the good cop on this one."

His comment made her laugh out loud. The idea of Greyson playing good cop was like dressing a pig in a tuxedo. It might be cute, but it was hard to imagine.

They found Barnett in his office smoking a cigarette, his feet propped up on a cheap pressboard desk that was more glue than wood. Cigarette butts littered a green linoleum floor that had likely been laid in the 1980s. The pattern had been popular at the time and more importantly cheap.

"Mr. Barnett, my name is Marcy Thomas, and this is my partner,

John Greyson. We're homicide detectives with the Memphis Police Department."

"Homicide, what do you want with me?" Barnett seemed genuinely baffled by the appearance of two murder cops in his office.

"You didn't hear that Judge Levitt was murdered night before last?" asked Marcy. "I find that hard to believe."

"I don't listen to the news anymore. It's all horrible."

"Where were you Friday night from six o'clock until two in the morning?"

"Am I a suspect?" asked Barnett turning to Greyson for confirmation."

"Why are you looking at him?" responded Marcy sharply, slamming her hand down on Barnett's desk to get his attention. "I'm asking the questions, and I'm not in a good mood. Nod if you understand me."

"I don't like your attitude, detective," responded the cycle shop owner with an angry scowl. "Yeah, I heard Levitt was dead. So what? That bitch got what she deserved. Now get the hell…"

Before he could finish the sentence, Greyson had grabbed Barnett by the throat and slammed him against the floor, his face contorted with rage.

"Say another word," he hissed squeezing harder, "and I'll personally rip your head off. Now answer Detective Thomas' question."

"You saw that!" screamed Barnett frantically looking at Marcy for help. "He can't do that; I know my rights!"

"I didn't see anything," replied the woman detective with a sly smile. "John, I need to use the restroom. Would you watch our suspect while I'm gone?"

"Okay, okay, I see where this is going," said Barnett throwing up his hands in surrender. "On Friday I left work a little before three. I think I got food poisoning and went home."

"You think you got food poisoning?" repeated Greyson. "What the hell does that mean?"

"Well, I didn't shit my pants, if that's what you're asking, but it was pretty damn close," came a smart-assed reply.

"He's not going to cooperate, John," commented Marcy reaching for her handcuffs. "Let's take him in."

"Someone needs to teach this bitch some manners," growled Barnett his hands balled into fists. "I had nothing to do with what happened to Levitt, and you know it. This is harassment."

Before Marcy could react, Greyson interceded. "We don't have time for this," he cautioned his partner. Looking back to Barnett, he asked, "Can anyone corroborate your story? That you were at home and didn't go out again?"

"I don't think so. I'm not married, and I live alone," responded Barnett.

"What a surprised," Marcy's derision oozed from each syllable. The comment earned a half smile from her partner.

"Did you go online or call anyone?" asked Greyson.

"No, I went home, took something for the shits, and went to bed. I felt better the next morning."

"What was your relationship with Judge Levitt?" asked Marcy.

He laughed before commenting. "There was no relationship. I was just another blue-collar bum in her eyes. I only went to college for one semester, and I didn't come from money. If you're looking for relationships, you should be talking to Ginny."

"What does that mean?" Greyson asked not liking where this was going.

"Ginny and I had our problems, but we were working through them until Levitt got involved. I made a mistake one night and hit Ginny, and you would have thought I'd shot the President. The next thing I know two cops come to the door and arrest me. I had to spend the next twenty-four hours in jail until a friend bailed me out. Next came a restraining order and then divorce papers. I found out later my wife had been sleeping with Levitt."

"That sounds like some made-up shit to me, Barnett," responded Marcy. "You can do better than that."

"I'm through talking," said the angry motorcycle shop owner. "I want an attorney."

"Okay, we can do it the hard way," commented Greyson smiling at Ginny Barnett's ex-husband. "We'll be back, and the next time we speak will be at our house. If I were you, I'd work on my alibi for Friday night."

***

"So, what do you think?" asked Marcy when they were back on the street.

"He doesn't like women in positions of authority…that's obvious. Did you see how he reacted when you threatened to take him in?"

"You know we'll break his alibi," commented Marcy as she looked back to see Barnett who was watching them walk away. "There's no way that ass-wipe wasn't out partying on a Friday night. He's the type to flash a little money and hope to get lucky pushing drinks on some bimbo in some low-rent bar. He likes attention, and that works in our favor. Somebody will remember him, and then we got him."

"That accusation about his ex-wife sleeping with Julia could muddy the waters," commented Greyson wearily. "I'm beginning to think I didn't know my friend as well as I thought."

"We all have secrets, John. I wouldn't worry about it, and I wouldn't put too much credence in anything Barnett said. If true, it provides him with more motive and strengthens our case against him as Julia's killer. I bet Barnett didn't consider that when he tried to slander the judge and his ex."

"I guess we need to visit Ginny Barnett," responded Greyson as he slid behind the wheel of his unmarked cruiser. "We were going to have to do it sooner or later anyway. I'll introduce you, and you conduct the interview. Considering the subject matter, she may feel more comfortable talking to another woman."

THINGS GET COMPLI-CATED

They stopped at Bosco's before continuing on to interview Barrnett's ex-wife. Marcy had skipped breakfast, and he could hear her stomach growling from his side of the car. As for himself, Greyson sensed the first signs of a coming migraine; sensitivity to light and smells, feeling sluggish, nausea. It was on the way. Sometimes caffeine helped with the severity of the attack, and sometimes it didn't. It was the oddest thing he thought. He'd never had migraines until his wife died unexpectedly. When he'd asked his doctor if the two could be related, Greyson had been assured they weren't, but he still wondered. Sue had been told she was in perfect health a few weeks before the heart attack, which proved medical professionals could be wrong. As they stepped inside the doorway, he could see the lunch crowd had long since vanished and been replaced by regulars who sat in groups around a long mahogany bar drinking beer and talking in low tones. No one seemed to notice Greyson and Thomas as a pretty young hostess seated them at a table looking out onto Madison Avenue.

"Your waiter's name is Walter, and he'll be with you momentarily," the hostess said. "Enjoy your meal."

"I wonder how she got her teeth so white?" Marcy said after the woman had gone. "Do they look natural to you?"

Greyson didn't respond as he read a text message on his phone.

"Do you have something?"

"Maybe," he mumbled his attention directed elsewhere. "The sub-poena for Julia's phone and credit card receipts has been served, and I received a message to call Dr. Vivian Gales."

"Who's Dr. Vivian Gales?" asked Marcy.

"Apparently, she's the older sister of Gene and Emilio Levitt. Her note says she might have information on who wanted her sister-in-law dead."

"Are you going to call her now? I can get something to go, or we can drive through a McDonalds."

"No, let's order and eat first. It looks like it's going to be a long day for us both."

Greyson ordered coffee, black of course, and a Ceasar salad after taking a handful of aspirin. Marcy went with the delta catfish, southern style greens, and hush puppies, with an extra order of hush puppies. She topped that off with a cast iron cookie and scoop of vanilla bean ice cream.

"How can you eat like that and stay so slim?" he'd asked after she'd finished.

"Two hours a day in the gym," she'd replied smiling. "You should try it sometimes, John."

He dropped seventy bucks on the table and said, "Let's get out of here. You drive."

***

Looking at the area code she'd called from, it appeared Vivian Gales lived in Nashville. Greyson returned her call and when no one answered, he left a message. The drive from Bosco's to the Barnett house took less than ten minutes. Marcy had just pulled to the curb when they saw the young woman walking in their direction, a rolled yoga mat under one arm. When she saw Greyson get out of the car, she smiled and waved.

"I didn't expect to see you so soon, detective. What can I do for you today?"

"Ginny, this is my colleague, Marcy Thomas. We met with David earlier this morning and have a few questions. It won't take long but is there someplace we could go to speak in private?"

"I guess so," came the tentative reply. She looked first at Greyson and then at Marcy. "What's this about? Am I in trouble?"

"No, absolutely not," replied Marcy. "We're simply trying to gather enough information to develop a profile on David. Other than your charge of domestic abuse, we have almost nothing on him."

"Okay, follow me," said Ginny breathing a sigh of relief. "We can talk in the kitchen."

"You two go," suggested Greyson. "I have a few calls to make. Marcy, I'll meet you at the car."

Marcy followed Barnett up a winding brick driveway lined by giant azaleas bushes and stepped into arguably the most amazing kitchen she'd ever seen before. It looked like something from an architectural magazine. When Ginny turned and saw the detective's expression, she laughed out loud.

"David claimed I bought the house because of the kitchen, which was cute but didn't make a lot of sense at the time. I have a hard time boiling water. The tiles and counter tops are supposedly over a hundred years old."

"It's perfect," declared Marcy happily. "I love to cook, and I wouldn't change a thing."

"What's going on, Marcy? Why did you and Greyson want to talk to me in private? What did David tell you?"

"He said you were sleeping with Judge Levitt."

"Wow, you don't pull your punches," came Ginny Barnett's reply. "No, I wasn't sleeping with Julia. That was David's fantasy, not mine. Julia was my friend, perhaps my best friend. She was there when I felt trapped and alone."

"What happened to your marriage?" asked Marcy as gently as possible.

"I made a bad decision, and after six years, I corrected it," she said biting her lower lip. "I married David on the rebound. I'd been dumped by a man I thought I'd grow old with, and David was the first person who made me feel special again. What a colossal fucking mistake that was. The abuse and infidelity started almost immediately, and the funny part is I thought it was my fault. One night my husband hit me hard enough to break my nose, and I ran to Julia's. We'd met at a yoga class in the park. She took charge and convinced me to call the police. The disgusting thing is David had hit me before, and I just took it. Julia found a class for battered women and attended every session with me. Who does something like that for someone they barely know? I filed for divorce citing abuse and irreconcilable differences, and it was granted. That's it, that's the whole story."

"I hate to ask, but is there any documentation of your husband's abuse? Medical records, trips to the emergency room, or anyone who can corroborate your story?"

"I can send you a copy of my divorce petition," said Barnett. "My attorney documented the number of times I was seen in the emergency room and collected statements from friends on David's abuse."

'What was your former husband's attitude toward Judge Levitt?"

"He didn't know she existed until the night I ran to her house and called the cops. After that, he couldn't stand Julia."

"Do you think David is capable of murder?" asked Marcy studying the face of the woman facing her.

"I don't know, maybe. David can be violent, but murder is something altogether different. It takes courage to kill someone."

"Do you know where your ex hangs out on the weekends?"

"I'd look at Thom's Place off Getwell Road or The Robber Baron downtown near Central Station. Both places are meat markets. If he's not there, check Danny's on Airways. It's supposedly a gentleman's club, so take Greyson with you if you go. You'll get less hassle that way."

"Have you been there before?" asked Marcy feeling that she had.

"David took me one time and wanted me to get up on stage. I took an Uber home instead."

"Is there anything you can tell me about the night Judge Levitt was murdered?"

"No, and I've been racking my brain. Leave your card, and I'll call if I remember something."

"Thanks for your time, Mrs. Barnett. I can see myself out," said Marcy.

***

"How did it go?" asked Greyson.

"I don't know. Barnett claims that she and Judge Levitt were just friends, but I'm not convinced. She didn't seem surprised or angry when I asked if they were lovers. I thought that was odd. I did get the names of several places her ex hangs out on the weekends, and one place is Danny's."

"He seems the type," grunted Greyson.

"What did you do while I was gone?" asked Marcy as she slid behind the wheel and started the car.

"I talked to Vivian Gales and discovered she's Gene and Emilio's older sister, and that the boys were twins."

"Did you know that?"

"No, I did not," replied Greyson.

"What else did you learn from her?"

"How much time do you have?" asked Greyson appearing tired and out of sorts. "Let's go to the Windjammer and get something to drink. Maybe it'll help this headache go away. Call Emily and see if she can meet us."

***

They were in a booth when Emily arrived looking as if she'd just rolled out of bed, her shoulder-length dark hair pulled into a loose bun. She'd added bright red lipstick and dark eyeliner to go with her ensemble for the day.

"God, what happened to you?" asked Marcy with a knowing smile.

"Shut up and order me a Bloody Mary. I've got to go to the bathroom."

"What's going on?" asked Greyson.

"Emily is seeing a guy she met at the gym, and I don't think she's getting much sleep."

All Greyson could think to say was, "Oh, okay."

She looked better when she returned.

"You guys do know I took today off, don't you? Even homicide detectives need to recharge occasionally."

"Why are the buttons on your blouse crooked?" teased Marcy trying hard not to laugh. "Did you do it all by yourself or did your boy toy do it for you?"

"Are you still seeing Murphy?" asked Emily not intending to answer her friend's questions. "If so, you're not getting laid enough. Leave me alone, and John why are we meeting?"

"I'm sorry, Emily," said Greyson sincerely. "I'm not with it today. Go home and go back to bed; we can do this in the morning."

"I'm here now. Let's get to it."

Greyson described to his two associates his search of Julia Levitt's house; the cannabis, sex toys, and the pornographic notes he found in the master bathroom. If they were surprised neither woman showed it. He then pivoted to the call he'd gotten from Vivian Gales.

"She's the older sister to Gene and Emilio, and she lives in Nashville," he began his narrative. "Like her brothers, she's also a psychiatrist and has a private practice in Franklin. She wanted to explain what it was like to live in the Levitt household as a kid. According to her, it wasn't ideal or something you'd find in a Norman Rockwell painting."

"Didn't you say she had information on who may have killed Judge Levitt?" asked Marcy interrupting.

"Yes, but I'll explain that later," said Greyson. "Let me finish and then you can ask your questions. As I was saying, growing up the kids didn't need for anything, except maybe a little love and attention from their parents. Their father worked for Standard Oil and lived on the road. Vivian described him as a shadow in their lives. They grew up in boarding schools and summer camps, coming home occasionally for the holidays. Vivian's brothers, who are twins, grew up as loners staying mainly to themselves. They weren't athletic or outgoing, so they were the perfect targets to be bullied. When their father died in a plane crash in New Mexico, Vivian was in college, and the boys were ten at the time. It was turbulent times for the family according to Dr. Gales, but her mother eventually pulled it together. Gene and Emilio finished school, followed her into psychiatry and opened separate practices in the same office building on Madison Avenue, near the UT Health Center. Dr Gales married another med student, Gene married Julia Allen, and her brother, Emilio, remained single."

"John, what the hell does this have to do with the murder of Judge Levitt?" asked Emily. "Just tell us why Dr. Gales called you."

"Most murders are committed by someone the victim knows," Greyson replied patiently. "You should know that, Emily. That means we look at the history surrounding the deceased. That's what I'm doing here. Dr. Gales also called to ask when Julia's body would be released from the coroner's office. Since her sister-in-law had no family and no children, she wanted to make sure there was a proper burial."

"I thought you said she might know who killed the judge," said Marcy.

"Since she had no proof, Dr. Gales suggested we discuss her suspicions after the funeral," came the reply from Greyson. "I'm to set up a meeting, and I expect you'll want to attend."

"Absolutely, let me know where and what time."

"I'm sorry, you're right, John," Emily said. "What else do you have for us?"

"Don't worry about it," Greyson said with a half-smile. "I'm sorry about asking you to join us when you obviously had more important things to do."

His comment had Marcy smiling.

"How old is this man-child, anyway?" she asked her friend.

"His name is Troy, he's twenty-seven, and he's a fireman," replied Emily with a smile of her own. "Okay, we're even, John. Go on with your story."

"Julia Allen had been one of Gene Levitt's patients. She'd been dealing with depression and anxiety after the death of her mother. According to Dr. Gales, her brother was captivated by his new patient, and the attraction only grew the more times they met. He finally told her how he felt and asked her out."

"That had to be creepy," commented Marcy. "You tell your doctor your deepest and darkest secrets, and he asks you out. Yuck!"

"Gene suggested Julia switch psychiatrists and see his brother, Emilio, who had a practice in the same building. She said no initially but changed her mind, and once she changed doctors, she and Gene started dating. Gene proposed six months later, and she said yes. It was a surprise to everyone."

"Why?" asked Maranda. "Did they hide the fact they were dating?"

"No, I guess it was the differences in age, and that they just didn't seem to fit. That's my take anyway. Gene was socially awkward, had no sense of humor, and he was kind of colorless. Julia was the opposite. Always up and ready for anything, a bright spot in the universe."

"What was Judge Levitt's background?" asked Emily.

"She was born in Memphis and raised by a single mother who usually worked two jobs to make ends meet. Julia never met her father. I know she was an athlete in high school and got her undergraduate degree while on a soccer scholarship. After earning a degree in political science, she took out loans to attend law school. Julia Allen finished at the top of her class at Memphis, was hired by the district attorney, and you know the rest of the story."

"What else did Dr. Gales tell you?" asked Marcy.

"That's about it. She said we'd talk more after the burial.

THE VELVET BOX

Blue was ready for their evening walk when he got home. He was on the small side for a pittie, but what he'd lacked in size he made up for in strength and enthusiasm.

"Okay, boy," said the detective as he bent down and rubbed his dog's belly. "Let me get a cup of coffee and find your leash."

Blue followed his master into the kitchen and waited patiently for the night's adventure to begin. Greyson started a pot of coffee, rinsed out the beat-up Brewer's thermos in the sink, found his dog's leash, and walked out the front door with twelve ounces of steaming hot java. It was Greyson's Achilles heel; he had to have it to function. They'd stop somewhere along the way for a refill, usually at Barksdale's, which according to the detective had the second-best coffee on the planet. Who was number one was anyone's guess. After their break, the two would continue their evening jaunt wandering aimlessly until they reached the gazebo in Peabody Park. That was the pivot point where they'd begin the trek home. Greyson used these long evening walks to decompress, and Blue helped him cope. He had found the pint-sized pitbull shot and abandoned in his backyard and had rushed him to a vet. That's how they'd ended up together. Whether it had been karma, fate, or whatever you want to call it, they'd found one another when each had needed a savior. Now they were inseparable, the dynamic duo patrolling their part of the hemisphere three hundred and sixty-five days a year.

"Which way do you want to go?" asked Greyson.

He'd put a little bourbon in his thermos to fight off the chill. Blue pulled ahead trotting towards City Coffee. At the corner, the two turned south in the direction of Copper-Young. It was a cool night with a light drizzle. No one was out; the streets were practically abandoned. That was fine with Greyson who wasn't looking for conversation. He kept thinking about the young woman who'd hunted him down after she'd been arrested and put in the backseat of his police cruiser.

"There you are," she'd said laughing. "I thought I'd bring you a peace offering. It's a slice of my mother's banana bread, and don't worry, I didn't poison it."

"How would I know," he'd replied.

With that Julia Allen had unwrapped the treat, taken a bite, and then another one all while smiling like the Cheshire cat.

"It was my mother's idea. She said I wasn't respectful enough towards the authorities. I bet her you wouldn't take it."

"I hope you can cover your bets," he'd responded, which elicited a big smile from the young, outgoing law student. Greyson had shared his sandwich and chips, and Julia had split the banana bread in two, handing him the bigger piece.

"I already had two bites," she'd teased.

Thinking about that moment left him furious, her death so senselessness. The walk with Blue should have helped, and it usually did, but not tonight. Small moments came flooding back like a tsunami casting a dark shroud over his soul. He was surprised when Blue stopped, and he was home again.

"Come on let's get you fed," he said.

***

He mixed a strong drink and made his way into the study carrying the velvet box he'd found in Julia's master bathroom. This was not something he wanted to do, but better him than a stranger. There were eleven notes in total, all with codes of some sort on the front and salacious handwritten notes on the back. Why keep these he asked himself. Were they from eleven different people?

"Souvenirs maybe?" he said out loud after taking a sip of his drink.

The cards were identical in size and appearance, printed on expensive paper with an orchid ensnared in the coils of a large snake on one side. What intrigued Greyson was the series of numbers printed neatly on the bottom of each card. The notes were graphic and raw, and signed in what appeared to be pseudonyms.

"Julia, what the hell did you get into?" he asked in a whisper.

Setting the cards aside, he began to study the box. It stood approximately five inches by eight, the interior was covered in suede, and the hinges and latch looked like they were made of brass. Luckily for him, a tag on the bottom identified the seller, *Bardo's Fine Jewelry, New York City*. At one time it was probably a jewelry box. It looked expensive and probably was. Julia loved things like this, something she never had growing up with a single mom. Greyson finished what remained of this drink, placed the cards back where they came from, and closed the lid. A quick note to MK Isoke, and he was ready for bed. Isoke was the top criminologist at the crime lab, and Greyson wanted him alone to do the analysis on the box and its contents.

"Come on, Blue," said a very tired detective. "Let's go to bed. Tomorrow is a good day to dig in the dirt."

DIGGING IN THE DIRT

He slept like shit tossing covers and pillows all night. Sometimes it happened like that for Greyson, especially when a case offended his sense of right and wrong. An elder couple gunned down doing nothing but trying to survive another day, or someone killed in a random shooting. Murdering Julia, his friend, had aroused something ugly inside him, something that wanted retribution. His psychiatrist had told him that dreams were often a way to process unresolved emotions, deal with past experiences, or to cope with current day stressors. It was a theory, but Greyson wasn't buying it, not this morning. He wanted revenge, the biblical eye for an eye. A quick walk with Blue helped, but he was in a bad mood again by the time he reached the crime lab. Isoke signed for Julia's jewelry box and its contents and promised to call him if he uncovered anything useful.

"Make sure you're the only one who touches those notes, MK," warned Greyson. "I can't tell you how pissed off I'll be if their contents becomes common knowledge."

"I got it, John. I'll let you know if something pops."

He took the stairs to his office, locked the door, and hit the brew button on a twenty-year-old Mr. Coffee that worked like new. After logging onto his computer, he pulled up a file with photos from the crime scene and Doc Richard's autopsy. He'd seen them earlier but now wanted to view them again. He took his time, made notes and was happy when he got to the last one. The photographer had done a good job; maybe too good he thought as he closed the file. Images of the wire-induced cut along Julia's neck, the black and blue bruising on her back, and her sallow skin coloring flashed as Greyson leaned back in his chair and rubbed his eyes.

He was beyond tired, but he could now put himself in the shoes of the killer. Crime scene photographs had captured everything. The broken lightbulb above the driveway, snapped azalea branches where the killer had hidden, mulch tracked into the mud room. He saw the killer waiting for Julia to arrive home, watching from an overgrown stand of wax-leaf privet and scraggly azaleas. It had been the perfect spot. It was near the door used to enter and leave the house, practically out of sight from the street. It had been dark and made darker when the driveway light was shattered. Its base was still in the socket.

The injuries Julia endured before she'd died made him angry; broken and bloody nails, a nasty almost surgical incision that ran laterally from ear to ear, and the discolored skin on her back where the killed planted his knee to hold her down. She hadn't gone down without a fight he thought. He could imagine the killer leaning back straining to end the life of his friend, but her fighting back. What had she done so egregious to merit something like that? He was deep in thought when a knock on his door snapped him back to the present.

"John, we're ready. I picked up coffee and bagels at Ugly Joe's."

"I'll be right out, Marcy. Give me a minute," he replied.

The pictures had been unsettling, and Greyson was feeling lost and empty, which was not what he wanted anyone to see. He had to treat this case like any other and keep everything in perspective. Like his old partner, Albert Leon Kelly, used to say.

"Do you know what time it is, John? It's time to start digging, that's where the worms are."

It made him smile thinking about his old friend and mentor.

"Rest in peace, buddy," Greyson muttered quietly before standing. "I have to go find some worms."

"Where's Officer Vale?" he asked as he entered the room.

"His wife went into labor early," replied Vale's partner. "It's another girl, their fourth. Bobby just knew this one would be a boy."

"How long do I have you, Hernandez?" Greyson asked.

"End of week and then I go back on patrol unless you can pull some strings…sorry," he said in earnest.

"Tell Vale congratulations and thanks. How much did you guys get done?"

"Not enough. I'm not going to finish by Friday, but I have an idea."

"Okay, shoot," said Greyson.

"We live in a two-income society where the husband and wife both work. At homes where no one answers the door, we leave a flyer with a hotline number. We ask the homeowner to call if they noticed anything unusual in the neighborhood. It isn't perfect, but it does the job."

"What do you think, Marcy?"

"I don't know," she replied, "but I know who does. I'll let you know something by the end of the day."

"I have an appointment at eight-thirty," said Greyson looking at his watch. "Marcy, take over the meeting. Status reports are due in the morning, keep it short and to the point. Good hunting."

"Have you heard anything from Horace?" asked Emily. "I miss that cantankerous, old SOB. We were partners longer than my second marriage."

"Not yet," came the response from Greyson.

***

A basic question in any murder investigation is who benefits from the death of the victim. The offices of Brown, Oswald, and McCutchen were in the Sterick Building, within easy walking distance for Greyson, and it was a good day to be outside. The sun was out with a warm wind from the south. Archibald McCutchen had agreed to meet and discuss Julia's will.

"It won't take long detective," the attorney told Greyson when ushering him inside his office. "All of Julia's immediate family are deceased."

"So, you expect no problems?" he asked.

"I didn't say that," replied McCutchen cautiously. "What do you know about the death of Gene Levitt and his will?"

"Nothing about the will. I know Julia's husband committed suicide according to the medical examiner."

"I'm surprised Julia didn't bring it up since she considered you a close friend. It took almost two years to finalize the terms of Gene's will, and I worked my ass off, pardon the French. Gene's brother, Emilio, was a pain in the ass and contested everything. I have to give the judge a lot of credit; she was more forgiving than I would have been under the same circumstances. She could have buried Emilio, but she didn't. Emil, as he likes to call himself these days, wanted everything; the house, cars, bank accounts, stocks, and the building where he and his brother had their practices. His problem was Gene's will was airtight, but that didn't matter to him and the shyster he hired to represent him. His main accusation was that Julia had driven his brother to suicide. He even demanded the police reopen the case and threatened to sue the medical examiner if he didn't change the cause of death."

"I didn't know any of this," Greyson murmured.

"If you're looking for suspects on who murdered Julia, I'd look at Emilio Levitt. He's nuttier than a pecan pie."

"And you think he'll contest Julia's will?"

"Oh yeah, it's almost a guarantee," replied the attorney, "but I like a fight. I'm the executor of the estate, so I'm going to do exactly what Julia wanted. She was my friend, too, Greyson. I don't know if you know it, but she talked about you a lot. You were the father she never had."

***

Marcy grabbed a bagel, smothered it in cream cheese, and hurried to her office. Subpoenas had been delivered to the bank and phone company, but she'd heard nothing back. Now it was time to find out why.

Sitting at her desk, she muttered under her breath, "I'm going to tear someone a new one. Don't these assholes know I'm trying to catch a killer?"

Her call to the bank exceeded all expectations. Within minutes the homicide detective had the judge's debit and credit card charges for the past six months, and the bank manager promised to hand deliver a hard copy to her office by the end of the day. With every positive outcome, you have to expect a negative one every now and then. Marcy's call to the phone company immediately ground her sleuthing to a standstill.

"What do you mean there's nothing you can do?" she said clenching her jaw. "You do know I'm investigating the murder of a criminal court judge, and you're in violation of an order to produce my victim's phone records?"

"We've forwarded your subpoena to our legal department in Atlanta, and they are studying it. You'll get Julia Levitt's phone records when I'm told to release them."

"Can you give me your last name, Charlotte? And your job title?"

"Why do you need my last name and job title?" asked the woman.

"You're impeding a murder investigation and ignoring a duly issued subpoena. I need your full name and job title to request a warrant for your arrest. Oh, and don't hang up now because I can find you."

"I…ah…wait a moment, please. I need to make a phone call." The phone company employee sounded noticeably worried now. "Don't hang up, I'll be right back."

Marcy was tempted to laugh but didn't. For her good manners, she ended up having to listen to a commercialized rendition of Neil Diamond's "Cracklin' Rosie", which nearly drove her crazy. Neil Diamond was a superstar, and his music was not to be messed with.

"Good news, Ms. Thomas," said the evidently relieved employee. "My boss has approved releasing Judge Levitt's phone records. Do you want me to put them in the mail?"

"It's detective," replied Marcy in a don't-fuck-with-me tone of voice. "I'll come by and pick them up. Make sure they're ready."

If Charlotte was nervous before, it was worse now.

"Of course, my apologies Detective Thomas. Just ask for my assistant, her name is Tess. I'm assuming you have our address."

Marcy hung up without responding. This woman was beginning to piss her off. As she reached for her keys, her phone rang.

"Homicide, Marcy Thomas," she answered.

"Detective Thomas, I think we found your 2020 black Mercedes.

It's in the parking lot of the Abe Goodman clubhouse in Overton Park."

"The APB was put out by Emily Morgan. Did you call her?"

"No, ma'am. My instructions were to contact you."

"Good work, officer. Keep everyone away and call CSI. Don't touch a thing."

"Yes, ma'am. We'll standby and await your arrival."

She called Greyson after hanging up.

"John, the judge's car has been found at Overton in the clubhouse parking lot. I'm tied up, what do you want to do?"

"Call Emily and tell her to meet me there," came the reply. "I just left Archibald McCutchen's office; he's Julia's attorney. We have someone else to add to our suspect list."

EMILY MORGAN

Emily was still a little pissed at Marcy for not saying their get-together at the Windjammer had been voluntary.

If Emily had known, she would have stayed in bed. She'd been working her ass off, especially lately, and it had been a long time since she'd met anyone like Troy. He was funny, could dance, and the sex was incredible. In fact, she'd left him in her bed when she rushed out the door looking like one of the undead. It had been a long dry spell for her, and sex at the beginning of any relationship was usually the best. The discovery of likes and dislikes, the spontaneity, the frequency, it was all perfect, and she wasn't ready for it to end. Unfortunately, his car was gone when she pulled into her driveway.

"Dammit, Marcy, I can't believe you did this to me. Just wait until I find out you're with Murphy."

She stripped as she made her way toward the bedroom dropping her clothes along the way. Slipping under cool sheets naked, she could smell him on her pillows and pulled them tight against her breast. In seconds, she was asleep dreaming dreams that would be R-rated if shown in a theater.

***

She woke to the rich, warm, complex smells of a dark roasted Columbian coffee…thank the gods. Emily stretched to the full length of her five-foot nine-inch frame and arched her back. Yesterday had been good, or most of it anyway, but now it was time to go back to work.

She was interviewing Judge Levitt's court clerk and her bailiff this morning, but first she had to get to the team's standing seven o'clock meeting. Greyson had been specific about being on time, and he was taking the death of his friend hard. Under that kick-ass, take-no-prisoners exterior he presented to most people, she'd seen another side, and she didn't want to let him down.

Before coffee and a bagel, she stepped into a hot, steamy shower water spilling down her back arousing all her senses. Twenty-four hours ago, she hadn't been alone and wished she wasn't alone now. Maybe later she thought lustfully. Troy was twenty-seven and she had just turned thirty-nine a month ago, but so far, the difference in age hadn't seemed to matter. He was fun, incredibly handsome, and they shared many of the same interests. Marriage was off the table, at least for the foreseeable future. She'd tried that twice and it hadn't taken. It wasn't that she hated the idea, but as her sisters loved to remind her, she had terrible taste in men. Truth be told, they were probably right. Emily's first trip down the aisle was with her high school sweetheart, and she liked to think of it as a test run that worked out the kinks. Then ten years later she married an attorney, who believed having a wife and girlfriend or several girlfriends was a good idea. It didn't take him long to realize that marrying a homicide detective wasn't ideal if you wanted to keep secrets. He ended up buying her the house she lived in now and called every now and then wanting to meet for drinks. Why? You didn't have to be a brain surgeon to figure it out; he was married again for the fourth time. He wasn't a bad guy; he just couldn't keep it in his pants. The sound of her alarm clock going off in the bedroom was her cue to get out of the shower and get dressed for work. The job wasn't going to do itself.

***

Thankfully, the seven o'clock meeting was short. Greyson had an appointment and couldn't stay long. She heard later he was meeting the judge's personal attorney. Marcy handed out assignments, cut everyone else loose, and rushed off to her office.

"You can run but you can't hide," she'd mumbled in a tone only she could hear. What should have been an evening of lovemaking had instead turned into a weak Bloody Mary and poor company. Marcy had to know payback was coming. Emily walked to the courthouse, which was a stone's throw away, where the judge's court clerk and bailiff were waiting to be interviewed. Both had worked for Levitt since her first day on the bench, and that had her a little worried. Lying or withholding information to protect their boss's reputation did nothing to honor her, and it could help a killer get away with murder. Terry Wells was sixty-two and looked ten years older. If she was nervous, Emily couldn't tell it.

"I hope this doesn't take long, detective," she'd said while looking at her watch. "I have a hair appointment in an hour and it's in Germantown.

"Mrs. Wells, I'll make this as quick possible, but I am investigating the murder of a criminal court judge. Let's start with you telling me about Judge Levitt, and how she got along with everyone at the courthouse. That includes other judges, attorneys, support staff, or anyone you consider relevant."

"It's Ms., I've never been married," responded the court clerk. "I've had my opportunities, but men are like roosters. They strut around the barnyard chasing any new hen in sight. No thank you, I don't need that in my life. I've got my cats and I'm happier than all my married friends."

"Good to know," commented the detective. "Now, what can you tell me about Judge Levitt's life here at the court?"

Terry Wells frowned before responding and looked at her watch again. "Everyone loved the judge. That includes Max, he's her bailiff, defense attorneys, prosecutors, even the janitors liked her. She had a great sense of humor and didn't lord over people. Judge Levitt could be stern, if the situation warranted it, but that didn't happen often, not in her courtroom. She was always prepared, and the attorneys knew they needed to be as well."

"What about threats?"

"All the judges I know have received threats, but none of them were serious. If Judge Levitt got anything, she turned it over to Max. You should ask him about that."

"What do you know about your boss's personal life?"

At the question, Terry Wells looked away briefly before answering. "I know her husband committed suicide a couple of years ago, and she'd occasionally meet friends for dinner or drinks. She didn't talk to me about her personal life."

"What about dating? In an earlier statement, you said Judge Levitt was meeting someone after work the night she was killed. I think you referred to it as a date and said she was dressed to party."

"She was a young, single woman," commented Wells. "What would you expect?"

"Do you know any of the people Julia Levitt dated?"

"No, I have no idea."

"Did she ever mention anyone's name?"

"No, I said she was a private person. Why would she talk to me about who she was going out with?"

"You worked with her since she was named to the bench, Ms. Wells. I find it hard to believe you've never overheard a private conversation or listened in on gossip about Judge Levitt's personal life. That's not how offices work."

"You've never worked in a courthouse, detective. What goes on here stays here. I'm not going to discuss the judge's personal life, and I'm not going to repeat gossip. Is there anything else I can do for you? If not, I have a hair appointment, and if I don't leave now, I'm going to miss it."

"We're through for now, but I'd ask you extend me a professional courtesy. The dead have no secrets and what you tell me will remain confidential. You have my word on it."

"I'm sure you believe that Detective Morgan, but I've been around long enough to know how the police operate. You share what you learn with someone else, maybe your boss for instance, and if there's anything salacious, it gets leaked, and reputations are ruined. I won't be a party to it."

She stood abruptly and walked out of the room never looking back.

"What are you hiding, Ms. Wells?" Emily asked to the now empty room.

***

Max Smith was a giant of a man who looked as if he'd been chiseled from a single piece of black onyx. He moved like a boxer confidently striding into the room. His eyes took in everything all at once before finally settling on Emily.

"Have a seat, this shouldn't take long," she said gesturing at the chair to her right.

"I saw Terry stalk out of here," replied Max Smith in a rich bass tone that resonated from someplace deep in his chest. "Did she give you that rooster shit about men strutting around? She's crazy, I don't know why the judge kept her on the job."

"What does that mean?" asked Emily.

"Julia Levitt replaced Judge Simpson after his stroke. He had Terry all but fired, but she didn't submit his documentation to personnel."

"Do you know why?"

"I think she wanted to give Terry a break and judge her performance for herself. Everyone knew Judge Simpson was a hard man to work for."

"Since Terry is still here, I'm assuming everything worked out," Emily said encouraging Max Smith to keep talking.

"I guess, but lately there's been a lot of tension around here. I was told to let the judge know when Terry talked to a certain defense attorney."

"Who's the attorney, and do you know why she was concerned?"

"His name is Sol Hammersham, and he's a regular in the judge's courtroom. The rumor on the street is he was trying to dig up dirt on Judge Levitt. I can't prove it, but the rumor mill around here is busy. And mostly accurate."

"And you think Terry Wells was helping him?"

"I didn't say that, but all-of-a-sudden Sol's her best friend, and he wouldn't give her the time of day before. Something changed," said the big bailiff.

"Terry told me any threats directed at the judge were funneled through you. Is that correct?"

"It is, but there was nothing serious taking place. If there had been threats, I would have alerted the police. Judge Levitt was fair, and she didn't belittle anyone, even those who deserved it. You'd get an outburst from an angry parent sometimes or an anonymous letter, but that was it. I logged every incident and the actions taken if you'd like a copy."

"I would," replied Emily. "What about men in Judge Levitt's life? She was an attractive, single woman so there had to be men."

"If there were, she didn't bring them down here," replied Max Smith. "Judge Levitt kept her business life and personal life separate."

"What about problems with other judges or law enforcement officers?"

"None that I know of," replied the big man. "I don't know of a single person who didn't like the judge, except maybe Sol Hammersham, and that's because she didn't let him get away with his bullshit in her court."

"Thanks for your help, Max. If you think of anything else, here's my business card," said Emily standing to end the interview.

"I know it's not possible, but if you catch this sonofabitch, I'd love ten minutes alone with him. He killed a fine person, and she didn't deserve it."

"No, she didn't, but don't worry, we're going to catch him, Max. You can count on it."

Walking out of the courthouse, Emily got a call from Marcy.

"Hey, we found the judge's car at the clubhouse in Overton Park. John wants you to meet him there."

"I just finished interviews with Levitt's court clerk and her bailiff," commented Emily. "I'll grab a sandwich at a burger joint on the way. You and I still need to talk about our little meeting at the Windjammer on my day off. I'm still pissed about it."

"Emily, I didn't know you'd requested a day off, but I have to tell you that issue with the buttons on your blouse was priceless. You should have seen your face when I mentioned it, and John couldn't look away fast enough," she said laughing. "I thought he was going to injure himself. I get it; I'm on your shit list, and you're plotting your revenge.

Whatever it is, it won't be as good as watching the two of you. I gotta go."

***

Two crime scene technicians were processing the car when Greyson arrived; he watched them from a distance. What they were doing was important, and they didn't need his help to do it. Emily parked next to his gray, unmarked Dodge Charger ten minutes later.

"Anything?" she asked staring toward the Mercedes.

"Not yet, but I just got here."

"I didn't know if you'd had anything to eat. I stopped at Dyer's," she said walking over and handing him a large brown paper bag and big soft drink. "When did they find the car?"

"About an hour ago," responded Greyson looking in the bag. "Thanks for the burger and fries. I didn't know it, but I just realized I'm starving."

Neither said much while Greyson dug into his food. When he finished, they spent the next half hour comparing the interviews they'd conducted that morning.

"The brother sounds like a nut," said Emily after listening to Greyson's recap. "Did you know about him and the problems he caused for the judge?"

"No, and Julia never said a word. What's your take on Terry Wells and the lawyer? What's his name again?"

"I made a few calls before I got here," explained Emily. "The name on his license is Solomon Hammersham, and he earned his degree from a defunct law school in California. My take is he was paying the judge's court clerk for dirt on her. Why, I don't know, but I'm going to find out. Have you seen his commercials? There're terrible."

"No, I don't watch a lot of TV," said Greyson.

"It's a rip-off from the old Perry Mason series with Hammersham sitting in a courtroom studying a stack of legal documents. An offscreen announcer asks – *Are you having legal problems? If so, you need Sol 'The Hammer' Hammersham. A Man of the People.* It ends when a judge strikes his desk with a hammer instead of a gavel and yells – *Not guilty!*"

"God, that does sound awful," replied Greyson shaking his head. "So, what's next?"

"I go back to Terry Wells and try to break her. Tell her that Judge Levitt had built a case to have her terminated for passing classified information to an unnamed defense attorney. She talks or I'll take the file to Personnel. If I get her, then I go after The Hammer and see what he knows. My gut tells me Judge Levitt's courtroom was not a happy one."

Before Greyson could ask more questions, one of the techs waved him over.

"This is an odd one, detective," the tech said in greeting. "Judge Levitt's key fob was left in the console and that almost never happens. We also found a card on the dashboard. I don't have a clue about it."

"Did it have an orchid and snake on one side?" asked Greyson fearing the worse.

"How did you know? I've never seen anything like it."

"I found something similar at the judge's house," responded the detective. "Was there a message on it?"

"No, it was blank."

"Make sure you take it directly to MK Isoke; he has the others," ordered Greyson. "Did you find anything else?"

"Some fingerprints and what I believe is cigarette ash. Do you know if Judge Levitt smoked?"

"She didn't, and she didn't let anyone smoke in her car," came the reply.

"Okay, thanks, detective. We're out of here; the judge's car will be towed to our shop. If we find anything significant, I'll let you know."

"What the hell?" cried Emily after the two crime scene technicians had gone. "The car was dumped in walking distance to the judge's house. Is this guy taunting us?"

"That and I don't believe he's finished," mused Greyson. "I can't explain it, but there's more at play here."

"One of your famous Greyson's hunches?" asked Emily.

"Probably" said Greyson, "and twenty years of working homicides.

The killer is screaming for attention and making a statement. I wouldn't be surprised if whoever did this didn't have some attachment to Mt. Moriah. It means something."

43

DAVID BARNETT

Thom's Place was practically empty except for a few old men seated along a cigarette-scarred bar drinking beer and talking in hushed tones. No one except the bartender moved when she let the door slam. The barkeep knew a cop when she saw one.

"Officer, my name is Marge Davis, and I own this place. What can I do for you?"

"I thought this was Thom's Place. Where's Thom McGraw?" asked Marcy. "His name is on the beer license."

"Oh," stuttered Davis caught off guard. "I guess I haven't gotten around to applying for it. It's just an oversight."

"A beer license isn't tied to the location; it's tied to the owner. You did know that didn't you? How long have you owned Thom's Place - don't lie to me because I'm going to check."

"Almost two years," came a meek reply. "Thom McGraw was my uncle, and I started running the place when he got sick. He left it to me in his will. I swear to God I'll apply for a new license first thing in the morning. Please don't shut me down; I'm barely keeping above water as it is."

"Okay, I'm going to cut you a break and look the other way. My name is Marcy Thomas, and I'm a homicide detective with MPD. I want you to look at a picture and see if you can identify the man. Can you do that?"

"I guess so," replied Davis.

Holding up a picture of Barnett, she asked, "Do you know him?"

Davis nodded.

When was the last time he was in your bar? I know he's a regular."

"Is David in trouble?" asked Davis, her eyes getting large. "Did he kill that judge?"

"Just answer my question," responded Marcy patiently. "When was he in your bar last?"

"Late Friday night, and he was with a dancer from Danny's. I had to drag her ass off a table to keep her from stripping. To make matters worse, the idiots in here were throwing dollar bills at the bitch trying to egg her on. I could have been shut down if the police had walked in."

"Why did you ask me if Barnett killed Judge Levitt?"

Davis looked almost pained, like she didn't want to answer. Eventually she said, "I don't want to get involved. That man scares me."

"You don't have anything to worry about," replied Marcy in a softer tone. "You let me handle him. Talk to me, Marge."

Davis said nothing for several seconds, trying to decide what to do.

"I'm not going away. You can answer my questions here or downtown. It's your choice."

"Okay, okay," replied the bar owner finally. "If I get killed, it's on you."

When Marcy didn't react, Davis continued. "Barnett's been badmouthing the judge for months telling everyone she'd pay for fucking up his life. A week before the murder, I overheard him tell Crazy Craig, one of our regulars, to watch the papers before staggering out the door. He was drunk and worked up, but I didn't think he'd do anything. That's all I know, I promise."

"Is Crazy Craig in here now?" asked the detective.

"No, he's at work. I won't see him until about six o'clock."

"Okay, thanks for your help, Marge. Don't say anything to anyone about our conversation. I'll see you later this afternoon."

"You're coming back?" asked Davis in a panic. "Barnett will know it's me who squealed on him. Oh, my god, I'm a dead woman."

"Calm down," replied Marcy. "He won't know because I'm going to set the table for you."

"What do you mean?" asked the bar owner.

"Don't bullshit me!" yelled Marcy, suddenly getting in Davis's face. "I know you're lying your ass off, and when I prove it, you're mine. Think about what I said, I'll be back later."

Marcy couldn't help but smile as she drove away. That acting job was an old trick to protect informants, and this bunch of professional drunks and underachievers would eat it up. Davis wasn't a dummy; she could manage this group on her worst day. One down and two to go. Thom's Place had been a hit. Now, she was off to the Robber Baron and Danny's. There was no rest for the weary she thought while laughing. She really loved this part of her job.

***

The Robber Baron had at one time been a bank, but that had been in better times for it and the neighborhood. Now it was a staging ground for drug deals and prostitution.

"Who would come to a place like this?" she whispered under her breath but knew the answer before she asked it. Men and women on the outskirts of the law and those who had lost their way. It made her sad, but it was the reality of life, especially in an old river city like Memphis. If Thom's Place had been dark and depressing, the Robber Baron was another story. It was hopping with people, bright colors, and loud music blaring from gigantic speakers hanging from the ceiling. Fifty heads turned to stare when the door closed behind Marcy, cutting off her only way out. That's also when the music stopped.

The bartender, a huge man with a shaved head and tattoos covering every exposed part of his body, signaled for her to come his way. When she was close, he said in a voice loud enough for everyone to hear. "You don't belong here, girly. That badge won't protect you from this bunch. Now get the fuck out!"

Smiling Marcy leaned in close and whispered, "Come with me, asshole. I want you to meet Brutus and Vice. Their handlers would love to turn them loose in this dump."

When he didn't respond quickly enough, she grabbed and twisted his arm behind his back guiding him through the front door and out into the parking lot. Two Belgium Malinois greeted him, their eyes laser-focused on the struggling man.

"Wait a minute, wait a minute," he pleaded with real fear in his cries. "I didn't mean anything. I don't want trouble."

"You get one opportunity at this. What's your name?"

"Jesse," he replied, never taking his eyes off the dogs.

"Okay, Jesse, I'm going to show you a picture, and you're going to tell me if you know the person or not. Nod if you understand me."

"No problem," he said his head bobbing up and down.

Marcy released his arm and took Barnett's DMV picture out of her hip pocket and handed it to the bartender.

"Do you know him?"

"His name is David Barnett, he's a regular," came the nervous reply.

"Did you see him Friday night and don't lie to me. I'll know it if you do."

"He was here about four or four-thirty," said Jesse turning to look at Marcy. "He came in right before the shift change at five."

"Did he have anyone with him?"

"No, he was alone. What's going on, what's David done?"

"Has he ever mentioned Julia Levitt?"

"Oh, man, did he kill that judge? I wondered about that when I saw the news the next morning."

"Why do you say that?" asked Marcy.

"He hated that woman, blamed her for his divorce. I warned him several times to let it go, but he couldn't do it. It was bad."

"How long was he here?"

"I don't know, a couple of hours. I heard him say something about going to Danny's. He likes the strips clubs."

"What else can you tell me about Barnett?"

"He was in here a few days after the news story, you know the one about the murder, and he was one happy dude. Bought a round of drinks for the house."

"Okay Jesse, you're going to write down everything you told me and give it to Officer Kelso. After you finish, you can go. One warning, if Barnett comes in here don't tell him we talked. Do you understand?"

"Yes, ma'am," he replied nodding. "I never liked that guy anyway."

***

Danny's was busy, even though the weekend was several days away. Its revolving neon sign out front flashed *Hot Girls – Hot Times – Hot Damn.* The newly paved parking lot was filled with a mix of pickup trucks, motorcycles, beaters and a variety of SUVs. Marcy grabbed her blazer from the back seat, slipped it on, and hung her badge from the front pocket. She wasn't anticipating trouble, but she was prepared for it if it showed up. A bouncer at the front door smiled and said, "Good evening, ma'am, can I help you?"

His greeting sounded normal enough even though Marcy felt he'd undressed her as she approached, his stare lingering longer than necessary on certain parts of her anatomy.

"Where's your boss?" she asked.

"Is there a problem?"

"No, not if you take me to whoever runs this place."

"Gotcha, give me a minute," he replied. "I'll be right back."

"That's okay, why don't I come with you? I've never been inside a place like this," responded Marcy. "It could be an educational experience."

"Suit yourself," he said with a shrug. "We have an amateur contest every Wednesday night at ten."

"Yeah, that's never going to happen," laughed Marcy, her eyes dancing. "Let's go."

The layout inside was uncomplicated and efficient; a DJ on one wall and three raised platforms placed strategically around the room. Opposite the DJ a long bar had been constructed where half-naked servers picked up drinks, mostly beer, and rushed them to tables surrounding the entertainment. The on-stage women swirled and clung to stripper poles, dollars bills dangling from garter belts and bikini bottoms. The women's dressing room and Danny's management offices were located on the second floor peering down on the activities below. In total, Marcy counted ten bouncers on the main floor alone all in black short-sleeved T-shirts with a company logo on the front and *BOUNCER* spelled out in block letters on the back.

"You guys take security seriously," she said, nodding at a lethal-looking man bent over a table talking to four guys who looked like they were being scolded by their professor.

"We have to," came the response. "Loud music, naked women and an abundance of alcohol can make for a volatile situation. Mac makes sure we stop trouble before it begins. That means having enough security to clear the place if we have to take things to the next level."

"Has that happened before?" asked Marcy interested in his answer.

"Only once since I've been here. A biker gang tried to break up the place. That didn't happen. Everyone Mac hires is a badass, and she makes sure we stay in shape. A gym membership and self-defense classes are perks of the job. You go or you don't work, and she checks."

"Mac is a woman?"

"Oh, yeah, wait until you meet her," replied Bobby, the bouncer. "Mac is a force of nature."

Force of nature didn't begin to describe Mackinzie Owens. Statuesque was a better term. She reminded Marcy of a picture she'd seen years ago of Amazon women warriors in a book on Greek mythology. Mac was dressed stylishly in tailored black slacks, three- inches heels, and a form fitting white blouse highlighted with a magnificent diamond dangling from a gold chain.

"Detective, what can we do for you?" Mac said to Marcy. "I know you didn't come here for the entertainment," she said with an amused smile.

"I'm confused, where's the previous owner? Where's Danny?" asked Marcy.

"Probably dead or in jail," came a light-hearted response. "Danny Kincaid hasn't been around for more than two decades. I'm the fifth person to own Danny's since it opened in 1952."

"1952?"

"Most people don't know the history of Danny's," replied Mac. "It's always been a little wild and unconventional. I bought it about three years ago."

"It looks like you've done well for yourself," responded the detective, her disapproval obvious.

"You don't like adult entertainment?" asked Mac as she leaned against her desk.

"This isn't entertainment. It's drugs and prostitution, exploitation, and abuse. Can you honestly tell me the women working here aren't being used?"

"It's a job, detective. Maybe the only one they can find. Most of the ladies at Danny's come to us abused, hooked on something, either drugs or alcohol, and without family or friends. If they're willing to follow my set of simple rules, they can stay and make lives for themselves. It may not be the life you would choose, but it's a life where they are safe, where they can save their money, and get an education. I don't allow drug users, prostitutes, or thieves at Danny's. My ladies are drug tested, are taught how to manage their money, and we help them find a safe place to live. If they break the rules, even once, they are out of here. I'd advise you to talk with Stu Ketchum in Vice or Father Pat at St Mary's. They can enlighten you on what we're trying to accomplish here. Now, what can I do for you?"

Marcy opened a portfolio and removed a picture handing it to the strip club's proprietor.

"Do you know this man?"

"His name is David Barnett," came a flat response. "He's in here a lot."

"When was the last time you saw him?" asked Marcy.

"I don't know, I haven't been on the floor lately. Bobby, look at this picture and tell me when David was in here last."

The muscled young man in the black T-shirt walked over and looked at the photo.

"I'd have to check our security tapes for an exact time, detective," he replied looking up, "but I'd guess Friday night between eight and nine o'clock."

"Did he have anyone with him?" asked Marcy.

"He did; one of our former employees. Her name is Anna Leigh Styles."

"What did he do?" asked Mac.

"I can't say for now," came Marcy's quick answer.

"I didn't get your name or department," stated the strip club owner now curious.

"My name is Marcy Thomas, and I'm a homicide detective."

"Interesting," remarked Owens.

THE MAN FROM ST PETERSBURG

It was after five when Horace walked out of the terminal in search of Greyson. He'd called him after his flight had landed and arranged to be picked up outside of baggage claims. Just as he was about to redial Greyson's number, a car horn grabbed his attention. He looked up to see his friend's Honda ease around a Ford F150 that had blocked two lanes of traffic.

"Where have you been?" asked Greyson as he hugged his old friend. "I had to circle the terminal three times to avoid getting a ticket."

"I thought flying into Memphis on Sunday would be a breeze, but every seat was taken. I appreciate the first-class ticket, by the way. How did you manage that?"

"I have connections," smiled Greyson. "Besides, what Director Edwards doesn't know won't hurt him."

"John, I can give you ninety days, but I need to go home after that. Why do you need me here? You've got more years in homicide than I do, and you're now chief of detectives."

"Let's get something to eat," responded Greyson looking at the traffic jam behind him. "I'll explain everything then."

As they were leaving the terminal, Greyson asked, "Where do you want to go?"

"How about Earnestine & Hazel's," replied Horace as he pushed his seat back as far as it would go. "Did you know that place is haunted?

It started out as a church in the late 1800s, then became a pharmacy, jazz joint, and brothel before it became a bar. There are a lot of dead spirits in that building. One night I'd ordered a burger and beer when I heard footsteps upstairs and then a piano started playing. I asked the bartender who was on the second floor, and he said no one. He said it was the ghost. I laughed and walked upstairs. John, as God is my witness, nobody was in that room just the piano. I could smell something sweet in the air like an overripe melon. I'm telling you it was a spirit."

All Greyson could think to say was, "Uh-huh," as he pulled away from the curb.

"Okay, talk, what's going on?" asked Horace, changing the subject. "Why am I here?"

"Two reasons…maybe three," came the answer. "One I'm swamped. I have twenty-three homicide detectives I'm responsible for, and we've been approved to add twelve more in the next three months. Two is I can't let Julia's murder go. I'm personally involved, and before you say anything, I know I should step away. I can't. Third is I'm thinking about stepping down after this case is over. I never wanted to be chief of detectives. Hell, I'm an investigator not a fucking manager. I hate my job, and Julia's death is giving me second thoughts about what I'm doing with my career."

"What do you need from me exactly?"

"A sounding board and another set of eyes," came the answer. "Horace, the director is letting me handle Julia's murder my way, but there are limits. Other cases can't suffer from my inattention. I play second fiddle to Marcy, and she runs the investigation. There are twelve new detectives coming onboard that start training in the next twelve weeks. That means they get paired up with an experienced investigator, but someone has to monitor their progress. I can't run down leads and spend all my time in the office. You know this job better than anyone I know. Do what you do best and be a second set of eyes for me. In other words, tell me if I'm screwing up."

Horace didn't say anything for several long seconds.

"Okay, John, I'll do what I can, but I'm not going to look the other way if you fuck up. I'm going to call it as I see it, and I expect you to listen. You don't have to do what I recommend, but I walk when you stop hearing what I say. Is it a deal?"

Greyson smiled and reached over to shake hands with a man he'd known and respected for twenty-five years. There was no person on the planet he trusted more than Horace Mann.

***

They ended the evening in Greyson's backyard sipping Fighting Cock bourbon and reminiscing about old friends and cold cases. A roaring fire, the flames reaching for the heavens, set an introspective mood for a good end to the day.

"Were you bullshitting me about the ghosts at Earnestine & Hazel's?" asked Greyson as he tossed the last few ice cubes from his glass into the fire. He was ready to go to bed. Blue had gone long ago.

"Maybe a little," snickered Horace, "but that shit about the piano is true."

"I'm going in; we have a quick debrief at seven."

"I have a suggestion about that," commented the old homicide cop as he poured another two fingers of the golden-brown elixir into his glass. "Sit down and let me tell you what I've been doing since I retired."

"It's almost midnight, so make it quick."

"I've been doing consulting work since I left MPD," said Horace. "It's part-time. I pick when I want to work and where I want to go. A company out of the UK contacted me about a year ago, and they do everything from setting up the consultation, providing support, travel accommodations …they quite literally do everything. What I do is leverage my thirty plus years of experience in law enforcement by looking at old cases and reviewing what went right and wrong, I cover a list of contacts and resources at organizations such as the FBI and Interpol, go over policy and procedures, and, of course, I toss in a few war stories to add flavor to the stew. My company has a new interactive program called Cyclops which I think you could use. You, as the originator, would designate who has access to enter and read case notes and forensic reports. Your team's reporting, logging, and activities gets compiled using artificial intelligence. In seconds everyone on your team is updated in real time. John, it's amazing, and I think I can get my boss to approve its use for free on a trial basis. All Director Edwards would have to do is make the request. We're looking for test cases."

"Can you give me a demonstration, not tonight, but maybe tomorrow?"

"Absolutely," replied Horace.

"I'm going to bed," stated Greyson after a big yawn. "Don't stay up too long, we have a busy day tomorrow. Everyone is looking forward to seeing you, especially your old partner."

"How's Emily doing?"

"She's one of the best investigators I've got," came the reply. "If I step down, I'm going to recommend her or Marcy take my place."

"A woman chief of detectives?" mused Horace. "That'll be a first, but I think it's about time."

***

His friend looked good after retiring and moving to Florida. He'd lost weight, and the stress lines around his eyes were gone. Maybe, Greyson thought quietly, he should do the same. After all, he'd seen enough death and destruction to last a dozen lifetimes. Horace had offered to help him get settled, and his daughter lived somewhere in Pinellas County. Was a reconciliation even possible he wondered? He hadn't talked to Lacinda and her younger brother James since the funeral and then not much had been said. It was his fault. Working too much - and for a time, drinking too much - had done nothing to endear him to his children. Sue had been the nurturer, not him. Always there to kiss a scrape or soothe a disappointment, she'd held the family together in an unbreakable bond, and in an instant that bond was broken, and she was gone. He missed her every day. Missed her singing in the garden, her rushing in to tell him the latest gossip, the gentle way she'd kiss him and hold him tight. The night she died, a part of him died, too. Not for the first time, he wondered why she had to go first. Why couldn't it have been him? He was In a reflective mood when Horace walked into the kitchen in his boxers and a T-shirt.

"Coffee made yet?" he asked. "John, I miss our nights together, my friend. I've got a little headache this morning, but nothing a handful of aspirin won't fix."

"Check the medicine cabinet," responded Greyson. "I thought we'd run around the corner to Barksdale's for breakfast. Is that okay with you?"

"Country ham and eggs with hash browns and biscuits, oh yeah, sounds like a slice of heaven. Give me thirty minutes to shower and shave."

***

The restaurant had both changed and stayed the same. New upholstery in the booths and chairs, a new kitchen and bathrooms, but the food was the same…delicious. They were getting their third cup of coffee when Emily walked in and rushed to their table.

"God, Horace, you look good," she squealed happily. "This is a treat."

"Hey, kid," he replied hugging her tight. "It's good to see you, too. Join us."

He couldn't help himself; Horace had called her before stepping into the shower. Horace Mann had been a pit bull on the force, and not many of his partners lasted long with his rambling demeanor and white-hot temper. Emily was the exception. They had the second highest case closure rate in the department, behind only Greyson and Alonzo Walker.

"How long are you here?" she asked.

"I told John I'd give him ninety days, then I'll go home again to my boat and country club."

Turning to Greyson, she said, "Isoke wants you to call him. He wouldn't tell me why."

"Hopefully he got something on the cards I found in Julia's house. Excuse me, I need to make a call," he said as he got up and walked outside.

"How's he doing?" asked Horace looking at his protégé. "Greyson looks like shit."

"It's got him rattled. I knew he and Judge Levitt were friends, but I've never seen Greyson so distracted. It's unsettling, and it has Marcy on alert."

"Where are we in the investigation?"

"At the beginning," came the reply. "We're gathering suspects and information but nowhere close to anything that's solid. Greyson thinks there'll be more murders."

"Don't bet against him," warned Horace. "He has some inner sense or connection to the spirit world that's more right than wrong."

Returning to their table, Greyson was animated.

"Emily, tell Marcy I won't be at the meeting this morning, I'll get with her later. Horace, you go with Emily. She'll make sure you have everything we have on Julia's murder. I hope to god you see something that we missed because we're swinging at air right now."

THE FIRST BREAK

MK Isoke was in his office glued to a computer screen when Greyson arrived. Isoke's desk was spotless everything in its place. That didn't surprise Greyson, as the scientist was known as a stickler for organization. Maybe that's why he'd advanced so quickly in the department; he was only twenty-six.

"Detective Greyson," he said standing. "As I said when you called, I could have emailed you my results on Judge Levitt's jewelry box."

"You got me out of a meeting," said the smiling detective. "I owe you one. What did you find, MK?"

"The jewelry box was purchased at Bardo's Fine Jewelry in New York City, but you know that. What you didn't know is it was one of fifty bought at the same time."

"Who was the purchaser?" asked Greyson hopeful for a break in the case.

"Oddly enough, Mr. Bardo didn't know."

"How is that possible?" asked the puzzled detective. "Even purchases made online require a name and a shipping address. What form of payment was used?"

"A wire transfer from a bank in Switzerland," said Isoke looking at his notes.

"How was the order placed?"

"By phone," said the crime scene specialist. "Mr. Bardo took a call from a woman, who he said had a slight accent, and she wanted to place an order for fifty jewelry boxes. He said she knew exactly what she wanted, which he thought was strange. He doesn't advertise online; he's strictly word of mouth. They agreed upon a price, and he received a wire transfer for the exact amount the next day, over forty-two thousand dollars."

"Who picked up the order? Or was it shipped?"

"You're not going to like my answer," replied Isoke calmly. "A man walked into Bardo's two weeks after the order was placed and identified himself as John Smith. He had the order number and a copy of the wire transfer. Mr. Bardo checked his identification, had him sign for the shipment, and helped him carry the packages to a town car parked outside his store."

"Damn it to hell," swore Greyson, "I'd hoped for something concrete. This shit is driving me crazy."

"I might have something for you on the stationery, detective," commented Isoke quickly. "The paper was produced in Japan, and there are only three distributors in the U.S. One of them is in New York City, another in Los Angeles, and the third in Nashville. I put together a list for you, including the phone number for Bardo's Fine Jewelry in New York City," he said, handing Greyson a folded piece of paper.

"That's a start," replied Greyson gruffly. "What about the notes. What can you tell me about them?"

"There were eleven cards signed into the crime lab, all written by different people. We think nine were from men, and two from women. The twelfth card found in Judge Levitt's abandoned car likely came from the same batch, but as you know, it was blank. I've been thinking," said Isoke in a cautious tone. "I wonder if Judge Levitt wasn't involved in some sort of sex club."

"What do you mean?" asked Greyson calmly. He'd given up the pretext of trying to analyze his friend's behavior. He'd known Julia was a complex woman; it was one of the things that had drawn him to her, but he'd discovered a side she'd kept hidden. A side that had him searching frantically for answers.

"The figure on the cards, an orchid ensnarled in the coils of a snake," explained Isoke. "In some cultures, the orchid is a symbol of beauty and femineity, the snake forbidden, sexual and masculine. Think of the serpent in the Garden of Eden," he continued. "It may be nothing, but the figures coupled with the pornographic messages from multiple partners sounds like something organized."

"Organized?"

"A place that matches men and women by sexual predilection and arranges for hook-ups. That could explain the numbers and letters on the front of the cards you found. If I remember correctly, there was a scandal several years ago where a company matched married men and women who would meet for casual sex. No commitment, no getting to know you, just sex. I think you're looking at something like that in this case, detective."

"Great, just great!" said an exasperated Greyson. "My suspect list just got a whole lot bigger. If you find anything else, let me know."

***

It was a break thought Greyson. A small one, but a break, nevertheless. The question was what next. One of the paper distributors was based in New York, the same city as Bardo's Fine Jewelry. To borrow from an old English idiom, travel to the Big Apple would be equivalent to killing two birds with one stone, but there was a problem with that idea. The budget was tight enough; a spending freeze was in place until the new fiscal year. Director Edwards would be hard-pressed to approve it. He thought for a moment about contacting the FBI, but just as quickly, discounted that idea. Once they got involved, it was impossible to get them to stand down and let the local police do its job. Walking to his car, he felt adrift. Julia's funeral was tomorrow, and he'd only scratched the surface on finding her killer. She deserved better he thought.

SAYING GOODBYE

The church was packed, and he'd been asked to say a few words. On a normal day, that wouldn't have bothered Greyson, but today was anything but normal. Flashbacks from better times kept creeping into his psyche. Julia's graduation from law school when he'd offered to take her to dinner but instead, they'd stopped at Krystal's, got an enormous bag of burgers and fries, and sat in Overton Park talking about life and what was to come. Her wedding to Gene Levitt when she'd asked him to walk her down the aisle, or the many times they cooked together in her kitchen her drinking wine and him bourbon. The laughs, pranks, just times spent together brought both smiles and tears.

Greyson saw that Dr. Vivian Gales was there, the dean of the law school, plus a dozen judges and an assortment of co-workers, but few friends. In that regard, she and Greyson were much the same. Maybe that's why it hurt so much that she was gone. When you have only a few loved ones, losing even one makes more of a hole in your life. The burial was in Elmwood Cemetery, the final resting place of generals, senators, madams and mayors. Julia would join the other 75,000 souls interred in the lush, park-like setting. One notable person who chose not to attend was Emilio Levitt.

"I'm sorry, detective," his sister had commented. "Emilio is difficult on a good day, and he didn't care for Julia. He thinks she turned Gene against him. He refused to see how good she was for him; how happy she made him."

"You mentioned knowing someone who wanted Julia dead," responded Greyson. "Is that person your brother?"

Gales nodded while dabbing tissue at the falling tears.

"Emilio is lost without his brother, and I think he could be violent. I wouldn't have thought that until recently and after our last conversation."

"What did you talk about?" asked the detective.

"Not now let's get through today first," came the response from Emilio's older sister. "What if we meet tomorrow for lunch? I'll tell you everything then and why I believe Emilio could be involved in Julia's murder."

***

It was a short service as Julia had directed thanks to her attorney, Archibald McCutchen. He'd stopped Greyson in the parking lot before everyone had arrived.

"We need to talk after the service," he said gripping the detective's arm. "Meet me at the bar on the ground floor in the Sterick Building. I need a drink after this is over."

"What's this about?"

"Just meet me, and I'll explain then," came a hurried response as he rushed away.

Julia had been very specific in what she wanted: a closed casket ceremony with the El Malei Rachamim prayer recited by her rabbi to end her Kevurah or burial. Afterward, a small reception had been arranged for her small circle of friends and her co-workers. Greyson didn't go. Instead, he walked the grounds of the manicured cemetery looking at old headstones and reflecting on what could have been. Julia had been at the height of her influence, and she would have made a difference in a city known for its poverty and perseverance. What had happened to his friend offended him and someone had to pay. That was his mindset as he walked into the Queen of Memphis Lounge on the ground floor of the Sterick Building to meet Archibald McCutchen at ten forty-five in the morning. The place opened at noon, but he watched as the attorney, his back turned to him, slammed a shot of something he suspected was scotch and then poured himself another one.

"It's a little early for that," remarked Greyson as he let the door close behind him.

"I'm going to get drunk, and then go home and fall in bed," came the attorney's remark. This obviously was not his first drink. "I have to tell you something first. Actually two things."

"What are they?"

"Emilio Levitt had something to do with Julia's murder."

"What else?" asked Greyson.

"I think I loved Julia from the moment I met her."

"Why do you believe her brother-in-law was involved? Do you have anything specific to go on?"

"The sonofabitch called me at the funeral home and wanted to know when he could move into Julia's house. He plans to contest the will, just as he tried to do when Gene died. He has motive and means. I want you to nail the bastard, Greyson."

"Let me call someone to take you home, Mr. McCutchen. We can discuss this again after you've had time to collect your thoughts."

"Talk to Vivian," he said with a slight slur. "She was there when I talked to the bastard, and she was furious with her brother. She thinks he did it, too. Ask her, goddamnit!"

***

Marcy was with him when he pulled into the Peabody Hotel's parking lot opting for valet parking.

"Aren't we being fancy?" commented his companion with a short laugh. "Where are we meeting Dr. Gales?"

"At the fountain, and then we're walking across the street for lunch."

"Do you know what she looks like?"

"Yes, I met her at the funeral," said Greyson. "Hurry up or we're going to be late."

"I'm sorry I couldn't make it; I had to sit for a last-minute deposition for a sleezy shyster who's going to get killed in court. If he was smart, he'd try to cut a deal."

"You didn't miss much," replied Greyson as he opened the door for his partner. "Julia wanted to keep it simple, and she got her wish."

Dr. Gales seemed irritated when they finally located her near the gift shop. In her mid-to-late seventies, she was well dressed, looked fit, and seemed intelligent.

"I'm sorry I must have misunderstood," apologized Greyson. "I thought we were meeting near the fountain."

"No, no, it's not you," came the doctor's reply. "It's my brother, Emilio. He's an insufferable ass."

"Doctor, this is my partner, Marcy Thomas. She's directing the investigation into your sisters-in-law's homicide."

Quick appraising eyes shifted to the woman detective standing to Greyson's left. After an awkward moment, Gales reached out to shake Marcy's hand.

"I hope you're good at your job, young lady," she commented while holding Marcy's stare. "Whoever killed Julia needs to be punished."

"I am," came the simple two-word reply. "There are few better."

That brought a smile to Gales's lips.

"There's an excellent restaurant across the street, and I know the manager," said Greyson. "We can talk undisturbed."

"Good," replied Gales. "I've got a lot to tell you."

***

It was busy, but they were seated at a table away from the crowd. After their drink order had been taken, Marcy asked, "Dr. Gales, how long will you be in Memphis and what's to be done with Judge Levitt's estate?"

"I'd intended to leave for Nashville tomorrow, but after talking with my brother, that's not going to happen. I don't know how long I'll be here."

"What's your brother have to do with you going home?" asked Greyson.

64

She laughed before answering. "Everything, detective. Emilio told me he plans to move into Julia's house this week, and I told him to go to hell. It's not going to happen."

"Why would he do that?" asked Marcy frowning. "The date for a reading of the will hasn't been scheduled."

"I need to give you a little family history," said Gales with a long sigh. "Maybe that will help. We were raised in what is now Julia's house, even though it looked much different then. My father bought it in 1945 before he married mom and at the end of World War II. The previous owner had been a pilot shot down over Germany the previous year and didn't return home. Dad married my mother in 1948; she was his second wife and a beauty queen. I was born in 1952, and the boys came along in 1962. As I've told Greyson, my father died in a plane crash in New Mexico. I was in college at the time, and I'd never contemplated returning to Memphis. My childhood was not the best, and I wanted to get as far away from it as possible. That left only the boys and my mother. Gene was always the dominate one and my mom's favorite. She struggled for a few years with alcohol and pills but finally found her balance. Gene and Emilio grew up and went away to college, and life moved on. When mother died, the estate was split three ways with one exception. Gene got the family home, and that was okay with me and Emilio – until Julia came along. From the start my brother hated our sister-in-law. I think he looked at her as an interloper, someone who had broken that special bond he had with his brother. Things got so bad, Gene had to finally step-in and put a stop to the attacks on his wife. Emilio didn't like it, but he would do anything for his older brother, so he toned it down. That didn't mean the hate vanished, it didn't, but he wasn't so upfront with it. Julia made repeated efforts to mend fences and befriend her brother-in-law, but nothing worked. It was like a truce had been signed, and the war was on again when Gene committed suicide. The long reply to your question, my brother believes the house should belong to him."

"Did Emilio blame Julia for your brother's death?" asked Marcy.

"Blame her? He wanted to have her arrested for murder. I tried to talk to Emilio, tried to get him to seek help, but he cut me off, too. It was him against the world, and he was determined to avenge his brother's death."

"You think he killed Julia," said Greyson as a statement of fact.

Instead of answering him, Dr. Gales nodded as her eyes filled with tears.

"Why were you upset a moment ago?" asked Marcy. "Did you talk to Emilio before we arrived?"

"He called and told me to get out of his house, or he'd throw me out," replied the doctor. "His house! Can you fucking believe it? Julia hasn't been in the ground twenty-four hours. When I tried to reason with him, he threatened me."

"What did he say?" Greyson asked shifting to his cop voice, "and be as specific as possible."

"He asked if I wanted to end up like Julia. It pissed me off, and I told him to go fuck himself. If he wants a good fight, I can give it to him. I'm moving into Julia's house tonight and staying until the will is finalized."

"That's enough to bring him in for questioning," said Marcy her voice low and serious.

"Maybe," said Greyson. "It's your call."

"Dr. Gales, if you believe your life is in danger, we can put extra patrols in the neighborhood, but your safety will still be at risk. I can give you the name of a private investigator that I recommend. He's not cheap, but he's very good."

Greyson didn't approve of private dicks, as he liked to call them, but he didn't say anything, not yet anyway. He especially didn't approve of Jack Murphy, the man his partner had in mind for the job.

"Give me his number, and I'll think about it," said Vivian Gales. "I do carry a gun, know how to use it, and I have a permit, but it might be a good idea to hire a professional. I don't know what Emilio is capable of anymore."

"I'd like to go back to your brother wanting Julia arrested for her husband's death," stated Greyson. "I read the coroner's report. According to colleagues Dr. Levitt had shown signs of severe depression before he took his own life, severe enough that he'd been approached by the assistant dean of the department concerned about his mental health. When the body was found, he'd left a note, and his office door had been locked from the inside. Toxicology reports indicated that he'd been off his medications long enough for only trace amounts to show in the lab results. How, in heaven's name, was Julia supposed to have killed Gene?"

"We believe what we want to believe," responded Dr. Gales. "My brother believes Julia drove Gene to kill himself by withholding her affections."

"How was their marriage?" asked Marcy.

"There was a twenty-year age difference when they married, and Gene made it clear from the onset that he wanted no children, but they made it work. If you're asking if theirs was a conventional marriage, I'd say no, but I've never seen my brother happier."

"You say it wasn't conventional, Dr. Gales. What does that mean?" asked Greyson.

"Oh, dear, this is going to sound bad, but they were two consenting adults. Sex was not important to Gene. Julia, on the other hand, was a young, vibrant woman when they wed, and Gene understood that. He and Julia worked out an arrangement."

"What kind of arrangement?" asked Marcy suspecting the answer before it was given.

"Julia could have her flings but nothing long-term, she had to practice safe sex, and never with the same man twice. I didn't like it and thought it foolish, but they didn't listen to me."

"How do you know this?" asked Marcy.

"Gene discussed it with me shortly after the wedding," responded Dr. Gales. "He loved Julia and didn't want to lose her. That meant making compromises."

"Did Emilio know about this arrangement?" asked Greyson.

"I honestly don't know. I didn't tell him."

"How did your sister-in-law do this? Meet men I mean." asked Marcy.

"The way you put it, it sounds so vulgar," replied Gales making a face. "I have no idea, detective."

***

Back in the car, Marcy looked at her partner and said, "This is screwed up, John. Our suspect list just grew exponentially."

"We need to look again at the jewelry box and what's written on those notes," said Greyson as he reached for his seatbelt. "Isoke believes Julia was involved in some variation of a swinger's club. He could be right."

"It makes as much sense as anything else," responded Marcy. "Maybe the FBI has something on the cards you discovered. I have a contact; I could make a call."

"Do it," said Greyson. "What about Emilio, are you going to bring him in for questioning?"

"Let's wait and see what else we can uncover on him. We'll only get one bite of the apple, and I don't want to screw it up by jumping the gun."

SOMEONE'S BEEN BUSY

Horace hadn't wasted time after arriving downtown at Police Head-quarters, which according to him hadn't changed one damn bit. He'd called Director Edwards and set up a working lunch. They were old friends and had ridden patrol together in North Memphis when he was a rookie. He needed to know two things: his marching orders from the top brass, and secondarily, the possibility of using his company's soft-ware in Judge Levitt's murder investigation. It would be their first live test trial, and Horace's boss was thrilled at the possibilities. The problem would be getting approval from legal and the mayor in time to find their killer. Time was never the friend of a murder investigation. Emily moved him into Alonzo's office, since Greyson's former partner was in a train-ing class, and a trip to IT got Horace access to their files and databases.

"I think you're ready to go, Horace," said Emily happily. "God, it seems like you've been gone forever."

"One year and five months, but who's counting," laughed the big former homicide detective. "Now get out of here and do your job. I have a lot of catching up to do."

Bent over Alonzo's desk, Horace studied each crime scene photo and report that was part of Julia Levitt's murder investigation. Using a red marker and yellow legal pad, he took copious notes circling any-thing that appeared vague or cryptic. It was a routine he'd developed long ago, and it worked for him, get the basics down first and tackle the intangibles later.

Emily had signed into the city's closed-circuit television system to look for the route the killer had taken in the judge's black Mercedes. Her car had vanished for hours after it turned onto old Hwy 78 before showing up in the Abe Goodman parking lot. She wanted to know where it had gone. After two hours of staring at a computer screen, her eyes dry and red she'd had enough.

Sticking her head into Alonzo's office, she said, "Horace, I'm about to go blind. I'm getting out of the office for a few hours. What are your plans for tonight?"

"I don't know," he answered without looking up. "You got my number, give me a call when you punch out."

That was just like him she thought. One hundred percent on the job and to hell with anything else.

"Marcy and Jack Murphy are grabbing a bite to eat at Alex's around six-thirty. Meet us there."

Instead of an answer, she got a wave. Whether it was an acknowledgement or not, she had no idea.

"If Greyson asks, I'm going to the courthouse to talk with Terry Wells. I want to ask her about Sol Hammersham, the attorney."

"Go, go, can't you see I'm busy," came a curt reply. "John's not going to ask, he trusts you, and I'll see you at six-thirty at Alex's. Now leave me alone so I can work."

***

The judge's court clerk was with two other women on a smoke break when Emily found her. Terry Wells frowned as she approached.

"What do you want now?"

"Let's go inside where we can talk in private," suggested the homicide cop.

"I have no secrets; you can talk in front of my friends," responded Wells in a tone that was less than friendly. "Besides, I'm on break, and I can't smoke in the building. I might offend someone."

Emily smiled and said loud enough for everyone to hear, "Sol Hammersham! Do you still want to do this here?"

"He's a friend. So what?" came Wells's dismissive retort.

"A friend?" laughed the detective, "That's rich. Terry, I think you're a backstabbing bitch who sold out your boss for a few dollars. You screwed someone who trusted you. Hammersham told us you came to him looking for money. How much did you get to betray Judge Levitt? What happened did she catch you? And you killed her to keep your job? Is that what happened?"

"Wait, wait," cried Wells now beginning to panic. "Maybe, I did pass information to Sol, but I had nothing to do with killing anyone. She'd promised to give me a raise, and the bitch reneged on it. I needed that money, and she stole it from me."

"Let's go," replied Emily without trying to hide her disgust. She'd gotten Wells's confession on body cam, and that's all she needed for the moment. She'd break her back at the station and then go after Hammersham. That's who she really wanted; he could lead her to their killer.

***

Horace had forgotten about lunch with the police director until the last minute. It hadn't taken him long to revert to old habits.

"Director, my apologies," he'd begun after reaching him by phone.

"Don't worry about it, Horace. Everybody in the mayor's office wants a piece of my ass today. Are you staying with Greyson?"

"Yes, sir," he'd answered, "John insisted."

"Good, I'll drop by later tonight after I beat off the wolves. Did you find anything interesting?"

"I don't know, I'm playing a hunch," responded the retired homicide detective. "Why was the judge's body dropped at Mt. Moriah Cemetery? One of the reports noted it was in a section that had been closed for a decade. I want to look for myself."

"Interesting," said Edwards. "Tell me about it later."

***

Mt. Moriah Cemetery was one of the biggest in the city having expanded into the suburbs after the original memorial gardens had closed due to running out of space. That was in 1963, and the new plot of ground had been developed in parcels described as Eternal Gardens. As one garden filled, the owners would develop the next new tract of real estate and sell it. As far as cemeteries went, this one was as good as any other Horace thought as he drove through the gate. He was meeting Jamie Hurtado, the man who had discovered the judge's body. Stopping his car in front of a low-slung stone and timber building that served as offices and chapel, he could see a Latino man in a side-by-side vehicle headed in his direction.

"Are you Jamie?" asked Horace, getting out of the car.

"Yes, sir," came an almost inaudible answer. "You want to see where I found the body?"

"That's right, and I want you to tell me everything you know about the cemetery."

"Hop in," said Hurtado with a weak smile. He seemed nervous to Horace his foot keeping beat with something only he could hear. "It's not far from here in the Garden of Peace," said the young man.

"Tell me about Mt Moriah and the Garden of Peace," said Horace as gently as possible. He could tell the young man was about to jump out of his skin.

"The original cemetery was in the city on Elvis Presley Boulevard, but it closed in the1970s. This is the company's second location. The Garden of Peace was one of the earlier parcels opened but I don't know the year. It was a long time ago before I started working here."

"Are the gates locked at night?" asked Horace.

"The front gates are, but sometimes we forget to lock the gate to the service road."

"So, it's fairly easy for someone to come onto the grounds after dark if they know the service gate isn't locked?"

The young man nodded.

"When you approached the body, did you see anything out of place, footprints for instance? It had been raining the night before."

"No, sir," said the cemetery worker. "Everything looked normal to me except for the body."

"Wait here," said Horace after they'd arrived at their destination. He took a stack of crime scene photos from an envelope and began comparing each photo to the area all while making his way to the grave where Julia's body had been found.

"Okay, come here," he said, motioning for the young man to join him. "Has anything unusual happened at Mt. Moriah lately? Someone hanging around that shouldn't be here or vandalism of any kind?"

"No, sir, not that I'm aware of," remarked Jamie Hurtado.

"What about new hires or someone who recently resigned or been terminated?"

"We haven't hired anyone in more than a year, but there have been several men fired the past few months. You should talk to Mr. Chester."

"Do you have the information I requested?" Horace asked.

"Yes, sir," said Hurtado, handing the detective a black folder with the name and crest of the funeral company on its cover.

"Tell me again the name of your cemetery director?" asked the former homicide detective.

"Mr. Cavendar," replied Jamie.

"Give him my thanks. We can head back to my car now; you've been a big help."

***

Horace parked his car on the street and slowly made his way up the driveway while keying notes into an iPad. At the top of the hill, he flipped it around and began to take pictures.

"This is private property," yelled Vivian Gales in a steely tone. "I'd advise you to get in your car and leave."

When he turned, the former detective noticed a woman holding a revolver. From her stance and demeanor, he knew she was not kidding.

"I thought the house was empty and…" began Horace only to be interrupted.

"Now, you know it isn't. Did Emilio send you?"

"I don't know an Emilio," said Horace with a shrug. He did not want to appear threatening and escalate a dangerous situation. "My name is Horace Mann, and I'm a former homicide detective that's been asked to consult on Judge Levitt's murder. You can call John Greyson and verify my identity."

"Wait in your car, and I'll call Greyson," said Gales, indicating the subject was not open for conversation.

"Yes, ma'am," said Horace. "Let me know when we can talk. I have a few questions, if you don't mind."

Gales's call to Greyson went to his voicemail. A few minutes later, she received a return call from his number.

"Dr. Gales, my name is Emily Morgan and I'm a detective working with Greyson on your sister-in-law's homicide. John is tied up now, but he asked that I call to verify Horace Mann's identity. I'm fifteen minutes from you and headed your way. Horace is a former homicide detective that we've asked to consult on your sister-in-law's murder."

"Okay, but he can wait in his car until you get here," said Gales. "You know it's proper to call before you barge onto someone's property. I could have shot him."

"Please don't do that, doctor. I'll be there as soon as possible."

***

He was glad to see Emily when she stepped out of her car.

"I don't know who that woman was," he said nodding toward the house, "but she is armed and dangerous. I have no doubt she would have shot me if I'd pushed the situation."

"Her name is Dr. Vivian Gales, the judge's sister-in-law," came Emily's reply. "Her brother recently threatened her. It's a long story."

"My money's on her," commented Horace, looking up the driveway. "I'm pretty sure she knows how to use a gun."

"Let's go talk to her," suggested Emily. "What are you doing here? I left you in the office looking over police reports."

"I wanted to see where the murder took place and talk to someone at Mt Moriah."

"You've been to the cemetery?"

"I have."

"Why?"

"Don't you think it's odd where the killer dumped Julia's body? He could have left it in the house or a dozen other places. I asked the funeral director for the names of people buried in the Garden of Peace."

"What did you find?"

"I don't know yet," responded Horace. "I came here after leaving the cemetery and haven't had time to look."

"Are you ready to talk to Dr. Gales?" asked Emily.

"I guess so, let's do it."

***

She was waiting for them on the porch. Emily approached, holding her badge and identification up like a shield.

"It's okay," called the doctor. "I just got off the phone with Greyson." The gun was resting in her lap.

"Doctor, can you give me your weapon?" asked Emily cautiously. "We don't need an accident."

"It's unloaded," said Gales reaching into her pocket and holding up five cartridges. "How about I give you the rounds, and I keep the gun?"

"I guess that works," replied the woman detective reluctantly. "Do you have a permit to carry a handgun?"

"I don't need a permit on my property, but yes, I have a permit, and I shoot regularly. It's a hobby of mine, a way to relax after a difficult day."

"I talked with Greyson briefly, and he said your brother had threatened you, but I don't know the specifics," commented Emily. "I can see you're taking his comments seriously."

"Unfortunately, Emilio has let the death of our brother distort his sense of reality. Yes, I'm taking him seriously when he says I could end up like my sister-in-law unless I let him move into her house. That's not going to happen, detective. Not without a fight. Now, what can I do for you?" said the doctor looking at Horace.

"Dr. Gales, I'd like to look around, if that's okay with you," he replied not wanting to make the situation worse with more questions. "I'm a visual person, and I need to see how your sister-in-law was attacked and killed. I've looked at police and weather reports, visited the cemetery where the body was discovered, and scoured the parking lot where the judge's car was found. This is my last stop, and I should be finished in half an hour or so."

"How do I address you since you aren't a police officer?

"Horace will do."

"Okay, Horace, do what you need to do. If you want to go inside the house, all the doors are locked except the front door. I'll wait here for you to finish."

"I'm going to stay and talk with Dr. Gales," explained Emily. "Let me know when you're ready to go."

***

"Would you like a glass of sweet tea?" asked Gales with a thin smile. The older woman looked stressed and exhausted.

"If it's not too much trouble," commented Emily.

"Come with me then. I have a pitcher made in the kitchen."

The last time Emily had been in this house it had felt lived in. Almost alive. A teacup in the sink, a sweater draped across the back of a rocker, light streaming through floor to ceiling windows. Now, it seemed to be dying, a coating of dust covering the furniture, its drapes closed to shut out the world. A stillness engulfed the entire household. It reminded her of someone holding their breath, waiting for something bad to happen.

"Doctor, what's going on? Talk to me and maybe I can help."

"Let's get something to drink and go sit on the front porch," replied Gales wearily. "What was your childhood like, detective? I'm curious."

"I had a great childhood," replied Emily. "Dad was a reporter for the evening newspaper, *The Press Scimitar*, and mom taught school until she started having children. We lived in a nice house in a middle-class neighborhood, took vacations in the summer, and I was happy."

"Must have been nice," commented Gales as she poured tea into a glass. "Do you have siblings?"

"Two sisters, I'm the one in the middle."

"What do your sisters do for a living, if I may ask?"

"Dorthy is a nurse, and Dot works as an HR manager for a transportation company. They're both happily married and have two children each."

"I don't see a ring on your hand," said the doctor. "Are you married?"

"I've been married twice, and neither one worked. My sisters say I have terrible taste in men. Why the questions?"

"Just curious," came the reply. "I have a bad habit of analyzing people. It's an occupational hazard I suppose. My childhood was not happy, nor were Gene and Emilio's childhoods. We were afraid of our father, and our mother was unstable. One minute she was the life of the party and the next suicidal. Today we would diagnose her as bipolar and put her on medication. She medicated herself with alcohol, drugs, and men."

"Did you father know?"

Gales laughed before answering.

"If he knew, he didn't care, detective. We would go for weeks, sometimes a month without seeing him, and when he was at home, we walked on eggshells. He started molesting me when I turned fifteen. We didn't have strong role models like you and your sisters. We had monsters pretending to be parents. I secretly celebrated after the headmaster called me into his office and told me my father had died. He thought I was hysterical. I wasn't."

"I thought you and your brothers were sent away to boarding schools and summer camps," stated Emily.

"I lied about that, and so did my bothers. It was a simpler explanation than what actually occurred."

"Why tell me now?"

"I don't know. I should, but I don't," muttered Gales in almost a whisper. "Maybe, I don't care anymore. I've run from demons my entire life, and I'm tired. It's been such a heavy load. Gene killed himself trying to deal with the trauma of his childhood, and I believe it's driven Emilio mad. He's spiraling out of control and has to be stopped."

"What was the relationship between Gene and Emilio?"

"Emilio idolized his brother. Gene was the first one born; Emilio came twenty minutes later. Whatever Gene wanted to do, so did Emilio. They were identical twins you know."

"So, Gene was the dominate brother?"

"Oh, definitely," responded Gales. "Remember, I was away in college when dad died. Mom fell apart, but Gene didn't. He stepped up and took charge. I hired a housekeeper, and a driver and Gene became the man of the house at ten taking care of his brother and our mother. I felt guilty about it, but I couldn't come home, not after mom let my father molest me."

"She knew?"

Gales smiled a sad smile before answering.

"She walked into my bedroom one night and caught us," said the doctor her eyes downcast. "Instead of being irate or calling the police, she backed out of the room and closed the door. It was never mentioned again."

"My God!" exclaimed Emily shocked to her core. "I'm so sorry, Vivian."

"What doesn't kill us makes us only stronger," responded Gales her words broken and drawn out. "At least that's what I've been telling myself."

"Did your father molest your brothers?"

"I don't believe so, but he screwed with them constantly. His favorite theme was that they were illegitimate bastards fathered by a syphilitic lowlife and an addict mother. How many ten-year-old boys know what syphilis is? It was disgusting, but I didn't do a damn thing about it. I'm sorry for that."

"Vivian, what happened wasn't your fault," consoled Emily gently taking the distraught woman's hands in her own. "You were young, and you'd been abused by your father, too. Did you ever talk to a mental health professional about any of this?"

A shake of her head told the detective what she expected.

"Why did Emilio hate his sister-in-law?" asked Emily changing the subject.

"She took his brother from him," whispered Gales trying desperately to regain some semblance of composure. "Emilio needed Gene; he was his North Star and had always been his constant. In an instant, everything changed, and he blamed Julia. Resentment grew to hate, and here we are now. Emilio is determined to retake what he believes was taken from him."

"You need more protection than we can provide," replied Emily.

"The other woman detective, I think her name was Mandy or Marcy, she gave me the name of someone to call."

"That would be Jack Murphy, and if you're going to stay here, I suggest you contact him now as opposed to later. He's very good."

"Can you call him for me?" asked Gales. "I don't know where I placed his card."

ALEX'S

In Emily's opinion, the best oldies-but-goodies jukebox in the South was at Alex's. The food was pretty damn good, too. Marcy and her on-again-off-again boyfriend, Jack Murphy, were here tonight as was Mike Cadera, Murphy's longtime friend and shadow.

Emily had called Horace and talked to him briefly. He was with the big boss, Police Director Johnson T. Edwards. Why, she didn't know or really care, but Horace had promised to show up and bring Greyson with him. Alex's was hopping, a symphony of sound, laughter, and the constant flow of people centered around only one thing – having a good time.

"Where's your new boy toy?" asked Marcy as she walked up and handed Emily a fresh beer. "I wanted Murphy to meet him."

"Un-huh," came a muted response.

"No, really," said Marcy her eyes dancing with mischief. "What did you say Todd's last name was?"

"I didn't."

"Don't be like that. I said I was sorry," laughed Marcy. "I even bought you a beer to make up for my little gaffe, or as the French like to say faux pas."

"Murphy, take this woman to bed. She's way too interested in my love life; she needs to get laid."

Marcy and Emily were a study in contrast. Emily was taller and built like a basketball player; Marcy was shorter, 5'6" in three-inch heels, and with more curves. Marcy was in her mid-30's, while Emily was about to turn 40 her next birthday. Apart from their physical differences, each approached the job from different points on the compass. Marcy was always in attack mode, the proverbial bull in a china shop. Her counterpart was more analytical and studious. While different in many aspects, they were the same in one thing. They were both lethal and not to be taken lightly.

At eight-thirty, Horace led Greyson into the popular watering hole to cheers from the small contingency that had gathered around the shuffleboard table to witness Emily go for the bumper match on a ten-dollar bet.

"Watch Stretch," warned Horace, using one of his many nicknames for his old partner. "She will take your last dollar."

As everyone looked on, Emily fired a red puck down the table obliterating Marcy's blocking shot. The puck spun to a stop a bare millimeter over the two-point line. She stuffed Marcy's ten-dollar bill into her hip pocket and then hugged her former partner and friend.

"Where the hell have you two been?" she asked as she hugged Greyson next.

"The director stopped by Greyson's house on his way home," responded Horace. "He's getting a lot of heat on Judge Levitt's homicide, and the mayor wants him to hand it off to the state. Don't get excited, he's got our back for now, but we need to produce."

"They don't know Memphis," said Marcy not happy with the prospects of being sidelined by the state investigative bureau. "John said something about an AI program, something you're familiar with Horace. What about it?"

"I wouldn't count on it. Everyone from the city council to the school board has to sign off and that's before it goes to legal. I discussed it with Director Edwards, and he's onboard, but it's an uphill battle for us. We're talking months before it'll be approved."

"Let's find somewhere quieter," suggested Greyson. "How about we go back to my house?"

Marcy pulled him aside in the parking lot.

"John, I know you don't like Murphy, but he's with me tonight. If he's not invited, I'll talk to you in the morning."

"Bring him," said Greyson without hesitation. "He may be of use."

*****

Emily stopped at a nearby corner convenience store and bought two cases of beer with five bags of ice and put them in the trunk of her car. The store clerk, who looked about eighty, smiled and said, "Laissez les bons temps rouler, Sugar. I get off at ten."

She tipped him the ten dollars she'd won from Marcy. Emily had never been to Greyson's house in Midtown. She knew the area, it was close to great restaurants and bars, but she didn't know what to expect. Her boss was notoriously private, even before the death of his wife, he kept his personal life personal. A Garabaldi's delivery vehicle was in the driveway, and the driver stood at the door as she pulled to the curb.

"Good deal," she whispered softly, "pizza and beer, what could be better."

Hurrying up the walkway, she could just catch the whiff of a fire somewhere in the neighborhood. It reminded her of her uncle's farm; the adults laughing and sipping whiskey while the kids roasted marshmallows and turned them into s'mores.

"Hey, someone give me a hand," she yelled after sticking her head in the door. "I have beer and a ton of ice in my truck."

"Take them to the mudroom," replied Greyson pointing. "Use my old cooler and the farm sink Sue bought at an estate sale. I almost threw it away, but it was made for this old house. It fit like a glove."

"I'll get a fire going," said Horace. "Murphy, why don't you, Marcy, and Emily get chairs out of the shed. Watch out for snakes."

"Snakes, seriously?" said Marcy, her eyes getting big. "I grew up in Chicago, and we didn't have snakes in Chicago."

"He's screwing with you," laughed Emily. "Come on, let's get this knocked out."

An hour after the small troop settled into Greyson's Midtown bungalow, he and his merry band of crime fighters plus one found themselves seated around a roaring fire, wolfing down the world's best pizza, and chasing it with a rich, full-bodied Mexican lager.

*****

"Don't you ever feed this dog?" asked Marcy as she handed Blue a piece of her pizza and watched him swallow it whole. "Poor baby, come to mommy."

"Watch it Murphy, I think that mommy hormone is beginning to wake up in your girlfriend," said Emily with a wicked smile.

Everyone laughed at the look on Murphy's face.

"Okay, let's talk about the case," announced Greyson bringing the group back to their shared purpose. "I'll start unless someone wants to go first."

When no one spoke up, he began.

"Here's what we know. Judge Levitt left her courtroom on Friday, March 21 at approximately five-thirty, and according to her court clerk, she was meeting someone. Correct me if I'm wrong, Emily, but Terry Wells said Julia was dressed to party."

"That's correct, John."

"Where she went or who she met is unknown. Marcy, did we get anything useful from Julia's bank or phone records?"

"Nothing unusual from her bank, and there are no red flags from the phone company, but it's possible the judge was using an encryption app. Apple has confirmed Judge Levitt downloaded the Guardian App six months ago."

"Can the phone company confirm the last time it was used?" asked Horace.

"Yes, but none of the details from the app itself. Judge Levitt's phone company says she used the Guardian app for seventeen minutes on the day she died."

"I've never heard of Guardian," commented Emily.

"They're a new player in encrypted messaging, but according to my sources, they have big bucks behind their name from a couple of tech billionaires."

"Did we ever find Julia's phone?" asked Greyson.

"No, but we're still looking," responded Marcy.

"According to phone records, we know Julia was alive at ten fifteen and that her body was found the next morning at approximately seven o'clock," continued Greyson, his facial features blurred by smoke from the fire pit. "Her body was dumped in Mt. Moriah Cemetery. Any ideas or comments?"

"I visited Mt. Moriah today," said Horace. "Judge Levitt's body was located in an old section of the cemetery that had closed. The last burial in the Garden of Peace was in June of 2017, almost nine years ago. The cemetery manager provided me with a list of the people buried in that section with the date of their interment. I'll start my research tomorrow morning."

"I think it's probable the killer has a connection to Mt. Moriah," said Marcy. "He knew about the service road and knew the gate would be unlocked."

"I'm not sure the killer used the service road," interrupted Greyson.

"It rained the night before, John," Marcy said. "Tire tracks would have washed away during the storm, and it's almost a hundred yards from the front entrance to the grave site where the judge's body was found. That's a long way to carry a body, even a small woman like the judge."

"The cemetery laid fresh gravel on the service road a week before the murder, and according to the grounds manager, it hadn't been used." Greyson paused to take a sip from his drink, then continued. "A prospective buyer was due from out of town to view the property, and the old owners wanted to make a good impression. I saw two car tracks in the gravel. One belonging to the responding officers and the other from Doc Richard's meat wagon. I'm not convinced the service road was used, but it's probably immaterial at this point in the investigation."

"Okay, let's move on," replied Marcy not convinced of her partner's logic.

"Emily, what did CSI get from Julia's house?" asked Greyson.

"Not much I'm afraid. Judge Levitt's housekeeper cleaned the house the day of the murder and took out the garbage, which had been picked up by a sanitation truck. Blood splatter in the mudroom was confirmed as coming from our victim, and only two sets of prints were found in the house. The judge's and those of her housekeeper. The area canvas conducted by Officers Vale and Hernadez only turned up a whiff of a lead."

"Which was?"

"A motorcycle was seen slowing down in front of the judge's house on several occasions before the attack. We got that piece of information from the door camera of a couple who lived across the street from Julia. The husband didn't want to get involved, but his wife called when he was out playing golf. He wasn't a happy camper when we showed up on his doorstep."

"Did you get a description of the driver?" asked Marcy.

"No, he was in leathers and wearing a face shield and gloves, but we think the bike was a Ducati Nightshift. There's not many like it."

"David Barnett has a motorcycle dealership," responded Greyson looking at Marcy for confirmation. "Does he sell Ducatis?"

"No, he has a Suzuki dealership, but he probably takes trade-ins on new sales."

"What about his alibi for Julia's murder?" asked Horace his words slightly slurred. He and Greyson had passed on beer, opting instead for a good Kentucky bourbon.

"He was at Danny's with a stripper named Anna Leigh Styles until nine," came Marcy's response. "I haven't talked to Anna Leigh, but we know Barnett has been lying to us. He told John and I that he was at home sick when the judge was murdered. I have witnesses at three bars who can dispute that."

"You have your next assignment," said Greyson. "Find Anna Leigh Styles and interview her. There's something else," he continued. "I found a velvet jewelry box at Julia's house, and in it were eleven cards. Each featuring a different colored orchid enmeshed in the coils of a large snake. Notes from eleven different people were scribbled on the back, nine men and two women. I can only describe the messages as pornographic in nature. A twelfth card was found on the dash of Julia's car after it was found at the Abe Goodman clubhouse in Overton Park. It was blank. Any ideas?"

"It sounds like a dating service to me," commented Murphy. "You meet someone in a public place, and you each have a card. If they match, you're free to take it to the next level."

"And you know this how" asked Marcy with a frown.

"He's too pretty to need a dating service," laughed Emily, reaching around and kissing Murphy on the lips.

"My partner, Mike Cadera, worked a case for the firm a few months back on a cheating husband. He was doing something similar."

Marcy didn't know who she was angrier with, Emily for laughing and kissing her boyfriend or Murphy for the smug look after the kiss.

"Well, look at you, Murphy. You finally added something useful without killing anyone," Greyson said teasing the private investigator. "Good job."

"Why wasn't a message found on the card left in Judge Levitt's car?" asked Horace thoughtfully. "Does anyone have an idea?"

The silence was deafening.

"We may never know the answer to that question," commented Greyson finally. "Let's move on. Julia was married to Gene Levitt, who was twenty years her senior. He had two siblings, an older sister and a twin brother. All three were psychiatrists. Vivian had a practice in Nashville, and Gene and Emilio in Memphis."

"Holiday conversations in that family had to be stimulating," commented Horace after taking another sip of his drink.

"Stay on subject, Horace, and put away the Fighting Cock whiskey, at least until we finish here."

"To say their childhoods were dysfunctional does a disservice to the definition of dysfunction, but they all survived. Gene's brother, Emilio, was not a fan of his new sister-in-law. In fact, he hated her. After Gene committed suicide, he tried to break his brother's will and disinherit Julia. He even went so far as to demand the police investigate her for murder. That went nowhere, and the will was airtight. That was two years ago. Now to the present. Marcy stop me if I miss something. This is where it gets a little complicated."

"You need a scorecard to keep up now," chided Horace. "Get with it, John."

"Two people have told me they suspect Emilio Levitt had something to do with the death of his sister-in-law. Her attorney, Archibald

McCutchen, and his sister, Dr. Vivian Gales. Both have stated that Emilio hated Julia and would benefit from her death."

"Is there any evidence he was involved?" asked Emily.

"Not really," said Greyson. "After the funeral, Emilio supposedly called his sister and told her he was moving into Julia's house and not to get in the way. When she asked him to wait until the will was finalized, he threatened her. Murphy, this is where you come in handy. Marcy gave Dr. Gales your business card and encouraged her to consider hiring private security. She may give you a call."

"She already has," replied the private investigator.

"Marcy, what am I missing?"

"Do you want to tell them about the marital arrangement between Julia and Gene?"

"You do it," replied Greyson as he bent over and picked up his drink. "I don't have the stomach for it."

"Dr. Levitt and his wife had an open relationship," said Marcy. "She could see other men, long-term relationships were forbidden, and safe sex was to be practiced at all times."

"What about him?" asked Murphy.

"Apparently, Dr. Levitt had little interested in sex."

"It kind of fits with what we know so far," commented Horace. "The date after work, the cards, use of an encryption app, and the secrecy."

"Okay, I think we've covered a lot of material tonight," Greyson said. "Let's end by going over what we do next, and I'll start. I'm going to interview Emilio Levitt. Marcy?"

"Locate Anna Leigh Styles and bring her in for questioning. If that turns out as I expect, I'll have another go at David Barnett."

"Don't push him too hard," warned Greyson. "You don't want him to lawyer up. Emily?"

"Find out who sells Ducati motorcycles in Memphis, and I still have to interview Sol Hammersham, the sleazebag attorney who was paying for dirt on the judge. I still don't know what he planned to do exactly."

"What about the court reporter, Terry Wells? What's going to happen to her?" asked Greyson.

"She's been suspended for now pending the outcome of an investigation. She'll be fired for cause if I can prove she'd took money from Hammersham. I hope she's working on her resume."

"Murphy, I'll make sure the area precinct commander knows you're providing security for Dr. Gales," said Greyson smiling. "I wouldn't want one of Memphis's finest to confuse you as a prowler. All that paperwork is a headache."

"I'm sure you'd be heartbroken."

"I'm sure I would," said Greyson. "Horace, you're next."

"I'm researching the people buried in the Garden of Peace where Julia Levitt's body was discovered. It means something to the killer. If I can find a connection, maybe I can find a name."

"Okay, we have a plan, good job everyone. Now, let the party begin."

"Just to be clear, it's okay to start drinking again?" inquired Horace, teasing his old friend.

"You never stopped," came the reply from Greyson. "It's dark outside but not that dark."

AN OUNCE OF PREVENTION

Unlike the last time the killer had been here, the weather was perfect. White, billowy clouds floated in a sea of blue with temperatures in the mid-seventies. People were out: walking their dogs, he could hear music coming from the Shell, and the area was alive with activity. He'd pulled his motorcycle behind a construction barrier at the College of Arts and leisurely strolled past the judge's house, as if he lived in the neighborhood. He'd even waved to the old couple at the end of the block. They didn't wave back. Today's mission was just another piece of the puzzle. Still, it had to be perfect, just like the night with Julia Levitt had been perfect. That meant he needed walk and observe. Maybe have lunch at the Crosstown Concourse and work his way back into the park after dark, somewhere near the bike plaza. From there he'd follow the limestone running trail to Rainbow Lake and cut across the Greensward to the College of Arts and end where he'd begun.

***

Vivian Gales had tried to talk to Emilio, but it only seemed to stoke her brother's paranoia. His threats and wild rantings had scared her; scared her enough to call Murphy. They were meeting at ten the next morning, and she planned to hire him no matter the cost.

Until then Vivian paced the darkened house. She checked and rechecked every door and window on the first floor more than once. No one was getting in tonight without her knowing it. It had been twenty years since she'd spent a single night in the home where she'd grown up, if you wanted to call it a home. So much had changed. Her brother and Julia had done a masterful job of bringing it into the twentieth-first century without losing its historic charm. The kitchen had Julia's fingerprints all over it; she loved to cook and host intimate dinners. It was three times larger than Vivian remembered, and the Viking appliances were a definite upgrade, as were the porcelain teacups she'd found in a beautifully handcrafted sideboard.

Vivian felt restless, sleep an adversary on this long night. She wandered downstairs for a cup of green tea and gingersnap cookies. Over the sink, she gazed at her own reflection in the blackened windowpanes. Suddenly, a faint face appeared out of the darkness. Predatory eyes stared into her very soul; the upturned corners of a mouth testified to the existence of evil. She screamed, desperately hoping to wake the neighbors, the neighborhood, the city. The face laughed. Then a man held up a long narrow knife turning it slowly until it was only thing she could see. An instant later, he was gone. Only then did she remember the gun and cell phone in her robe.

"This is the 911 operator, what is the nature of your emergency?"

"He's after me," screamed Gales in a mix of tears and hysteria.

"Is an intruder in your house?" asked the operator in a calm voice.

"How the fuck do I know? Someone was staring in my window, and he had a knife."

"The police are on their way; stay on the phone with me. Is there a room where you can lock the door from the inside, someplace secure?"

"Maybe the bathroom," cried Gales frantic with fear. "I have a gun."

"Okay, a gun is a bad idea. Go in your bathroom and lock the door. The police are minutes away. Do not fire that gun, in fact, unload it now."

"Screw that!" shouted Gales as the panic began to be replaced by anger. "I'll unload it when I know I'm safe. Call John Greyson, he knows what's going on. My name is Dr. Vivian Gales and Judge Julia Levitt was my sister-in-law."

***

Surprisingly, the first patrol car didn't arrive for more than twenty minutes, which only aggravated Vivian Gales more. She hung up on the 911 operator at the ten-minute mark and called Murphy, who luckily was at home with Marcy.

"Someone was looking in my window, and he had a knife," said Gales in a wail. "I called the 911 number, but the operator was worthless."

"I'm on my way," said the private investigator, motioning for Marcy to follow him. "I'll be there as soon as possible. Lock yourself in your bedroom, I'll call when I'm at your door. Don't answer it for anyone but me."

Murphy explained the call to Marcy as they jumped in his truck and backed down his driveway.

"Motherfucker!" Marcy exclaimed. "I'm calling Greyson. He's five minutes from the Levitt house."

Marcy, Murphy, and Greyson arrived at the same time and were surprised no patrol cars had responded. Murphy called the doctor's phone from the street, and she met him at the door. Vivian threw her arms around his neck in tears.

"I thought I was dead," she cried. "He had this cruel smile and held up a long, thin knife for me to see, for me to know it was meant for me. Oh, God, what makes people like that?"

"It's okay, I'm not leaving" said Murphy gently. "Let's go inside and sit down. The police will want a description of what you saw. Think about it; it's important."

Greyson was furious, and Marcy was only slightly less so.

"I ordered extra patrols on this house," Greyson growled.

As he paced, a patrol car pulled up in front of the house, its tires scrapping the curb.

"What the hell happened, and why did it take you more than twenty minutes to get here?" Greyson asked looking at his watch.

"Sir, we were dispatched to a home invasion in Hein Park. When we arrived, the homeowner said he didn't make the call. We had to investigate."

"What about other cars in the area?" asked Greyson, beginning to calm down.

"We've had a busy night, detective. I'd suggest you talk to someone in dispatch. From the radio chatter, it sounds like there's been a lot of crank calls tonight."

He joined Marcy and Murphy inside the house where Dr. Gales was describing her ordeal.

"I couldn't sleep, so I came downstairs to make myself a cup of tea. I was looking out a window over the sink waiting for the water to boil. Suddenly, a face appeared seemingly out of nowhere. It was terrifying."

"Can you describe him?" asked Marcy her notebook and pen out to take notes.

"No, I'm afraid not," responded Gales after taking a sip of water. "He was wearing a black hood with the eyes and mouth cut out. I could tell he was white, but that's all."

"Was there anything particular about the mask, a logo maybe?"

"No, I don't think so," said the doctor after a pause. "I was just so startled, I couldn't move for a moment or two. He just stood there, an evil grin on his face, and then he showed me the knife. That's when I screamed."

"Murphy, can you stay with Dr. Gales while Marcy and I check outside?"

"Not a problem."

"What do you think?" asked Greyson once he and Marcy were out of earshot. "Did she see someone or was it her imagination? The responding officers checked around the house before I joined you. There was nothing out of place, no footprints, nothing."

"I think someone was here," replied Marcy. "The knife does it for me. It's too specific for it not to be real."

"The officers who arrived after we did said there's been an unusually high number of crank 911 calls tonight. That's why it took them so long to get here."

"That adds a little intrigue to the situation."

"Yeah, it does," agreed Greyson.

"Murphy is staying the night," said Marcy. "Cadera will take his place in the morning. I think it's a little overkill, but Gales insisted. She wants around-the-clock protection."

"We need to bring Emilio in for an interview. What do you think?" asked Greyson, trying to hold back a yawn.

"That's not a bad idea. You handle him, and I'll do the same with David Barnett, after I issue an APB on Anna Leigh Styles," said Marcy. "Can you give me a lift to my car? It's at Murphy's.'

"Are you guys a couple again?" asked Greyson.

"Maybe," she said. "I love the big jerk, but trust goes a long way with me. Time will tell."

***

Killing Julia Levitt had made him feel like Superman and Batman rolled into one, a super superhero, but the look on Gales's face tonight had taken him back to that moment in time. It had been exhilarating. Next time he'd bring a camera, the kind that fit on your head. He smiled at the idea. The bogus calls to 911 had worked like a charm. He had seen a segment on a true crime show where the killer had done something similar, but that idiot had screwed up and been caught. That's what happened when you didn't make contingency plans. Something always went wrong in those documentaries, so tonight he'd been careful. That was the purpose of his reconnaissance trip earlier in the day. Running through backyards, he'd been able to get to his motorcycle in minutes, take the Sam Cooper Boulevard, and be miles away before the first patrol car rolled to a stop in front of Levitt's house. It had been a good plan, and it had worked as he'd expected.

INTERVIEWS

Greyson started his morning in police dispatch where he poured over transcripts and listened to the previous night's 911 calls. The similarities in the caller's voice, the condensed window when the calls were received, and the area where the disturbances were reported all led to one conclusion. Someone wanted to clear police coverage from around Julia's house, and he knew why. If confirmation was needed that Dr. Gales had witnessed an intruder, this was it. He ordered copies of eight 911 calls to be forwarded to MK Isoke at the crime lab. It was a longshot, but maybe the super sleuth could triangulate where the calls had been made. With the growing number of security cameras around the city, a location might lead to an identification. He'd also called Emilio Levitt's office number to schedule an interview. Instead of talking to a receptionist or the doctor himself, a recording explained that the office had been closed due to a personal emergency. Another psychiatrist, Dr. Gary Wong, was to be contacted in case of emergency. Things got stranger when Greyson called Gary Wong, and Wong sounded confused about the referral.

"I think I've met the man once or twice, but that's about it," he told the detective. "Emilio didn't talk to me about this."

"What can you tell me about him?" asked Greyson, desperate for information.

"I think he has an office on Madison Avenue. I knew his brother fairly well; he was an outstanding psychiatrist. His death was a real loss, but suicide happens in our profession."

"Thank you, doctor," stated Greyson. "I appreciate your help."

"Tell Dr. Levitt to call me when you find him. I don't appreciate him referring people to me without consulting me first. It's unprofessional and dangerous for his patients."

***

Greyson called Emily when he got to the office; he wanted someone with him when he picked up Emilio. They agreed to meet at Ugly Joe's Coffee at nine-thirty, a ten-minute drive from the doctor's house in Belle Meade.

"I'm available," Emily said happily. "I'm clear until one-thirty when Sol Hammersham is coming in for a chat."

"Let me know what he says," commented Greyson as he looked out his office window and watched the shift change at Cop Central. "If Hammersham was planning to blackmail Julia, he didn't know her. There's not a way in hell she'd give in to his demands. She might kick his ass, but she wouldn't give him the time of day."

As he pulled into the parking lot at Ugly Joe's, Emily walked out carrying two large coffees in a flimsy cardboard tray.

"Coffee black. Yours is the one without a lid."

"No sugar, right?"

"Right," Emily replied with a smile. "Me, I'm a double shot girl, I need that boost of energy."

"It gives me the jitters," said Greyson after taking a sip from his cup. "I can drink coffee all day but toss in a couple shots of caffeine and my nervous system goes berserk. Where's your car?"

"I walked. My house is only four blocks from here, and Todd is picking me up later this afternoon. How do you want to handle Emilio?"

"I'm not sure; I don't know what we're walking into. Just keep your body camera on and play it by ear."

Belle Meade was a mixed neighborhood of three-million-dollar homes and two hundred-thousand-dollar condos. The movie *The Firm* had *featured* a house in Belle Meade. For the most part, it was a quiet community of manicured lawns and majestic oak trees. The exception being the home belonging to Dr. Emilio Levitt. His yard was full of weeds and probably hadn't been cut since last summer. There were more dead shrubs than alive, and a dozen newspapers littered the driveway. Greyson parked on the street and the two detectives walked to the door.

"It looks like someone backed over the good doctor's mailbox and propped it up with a two-by-four," said Emily nodding to her left. "Do you want me to check it out?"

"No, there's a security camera over the front door, let's play this one by the book."

Greyson knocked and waited. A sign warned that the doorbell didn't work, but the intercom apparently did.

"Who is it?" squawked a mechanical voice from somewhere in the house. "If you're selling something, I'm not interested."

"Dr. Levitt, my name is John Greyson, and I'm a homicide detective with the Memphis Police Department. With me is Detective Emily Morgan. We'd like to talk to you about the murder of your sister-in-law, Judge Julia Levitt."

"I don't know anything about it. Go away!"

"Sir, we can talk here or downtown. It's your choice, but we're not leaving."

Levitt was red-faced and close to hyperventilating when he answered the door a hammer in his hand. Emily quickly slammed him onto the stoop while Greyson snapped cuffs around his wrists.

"You can't do this; you can't do this!" screamed the handcuffed man trying to squirm away from the woman cop restraining him.

"Stop fighting us," said Greyson in his ear. "You're making things worse for yourself, doctor. We only want to talk."

As if hitting a switch, Emilio Levitt stopped moving and started crying.

"John, I think this guy is on something. We need to call an ambulance," uttered Emily as she loosened her grip.

"Shit, I'm on it," came the reply as Greyson reached for the radio on his belt.

***

It was almost one o'clock when Emily finished her incident report and filed it. Greyson had called from the hospital; they were admitting their suspect. Ketamine and a host of other recreational drugs had been detected in his system.

"He'll be there for several days," stated Greyson. "Do you want to guess who he named as his emergency contact?"

"His sister," stated Emily with conviction.

"That's right, and she's on her way as we speak."

"God, this is one fucked up family."

"Which families aren't?" was his reply. "I have two children, and I haven't seen them in over a year. I wish I could change things, but unfortunately that ship has sailed."

Emily didn't know what to say so she didn't say anything. Her boss was not one to discuss his private life. All the department's detectives knew was that his wife had died and that he'd served in the Marine Corps Reserve, but that was about it outside of work. He only let a few people into his inner circle.

"I'm going to stay a little longer and work from home for the rest of the day," he continued. "Tell Horace I'll see him there."

She'd wanted to pick Greyson's brain about this new wrinkle with Emilio, but she had an interview to conduct. Sol Hammersham was early and waiting for her in Interview B.

***

Hammersham was like nothing she'd imagined. He sat with his legs crossed, leaning back in his chair. He was a small, smug man dressed in a well-tailored suit, and his head shaved to hide what was probably male pattern baldness. Emily could see stubble along the ridges of his head. He didn't stand when she entered the room.

"Mr. Hammersham, thanks for coming in today. If you don't mind, I'll get right to the point. I have a written statement from Terry Wells that you paid her to get malicious information on her boss. What were you planning to do with that information?"

"Detective, I don't believe I have to answer that question. It isn't illegal to pay someone to spy on their boss. It might be unethical, but it isn't illegal."

"It is if you intended to use that information for the purposes of blackmail."

"I suppose you have proof of that allegation?" countered Hammersham, still smiling.

"What other purpose could it be, counselor? A career change? You want to be a journalist or you're writing a book. Ask yourself this. How are you going to explain your behavior to the Board of Professional Responsibility when I file a formal complaint? Even if you get a slap on the wrist, every single judge in this city is going to consider you a courtroom pariah. Now, if you have an explanation, I'm listening."

Hammersham wasn't smiling now. "What I did was perfectly legal!" he exclaimed.

"Why don't we let the Professional Responsibility Board make that determination," countered Emily.

"I was working for a client and following his explicit instructions."

"Who was the client?"

"That's attorney/client privilege. I don't have to give you squat, sweetie."

"You do know I'm investigating the murder of a criminal court judge," responded Emily in a hard tone of voice. "If your client had anything to do with the murder of Judge Levitt and you cover for him, I'm going to arrest you as an accessory and for obstruction of justice. This is your *get out of jail free card*, counselor. I'd suggest you take it."

"And if I cooperate?" asked Hammersham, considering his options.

"You're done with me, but you might have a problem with Terry Wells," responded Emily. "She's being terminated this afternoon at three o'clock."

"Okay, I can handle her. My client was Emilio Levitt."

"What were you instructed to do?"

"Dr. Levitt was convinced the judge had something to do with the death of his brother. My job was to find proof of that…and anything else to discredit her. I hired a private investigator and started paying for dirt on the bitch, the doctor's favorite term for his sister-in-law. He despised that woman."

"Who was the investigator?" asked Emily feeling an adrenaline rush that she'd uncovered something big. Maybe, something big enough to break the case wide open.

"Sammy Hankins I've used him before. He's discreet and good at what he does."

"I want everything you dug up," said Emily.

"I don't have anything. That was one condition my client insisted on – only he would have the collected information. No duplicates either. I can show you our contract if you'd like."

"When did you start working for Dr. Levitt?"

"Maybe nine or ten months ago; I can check my records for an exact date."

"Do that. What about Hankins?"

"What about him?" asked Hammersham confused by the question.

"Did he retain copies of his investigation on Judge Levitt?"

"I didn't check, but knowing Sammy I'd say maybe. My arrangement with him was I get everything. After that I didn't care."

"I think we're done for now," said Emily. "Don't call Sammy Hankins. Is that clear?"

"Crystal clear," responded the attorney rising from his chair. "I'll call you later on the date I began representing Dr. Levitt."

"Why did he come to you?" asked Emily with one more question. "Why not go to a detective instead?"

"I asked him the same thing," responded Hammersham. "He told me that it was none of my business."

BACKYARD CONVERSATIONS

Horace called as he was leaving work. "I'm bringing Emily home with me. Do I need to stop at the grocery?"

"I thought Emily's boyfriend was supposed to pick her up," said Greyson.

"Apparently something changed," Horace responded.

"Then yes, pick up a good ribeye and a bottle of white wine. The good stuff not the syrup you drink." After a long pause, he asked, "What's up?"

"I'm going to let her tell you. Emily did good today, John. You're going to be pleased."

"Okay, I'll see you when you get here. I'm starting the grill."

"Have a drink waiting," replied Greyson's oldest friend. "Three inches of caramel brown elixir gently poured over sparkling cubes of blue ice. I can almost taste it now."

"I think you have an unusual relationship with alcohol," laughed Greyson after taking a sip of his Blanton's neat. "See you when you get here."

***

Emily had gotten a ride home and changed into jeans and a blue linen blouse she left untucked. Her mousy brown hair fell loose to her shoulders. It was a good look for her.

Greyson answered the door and found her there, holding a mixed bouquet of camellias, dogwood, and daffodils.

"I cut these from my garden," she said handing Greyson the arrangement. "Is Horace here yet?"

"He's out back tending to the steaks. Come on in. You remember Blue, don't you?" he asked as his four-legged companion sniffed his guest's leg.

"I do," said Emily as she reached down to scratch the little pittie's ears.

"Wine is in the refrigerator - help yourself. Horace picked it out, so I hope it's decent."

Horace was a big man, standing six feet six in his stocking feet. He'd aged well with a full head of salt-and-pepper hair, and he'd kept his weight under control. He moved like a much younger man due to a lifetime habit of Tai Chi and Pilates. He turned when Greyson and Emily joined him and grabbed his old partner in a bear hug. He didn't miss the job, but he did miss some of the people, meaning he missed Emily and Greyson and maybe a few others. Whether those few others missed him was unclear; Horace was a notoriously difficult colleague and had gone through a litany of partners in his career at MPD.

"I got something for you," said Emily to Horace, a mischievous smile flickering across his face.

She opened her purse and pulled out an eight-by-ten envelope and handed it to him.

"It's my favorite photo," she said, cutting her eyes at Greyson.

Horace laughed out loud after looking at the picture.

"You told me you destroyed this."

"I lied," laughed his old partner.

Greyson moved closer to look over his friend's shoulder, but Horace blocked his view.

"Nope, it's not going to happen," laughed the big man. "You should be ashamed of yourself, Emily. This could be considered elder abuse."

Changing the subject, Horace's old partner asked, "Where's Marcy?"

"She's looking for David Barnett. Apparently, his motorcycle dealership was in foreclosure the first time we met him and shut down when she returned. He'd also moved from his apartment. Marcy is hitting the dive bars he frequents."

"Is he a serious suspect?" asked Emily after taking a sip of her wine.

"He lied to us, Greyson said. "He doesn't have an alibi for the time when Julia was murdered, and he threatened the judge on multiple occasions. Yeah, I think he's a suspect, at least until we clear him or find someone else who looks better."

"I may be able to help you there," commented the woman detective.

"Let's eat first," announced Horace as he tossed three sizzling ten-ounce steaks on a platter and covered them with tinfoil. "Baked potatoes, corn on the cob, and a tossed salad are in the kitchen. Help yourself."

***

Greyson had built a huge fire that could probably be seen from the space station as it passed over Memphis. The food was excellent, but the company was better. It was only the second time Emily had been around Greyson in a non-business setting, and she was pleasantly surprised by her boss's dry sense of humor. It was a side of him that she'd occasionally caught glimpses of but had not truly experienced. He was at ease in his old Midtown fixer-upper; the one he'd purchased after the death of his wife. The house had been decorated in warm browns and deep greens throughout, and Greyson had used colorful wool and flat-weave rugs to define different living spaces. It seemed to Emily like a setting meant to wash away the stress and worries of everyday life. She now understood why he spoke so lovingly about his old bungalow in the Idlewild Historic District. It was his Fortress of Solitude; a place he could go to rejuvenate after viewing the worst of humanity.

After dinner, the guys pulled out cigars and Emily found a can of Dos Equis Mexican Lager in the back of the vegetable crisper and joined them around the fire. It was time to get back to the case.

"Okay, spill the beans," said Greyson, looking directly at her. "What's going on? Horace implied you're on to something."

Emily launched into her discoveries from her interview with Hammersham: Emilio hiring him, what his client wanted him to do, and him hiring a private investigator. When she mentioned the name Sammy Hankins, Horace shifted in his seat.

"Do you know him?" Emily asked.

"Oh, yeah, I know Sammy. John, remember a few years back the Blackstone Case. Hankins was on Mayor Graham's payroll. There wasn't enough for an arrest, but he was dirty."

"I know him," answered Greyson his jaw tight as he stared into the raging fire. "Horace, can you go with Emily tomorrow? Lean on Hankins and make sure he understands it's in his best interest to cooperate."

"Is his office still on Summer Avenue near the drive-in theater?"

"It is, and I want to grab him early, maybe around eight-thirty," replied Emily.

"Come by and pick me up. I'll have coffee ready," said the retired homicide cop.

"What else did Hammersham tell you?" Greyson asked Emily.

"That his agreement with Dr. Levitt stipulated he hand over everything he uncovered, meaning no copies."

"That's bullshit," interjected Horace as he tossed ice from his glass into the fire.

"Did Sammy have the same arrangement?" asked Greyson.

"He did," came the response, "but Hammersham had no way of knowing if he kept some of the material or not."

"If that dirtbag could use it or sell it, I can guarantee Hankins kept it," said Horace with certainty. "The guy's a weasel; he'd steal from his mother."

"Do you think we have enough for a search warrant?" Greyson asked his old friend.

"With the right judge, I'd say so."

"I can try Judge Kennedy," responded Emily. "He and Judge Levitt were close friends."

"Do it," said Greyson standing. "I'm going to bed; I've got a splitting headache."

"I'll put out the fire after Emily leaves," said Horace. "We've still got a little catching up to do."

DOWN THE RABBIT HOLE

The crushing sound of a bass guitar thundered in the background making it almost impossible for Marcy to hear through the phone.

"Can I speak to Mackinzie Owens?" she shouted into the receiver for the third time. "This is Marcy Thomas."

"Hold on a second, and I'll check. I think she's in."

The owner of Danny's Cabaret answered almost immediately.

"I thought I'd hear from you again," laughed Owens in a playful, teasing tone. "What can I do for you, detective?"

"I'm looking for David Barnett. Have you seen him?"

"As a matter of fact, I have. He was tossed out of here two nights ago after groping one of my dancers. I don't put up with that type of behavior."

"Did he mention where he was going? I've looked and I can't find him."

"Let me ask around, and I'll call you one way or the other. How can I reach you?"

Marcy recited her phone number and thanked the strip club owner for her help.

"Did you ask Stu Kellum about me?" asked Owens before the call ended.

"I did and I called Father Pat at St. Mary's," said Marcy. "I may have misjudged you, Ms. Owens. I don't like your business, but from what I've been told, you're helping a lot of lost souls."

"Call me Mac," said Owens. "Drop by one night, detective, and I'll buy you a cup of coffee. We probably have more in common that you realize."

"I might do that," said Marcy. "Call me if you hear anything on Barnett."

"Do you think he killed that woman? The judge I mean?"

"I don't know," came Marcy's reply. "He had motive, he made threats, and as far as I know, he doesn't have an alibi for the time when she was murdered. He's high on our list of suspects. I'd be careful around him if I were you."

"I guess you never know what people are capable of," commented Mackinzie. "I always pictured Barnett as kind of a blowhard. I'm surprised he had the courage to kill someone in cold blood. That takes balls I didn't know he had."

The strip club owner's last comment corresponded with Marcy's impression of Barnett, but with one exception. He didn't like women he couldn't control. That was his hot button. The one thing he couldn't tolerate. He'd browbeat and physically abuse his wife until she'd finally stood her ground and divorced him. She could see him blaming Judge Levitt for everything, for him being kicked out of his house, and for being cut off from his wife's money. It wasn't his fault it was that fucking bitch's fault. That's how he'd frame his predicament, and now the bastard had gone down the rabbit hole, but she'd find him. It might take time, but Marcy would gladly put him in a cage if she could prove he had anything to do with the brutal murder of Greyson's friend.

***

At two in the morning, Marcy decided to throw in the towel and grab something to eat at CK's. Murphy lived nearby, so she called and woke him up. Company would be good after a frustrating night of wading through smoke-filled dive bars and having to enduring salacious leers from drunks and losers. Maybe a hot shower could wash away the stink. The bartender at the Robber Baron had been a dick, but he'd decided it was better to cooperate than having Vice flood the area and chase away his customers.

"Listen, you're hurting my business," he'd complained. "Everyone knows you're a cop, and that means they want to get as far away from you as possible. I haven't seen Barnett. I'll call you when I do."

"Fair enough," Marcy had replied. "Do you know his stripper girl-friend?"

"Anna Leigh? Sure, I know her, but I haven't seen her either."

"Add her to my call list," said Marcy.

"Okay, but can you get out of here? I've seen ten people walk out since we've been talking."

That's how Marcy's night had gone. It was the bane of all police work, the tedious footwork before ending the hunt.

***

She was in a side booth sipping probably the best coffee she'd tasted all day when Murphy's big F-150 parked outside. He looked like a cowboy in jeans, a dark blue t-shirt, and boots. All he needed was the hat. God, he looked good thought Marcy.

"You're out late," he said as he slipped into the booth and kissed her.

"The grind never stops in Grind City. What's the latest on Vivian Gales?"

"She's thinking about going home. You know she rushed to the hospital after her brother was admitted. It didn't go well."

"What happened?"

"Emilio went berserk and tried to attack her. He would have been successful, too, if an attendant hadn't been in the room."

"God, this is crazy."

"Could it be an act? Could little brother be setting up an insanity defense?"

"I don't think so," replied Marcy after taking another sip of her coffee. "Greyson and Emily both said Emilio was high on something when they found him."

"It was just an idea. Is he your top suspect?"

"Him and a guy named David Barnett. That's who I was hunting tonight, and he's gone underground. Apartment cleared out, business closed down, he's in the wind."

The small restaurant at the corner of Evergreen and Poplar was filling up fast as the bars closed down for the night. Mama June was dressed in her splendor tonight wearing bright yellow tennis shoes, and a tomato-red top with matching lip stick.

"What can I get for you two lovebirds?" she gushed with a smile as wide as the Mississippi River.

"Two eggs over easy, hash browns, sausage patties and more coffee," replied the woman cop.

"Wheat toast and honey," commented Murphy. "I gotta watch my waistline."

His comment drew a harsh stare from Marcy who usually ate like a horse. She leaned over and whispered, "I was going to suggest we go to your house and burn off a few calories, but I wouldn't want you to get too skinny."

He caught an elbow in the ribs when he laughed.

"Okay, why are you so stressed looking for Barnett?" asked Murphy. "You'll get him eventually."

"It's not stress. I just want this case closed and the killer put away. It's eating Greyson from the inside out. Julia Levitt was like a daughter to him."

"What can I do to help?"

"You know a lot of street people. Put out the word, I need to find David Barnett."

"I can do that. Are you making any progress?"

"I think so," replied Marcy as she scarfed down her food. "Did I tell you about Judge Levitt's court clerk being paid to dig up dirt on her?"

"You did," came the response. "Emily interviewed the attorney who was paying her, and it turns out he was working for a client. That client was Emilio Levitt. When are you going to arrest him.?"

"That's a good question. Right now Emilio is as crazy as a loon and not competent. I'll wait until he gets out of the hospital."

"So, he and Burnett are your top suspects. Anyone else?"

"I'm going to look at Barnett's ex-wife, Ginny. Something about her seems off to me. I'm pretty sure she lied to me about sleeping with Judge Levitt."

"This is beginning to sound like something from one of those cable crime shows. Come on, let's go to my house. You're exhausted and need to close your eyes for a couple of hours."

"Can I get a rain check on my earlier idea?"

"What idea?"

"About burning calories," she replied as she leaned over and kissed him.

"Not if you do that again," laughed Murphy. "I'll get the bill and see you at my house."

SAMMY HANKINS, PRIVATE INVESTIGATOR

"What can you tell me about this guy?" asked Emily as she sat in Greyson's small kitchen talking to Horace.

"He's a former cop with about three years on the force. Sammy was fired for insubordination, but it could have been for a score of other charges. He was dirty."

"Will he cooperate with us?"

"He will if it benefits him," came the stark reply. "Sammy and the truth seldom ride in the same car. Let me take the lead this morning. Hankins knows me and knows I won't take his crap. If I ask you to step out of the room, don't be surprised."

"It's almost nine o'clock we need to go," said Emily, putting her coffee cup in the sink. "If he's not in his office, I have his home address."

"He'll be there but by two or three o'clock Sammy will be at his county club. He claims to be a scratch golfer."

The drive down Summer Avenue was a big departure from the eclectic mix of old Memphis neighborhoods, popular restaurants, and bohemian shops that adorned Midtown. The Summer Avenue corridor was more commercial and always had been. Hankins's office was in a strip mall adjacent to the interstate and within eyesight of a gentleman's club. As Horace had predicted, the P.I. was in his office when they arrived.

"Damn Horace, I heard you were dead," roared the bemused P.I. as he pushed out of his chair sporting a big grin.

"You wish, Sammy," came the reply. "How someone hasn't killed you yet is a mystery to me."

The two men shook hands as the retired detective glanced around the room. It was sparsely furnished but somehow felt claustrophobic in the small, confined space. The entire office consisted of a desk, filing cabinet, and three-tier coffee station with a single chair for Hankins's clients.

"Why did you move out of your office on Jackson Avenue?" asked Horace. "You had three times the space and I know you paid less rent."

"Too many break-ins," responded Hankins with a shrug. "That area was a war zone, and I'm getting too old for that shit. I was expecting the police, but you're a surprise, big guy. I thought you'd moved to somewhere in Florida."

"I did, but Greyson asked me to lend a hand in the Levitt homicide, plus I missed you, Sammy."

That comment got a big laugh from the private investigator.

"Horace, we never liked each other, but I hope there's still some respect. I know why you're here; I got a heads-up from Hammersham. He told me to shred what I'd kept on Levitt, but I didn't do it."

"And why is that?" asked Emily in her cop voice.

Hankins seemed surprised that someone else was in the room. "Well, you're not bad on the eyes," he replied in suggestive tone. "What are you 5'8" or 5'9" maybe 36 C or D cup?"

Emily didn't bite on the taunt.

"I'm 5'9" you creep, now answer my fucking question."

"Oh, Horace, I'm think I'm in love. Who is this bewitching creature?"

"Emily Morgan meet Sammy Hankins," said the retired detective. "Sammy, a piece of advice. Answer her fucking question."

"God, I miss you, Horace," he said as he ogled the woman standing in front of him. "Do you play golf, honey?"

"Emily, why don't you wait for me in the car? This shouldn't take too long."

"No, that's not necessary. Levitt's file is on my desk," said the private investigator while nodding to his right. "It's yours free of charge."

"Give me the *Reader's Digest* version, Sammy," commented Emily as she picked up a wide envelope marked *JL*.

"I followed Levitt for about nine months; here are the highlights. She smoked a little weed; her dealer was a retired cop name Spruce. I think his first name is Al, but I could be wrong about that. He left the department in 2015 on disability…something about a high-speed chase that killed a couple of people. The judge socialized some, mainly with co-workers. Nothing big, drinks after work, small dinners, that kind of thing. Levitt didn't date in the normal sense of the word. Here's where it gets weird. Every three weeks or so, she would dress up and meet a different person, usually a man, for dinner and spend the next night with them at a discreet location. I never saw anyone pick her up at her house."

"By discreet location do you mean hotel? Or something else?" interrupted Horace.

"I'm talking high rent digs; a house on the South Bluffs overlooking the river, a mini mansion off Johnson Road, a place in Hyde Park near Rhodes College. The routine never changed. The next morning, Judge Levitt would leave her lover's nest, go home and change, and go about her business as if nothing had happened."

"You said usually men," began Emily. "How many women and did one of them live down the street from her?"

"I saw three women, and they were lookers, too. Yeah, one of Levitt's hook-ups lived in a house down the street. It had a big magnolia tree in the front yard. It's all in my report. Dates, times, addresses, and pictures."

"Why are you doing this?" asked Horace as he closed his notebook and put it in his jacket pocket. "What are you getting out of this?"

The P.I. smiled before answering.

"Hammersham welched on our deal. We had an agreement, I held up my end of the bargain, and he didn't pay in full."

"How much of what's in the envelope did you give Hammersham?" asked Emily.

"Enough for him to know what the judge was up to."

Looking at Horace, Emily asked, "Do you think this could have pushed Emilio over the edge and given him a reason to kill his sister-in-law?"

"It's not what I think, it's what I can prove," remarked the retired detective. "Anything else, Sammy?"

"I don't think so, but it's been good seeing you, Horace. Drop in again and bring your golf clubs next time. I'll take you to my club."

"I just might do that," said Horace. "Keep your nose clean, Sammy."

***

"Quick, let's go somewhere and look at what's in that envelope," said Horace as he put on his seatbelt. "Jesus Christ, what the hell was Julia Levitt thinking? She should have known better."

"There's a police station on Tillman," suggested Emily. "I can be there in fifteen minutes."

"Go, I'll call John. He's not going to be happy."

ROADBLOCKS AND FRUSTRATIONS

"How many times do I have to say this? You can't talk to Levitt until it's cleared by his doctor."

"That could be months," moaned Greyson frustrated by the slow wheels of justice. He was in the district attorney's office accompanied by the police director. "We're talking about the murder of a criminal court judge."

"We do have grounds to charge Dr. Levitt for assault," interjected Director Edwards. "I've seen the video clip from Detective Morgan's bodycam. He charged Greyson and Morgan while brandishing a hammer."

"What about a search warrant for his house?" asked Greyson.

"Based on what, a hunch? No thanks!" declared the attorney. "If Levitt did kill his sister-in-law, I'm not giving him grounds to toss the evidence at trial."

"You won't have to worry about that!" exploded Greyson angrily. "We'll never be able to charge the bastard unless we're allowed to do our jobs. Grow a set a balls for god's sake."

In the hallway, Edwards patted him on the shoulder and kept walking. At the elevator, he turned and said to Greyson, "Keep following the evidence, John. It's what you do best. The DA's right on this one. Slow is better than reckless."

***

Greyson had just sat down at his desk when his phone rang.

"Homicide, this is Greyson," he said

"Is Marcy with you?" asked Horace.

"I saw her a few minutes ago. Why?"

"Emily and I are at the Tillman Station. You need to get over here and bring Marcy with you. Sammy Hankins handed us a treasure trove of information."

"Okay, I'm on my way. Give me half an hour."

Treasure trove was an apt description of what was in the envelope they'd gotten from the private investigator. Dates, pictures, addresses, names, it was all there.

"Sammy would have made one hell of a detective," declared Horace. "Too bad he lacked self-control. He's a lot like that guy Marcy is diddling, you know Murphy."

"Diddling?" repeated Emily before bursting out laughing. "What is it with you old guys? You mean fucking."

"I don't like that term, it's crass."

"And diddling sounds like a blues guitarist."

"We're getting off the subject. Murphy can be charming but there's an undercurrent of violence to him. Sammy was like that, but Murphy has self-control and acts out of necessity. With Hankins it was all emotion and anger, and it cost him a promising career. By the way, John and Marcy will be here in the next half-hour."

Horace separated the material Hankins had collected into two bundles: pictures in one, addresses and reports in another. Emily sorted everything beginning with the earliest date. When they'd finished, they had the names and addresses of nine people the judge had met in the last nine months. A partner in one of the largest law firms in the city, the CEO of a regional non-profit, a ballerina, and Ginny Barnett to name a few.

"What do you think?" asked Emily.

"I think Julia Levitt had good taste," came Horace's reply. "All of these people could be models."

"Some of them have juice, too," added Emily. "They're not going to like us asking questions."

"Yeah, but they'll talk to us to avoid negative publicity."

"It's going to be hard keeping this under wraps. The public loves this stuff."

"We do what we can do."

***

Horace had just stepped out of the small conference room they'd commandeered when he spied Greyson and Marcy pull into the visitor's parking lot. Greyson's face was set and intense like a man on a mission. Horace met them at the door.

"John, I think we got something," he said. Looking at Marcy, he continued, "I think you need to go back and talk to Ginny Barnett. She lied to you."

"I knew it!" exclaimed Marcy. "I knew she was sleeping with Levitt."

"At least one time we can prove," replied Horace. "She met Barnett for an intimate dinner at the Four Flames. The next night Julia walked down the street and spent the night at Barett's house. That's the pattern. Meet her date for dinner and if it goes well, you know the rest."

"How many others?" asked Greyson.

"Nine total and most are well known. I expect they all have money. This could get out of hand if not handled properly."

"What do you suggest?"

"Marcy needs to reinterview Ginny Barnett as soon as possible and pump her for information. Find something we can use as leverage on the others."

"Anything else?" asked Greyson nodding his approval.

"We interview the others away from Cop Central unless they refuse to cooperate. Lower the anxiety as much as possible."

"Okay, I like it," came Greyson's response. "Let's see what you got."

"Before we start, Hammersham knows about Julia's extracurricular activities," said the retired cop. "That means Emilio Levitt knows it as well."

"Well, shit! That's just great."

"The good news is he doesn't have what we have, according to Sammy. He doesn't have the pictures or addresses. That gives us a leg up."

***

Horace hadn't lied, Greyson thought moodily. They'd uncovered an explosive dossier of his friend's personal life, and he hated it. Hated that it would probably become public knowledge and hated that it would diminish who she was as a person. Judge Julia Levitt would become just another headline here today and gone tomorrow.

"John, you're as white as a sheet. Get out of here, I can handle the rest," said Marcy putting her hand on her partner's shoulder. "I'll get a ride with Horace and Emily."

"Good idea," said Greyson wearily. "God, this is going to turn ugly, and there's not a damn thing I can do about it."

After he'd gone, Marcy asked Horace, "Is he going to be okay? You've known Greyson longer than me."

"I think so. Remember Julia was like a daughter to Greyson. Her death and now something like this is hard for him to take. He savagely protects what he loves, and he wants to protect Julia's reputation. I'll talk to him tonight," continued Horace. "Right now the best way to help John is to close this clusterfuck. Let's get to work. How do you want to proceed?"

"Start setting up interviews," Marcy said. "We can go to them unless they play dumb. If you get pushback, bring them in and let me know. I'm going to have a little talk with Ginny Barnett."

GINNY BARNETT AND OTHERS

Marcy and Ginny's conversation started with, "You lied to me. Why?"

"What are you talking about?" asked Ginny.

Instead of answering the question, Marcy dropped three photographs on Barnett's kitchen counter.

"Is this how you greet someone who comes for a visit? You stick your tongue down their throat and feel them up. Tell me you weren't sleeping with Julia Levitt."

"Where did you get these?" asked Ginny, her face flushed.

"Just answer my question and don't lie to me this time. Did you kill Judge Levitt?"

"No, no, I would never hurt Julia. I loved her but not how you think. I've never been intimate with another woman."

"No? Then explain these pictures. They were taken on your doorstep, and we know the judge spent the night. There are more pictures of her leaving your house the next morning."

"I thought I wanted that kind of relationship, but I was wrong. She showed me that; Julia was so patient with me."

"Are you telling me that nothing happened?"

"Nothing happened except we became closer as friends. The night those three pictures were taken," said Ginny picking them up off her kitchen counter and staring at them, "I expected to have sex with Julia. We'd had dinner the night before and agreed to meet at my house the next night. After a few glasses of wine and a lot of talk, Julia made me realize I was looking for someone else to make me feel good about myself. It was a repeat of my marriage to David, only this time I wanted Julia to save me. We spent the night talking and watched an old rom-com. In the morning, she went home. That was it. Detective, I've never been a confident person. I know I'm considered cute, but I don't see it. I see every flaw."

"That's one hell of a story, Ginny. Now tell it to someone who believes you."

"Why are you doing this?" Ginny said her eyes filling with tears. "Julia was the only person who ever believed in me and wanted nothing in return. If we'd had sex, we could no longer be friends. That's what she said, and I couldn't stand the idea of that."

"Why couldn't you be friends if you'd slept together?" asked Marcy.

"Because of her dead husband," cried Barnett the tears streaming down her face. "It was a promise she'd made to him when he was alive. She could have sex with anyone with one stipulation. She could only sleep with that person once. I tried to tell her Gene was dead, that her promise to him no longer mattered, but she wouldn't listen."

"She told you this?" asked Marcy staring intently at Ginny.

"She said it was the way she lived her life. Then she told me to make a choice. We could have sex, but then our relationship would be altered for good."

"Did your ex know about this?"

"No, it happened after the divorce. Why?"

"Is there any way he could have found out about you and Julia?"

"I don't see how. What's this about?"

"David has disappeared. His apartment is empty, and his business shut down. We know he blamed Julia for your divorce. We know he'd threated her on numerous occasions, and we know he lied to us about being home all night on the night of the murder. That makes him a prime suspect in this case. Can you think of any other place he might have gone other than what you told us earlier?"

"His father has an old fishing camp on the Tennessee River near Dover. David and a few friends use to go there to drink beer and shoot guns. I went once and swore I'd never go back."

"Can you find it on the map?" asked Marcy.

"I don't think so, but I may have something better. David's dad stopped paying taxes on the property. My shit-for-brains ex decided to do it for him, and I may have a copy of the tax receipt. Do you have time to wait while I look?"

***

Horace and Emily took four addresses each off Hankin's list of names and called them. In each case, the response was the same: *I don't know what you're talking about.*

"What do you want to do now?" Emily asked Horace after striking out again. "The people I called are educated and have money. They'll lawyer up as soon as we take them downtown for questioning. There has to be a better way."

"Let's pick one and try again," suggested Horace. "If these people are somehow connected - and I suspect they are - the phone lines are smoking right now. We just need one to talk."

"Okay, who?"

"I like the attorney, the partner at Fitch, Smith and Turner."

"Why him?"

"Fitch, Smith and Turner is a criminal defense firm. They'll do anything to avoid being linked to the murder of a criminal court judge. He'll talk to us."

"Do you want to make the appointment, or do you want me to do it?"

"I will. At one time, I knew someone who worked there."

"When?" asked Emily.

"There's nothing like the present. Can you run out and get us something to eat? I'm starving. My treat."

Horace called the main number for Fitch, Smith and Turner and asked for Rose Stevens. She was a friend of his wife and had been to their house many times before the death of her husband. After Glen died in an automobile accident, they had drifted apart.

When she picked up the phone, he said, "How are you doing Rose? This is Horace Mann."

"Horace, it's been a long time. I heard you and Barb retired and moved to Florida."

"St. Petersburg, you should come for a visit."

"Did you hear I got remarried to the most amazing man? His name is Jerry."

"I didn't, but congratulations. Come down and bring Jerry with you. Barb would be delighted."

"I know you didn't call to catch up on old times. What can I do for you?"

"I need to make an appointment to see Jordon Sellers, and the sooner the better. It's police business."

"I thought you'd retired," said Rose.

"I've been brought in to consult on a murder investigation. Mr. Sellers may have tangential information that can help us."

"What case?"

"I'm not at liberty to say, but if I could talk to Mr. Sellers for one moment."

"Does he need another attorney present?"

"That's his decision to make, but he's not considered a suspect."

"Okay, let me see if he has an opening. Hold on."

A minute late, she was back. "Mr. Sellers will talk to you now, Horace. Hold on while I transfer your call. I told him he could trust you, so don't make a liar out of me."

"I won't, and please bring Jerry for a visit. Barb would love to see you."

Jordon Sellers had a deep resonate voice that would play well in a courtroom. He came right to the point.

"I talked to Detective Morgan. I have nothing to say to you people."

"Okay, don't say anything. Just listen," replied the retired detective. "We are in receipt of pictures of you and Julia Levitt at dinner at the

Ninety-First Bomber Squadron, and don't pretend this was a business meeting. You were all over the judge. We've also collaborated the authenticity of the photos by interviewing your waitress."

When Jordon Sellers didn't respond, Horace continued.

"The next night the judge arrived at your house at eight in the evening and stayed the night. She was carrying an overnight bag. Would you like me to continue?"

"Not really, I could care less," said Sellers, getting angry. "It isn't against the law to have dinner with someone or for them to spend the night. Nice try, but we're through having this conversation."

"This is the murder investigation of a sitting criminal court judge. Just so you know, I'll be at your office tomorrow morning to bring you in for questioning. I'll try to keep this from becoming a perp walk, but I can't control the press."

"You sonofabitch. You're enjoying this, aren't you?"

"No sir, I can assure you I'm not and I'm trying to give you a way out."

"How?"

"Meet me this afternoon. You pick the spot and answer a few questions. You have my word that anything you say will not be used against you unless you had something to do with the murder of Julia Levitt."

"Zinnie's East at six o'clock," said the attorney, clearly not happy with how the conversation had gone.

"If you want to bring your attorney that's fine."

"Just us," said Sellers with attitude.

***

Greyson needed to think. He felt like they were missing something or someone. All their focus had been on the brother-in-law and low-rent ex-husband, but they alone didn't fill in all the spaces - why the body was left in a cemetery or explain the erotic cards he'd found in Julia's master bathroom. Were the cards a keepsake or something altogether different, and what did the numbers of them mean? Maybe Horace and Emily would stumble upon a clue using the stuff they'd gotten from

Sammy Hankins, but he didn't trust the private investigator. In fact, he didn't trust any P.I., including Marcy's boyfriend, Jack Murphy. Greyson hooked Blue's leash to his harness and headed out the door.

It was a good evening to be outside. Memorial Day was in a few days, and spring had sprung. Trees were budding, flower beds coming back to life, and the wind had shifted from the north to the south bringing warmer temperatures and gentle rains. Blue, as always, was up for another adventure in their tiny kingdom. For his part, Greyson had donned a light rain slicker, Brewer's ballcap, and coffee mug topped off with a splash of Blanton's. A small flask was in his hip pocket. He was planning for a long outing and like a good scout, he wanted to be prepared for all contingencies. Blue led them into the depths of Central Gardens as if on a mission, his tail keeping beat to the music of the universe. Pushing west down Cowden, the duo crossed into new territory at South Belvedere and kept going. As they entered this new land, a light drizzle began to fall, but it didn't dampen their enthusiasm. In fact, it was a welcomed relief. Blue was in his element, and the detective felt happy to see everyone head indoors. He needed to think, not talk. At Melrose they turned north for five blocks, crossed Peabody, and changed directions again at Linden.

They needed to widen the investigation. Go back to the cemetery, revisit the crime scene, look again at the closed-circuit television cameras close to Julia's house. Just one break was all they needed. Someone had to see this sonofabitch, he thought. No crime was perfect. The earlier light drizzle changed to a steady downpour as Greyson and Blue approached Barksdale's. As he considered whether to go home, or step inside to look for his favorite waitress, he spied another one of his favorite Midtown people trudging in his direction.

"Bert, what the hell are you doing out in this downpour?"

"Someone just stole my bike, and I tried to run them down. It was chained to a post next to the front door."

***

Back at home, Greyson unhooked Blue's harness and began to towel him off. That task ended when his best friend performed a whole-body shake that sent water flying in all directions.

"Okay, then," said the detective smiling. "dry yourself off. Let's get you something to eat."

He was pouring himself a strong drink when his phone vibrated and a message appeared.

The text read: *Will be late, meeting one of Julia's dates, keep your fingers crossed…Horace.*

A PLACE IN THE WOODS

Marcy was a city girl raised on the South Side of Chicago. She had no idea where to begin after Ginny Barnett gave her the tax receipt to her ex father-in-law's fishing camp, but she knew someone who did. Two phone calls later and after buying a Delorme Atlas and a Gazetteer map, she signed into Google Maps. Emily had agreed to tag along after a little arm twisting, which was a relief. Marcy didn't like the country with its overabundance of crawly creatures and all that open space, but her friend had practically grown up on a farm. Emily had an uncle in Mississippi and rode horses when she could get away from standing over dead bodies. That was becoming harder and harder to do when everyone carried a gun and had adopted a *I don't give a fuck* attitude. With a little luck, they would be on the road early the next morning and get to the camp well before noon. Hopefully, the Houston County Sheriff's Office would provide back-up, after all it was their jurisdiction, and they knew the area. Still, Marcy would wait to call them when they reached the Tennessee River. She didn't want some rookie cop stumbling all over their investigation in an attempt to get his name in the paper.

At six her phone rang. It was Murphy.

"When are you getting out of there? Cadera and his new girlfriend just got here, and I have steaks ready for the grill."

"Give me another ten minutes," said Marcy. "I'll be at your house soon."

"Are you spending the night?"

"Not this time, cowboy. Emily is picking me up at my house at five."

"See you in a few…love you," he managed to say. That *love you* was new and something hard for Murphy. He didn't go overboard expressing his emotions, unless it was to kick someone's ass.

"Love you, too," said Marcy. "Have a gin and tonic ready when I get there."

***

It was a perfect day to travel. Sunrise was at least a half hour away with temperatures in the low sixties. A high of seventy-four degrees had been forecast for later in the day. Emily pulled into Marcy's driveway and honked her horn. She wanted to get this safari behind her; she was meeting Todd later today. He'd called and asked her out after she'd agreed to accompany Marcy to Barnett's fish camp. She couldn't back out now.

"Where did you get a truck?" asked Marcy as she used a grab handle to pull herself into the cab. "God, I'm high off the ground."

"It was my uncle's; he left it to me when he died a few months ago. I need to get it out more often."

"I didn't know about your uncle. I'm sorry."

"He was a hoot and lived a big life. There's a Mickey D's on Poplar, right before we hop on the interstate. I think it's open 24/7. Let's get something for the road."

With minimum traffic, the dynamic duo made good time. Before they knew it, the big Ford truck had thundered across the Tennessee River over the Jimmy Mann Evans Memorial Bridge, taken the Linden Exit, and made it to Waverly using Tennessee State Highway 13. That's where they were meeting R.J. Rawlings at a Sonic Drive-in. He would lead them to Barnett's fish camp. As promised, he was waiting when they arrived. Rawlings wasn't a rookie; in fact, he was the senior officer in the Houston County Sheriff's Office. If he was surprised at seeing two good-looking Memphis detectives slide out of the truck, he didn't show it.

"Who's Thomas?" asked the squared-away cop as he adjusted his sunglasses.

"That's me," replied Marcy. "Officer Rawlins, this is my partner Emily Morgan. I appreciate your help today."

"I understand you're looking for a murder suspect?" he said, getting to the point.

"That's right, the murder of a criminal court judge."

"So the person you're looking for could be armed?"

"It's possible."

"Okay, follow me," said Rawlins as he turned to get in his car.

They traveled up Route 13 and turned onto State Highway 49 into Erin, then they continued west on 49 headed toward Cane Creek. Outside Stewart the roads changed to a single-lane and the going slowed down considerably. A few minutes shy of an hour, Rawlins pulled over on the shoulder of the road and got out of his car.

"The fishing camp is at the end of this gravel road," he said while pointing. "I'm assuming you're armed."

"We are," replied Emily. "Give us a minute to get our vests from the back of the truck."

When they were ready, the Houston County cop took the lead, and they eased their way forward toward what could only be described as a shack. Ten feet away from the building, Rawlins stopped.

"Do you smell that?" he asked, his eyes fixed on the structure.

"Decomp," replied Marcy. "Jesus, it's bad, too."

"Wait here, I've got Vicks and cotton balls in my car," said Rawlins as he turned and ran back up the road.

An old Pontiac Grand Prix, held together with Bondo and rust, sat ten feet from the front door of the shack, the driver's side window shattered.

"Emily, check the car," said Marcy. Her eyes were fixed on the front door, her gun pointed downwind.

"Gotcha," she grunted, already on the move.

Rawlins appeared and handed Marcy a jar of Vicks and a couple of cotton balls which she promptly put to use.

"This is a bad one," whispered the sheriff's deputy."

"Anyone in the shack come out with your hands in the air. This is the police!" yelled Marcy. "Barnett, we know you're in there. Come out now!"

Nothing moved; even the birds and crickets had gone silent.

"There's only one way in and one way out," said Rawlins. "Who's going to do it?"

"Shit! I guess it's me," declared Marcy. "Watch my back."

"Go," said Rawlins, "I'm right behind you, so don't stop until you get through the door."

"Cover us, Emily," shouted Marcy as she ran toward the building, Rawlins a step behind.

"Here goes, "grunted Marcy as she kicked open the door only to be engulfed in the fetid order of death.

On a far wall lay a woman's bloated body. The small space was filled with thousands of blowflies that had been feasting on the dead.

"Stay back, Emily. This is bad," yelled Marcy as she stepped back and vomited. Rawlins did the same moments later.

"Who the hell was that?" asked the local cop.

"I suspect it's Anna Leigh Styles. She was a stripper and Barnett's girlfriend."

"Not anymore she ain't." Rawlins said before throwing up again, "Do you want this one, or do I call our M.E.?"

"I got it, but it'll take time for Doc Richards to get someone here. Can you guys lead them in and watch this place until they arrive?"

"Sure, as long as no one has to go inside that hell hole again," replied the greening Rawlins. "I hate calls like this," he said. They keep me up at night."

"I know what you mean," said Emily from the doorway, her hand over her nose and mouth.

"I called Doc, and he'll have someone here this afternoon. I told him they'll need PPE. Was it Barnett?"

"No, it's a woman. I suspect it's Anna Leigh Styles," replied Marcy.

"Do we want to check the cabin?" asked Rawlins.

"No, we let the removal team take the body first. Unfortunately, that means I'll be back early in the morning. Emily I know you have a date with Todd, so I got this."

"Thanks, that makes us almost even after that crap you pulled at the Windjammer."

The comment had them both laughing and Rawlins trying to figure out the joke.

"RJ, it's been a pleasure but let's meet under better circumstances next time," said Marcy. "Here's my business card, call me if you get to Memphis."

"Sure thing," replied Rawlins. "You two handled yourselves well today. I'm impressed."

Emily hugged the big cop and handed him her business card, too. "Come see us, we'll show you a good time."

***

The drive home was more subdued than their early morning excursion to Cane Creek with RJ Rawlins in the lead.

"What'd you think about that Houston County Deputy?" asked Emily as they approached the Tennessee River.

"He was alright. Why?"

"I thought he was cute, and I love a man with a mustache."

"What about Todd? I thought you were head-over-heels in lust with him."

"My relationship with Todd has an expiration date. He's a little young for me, but the sex is to die for."

"Well, that's something, I guess," responded Marcy with a shrug.

"If he didn't talk, I could make it work, but Todd talks a lot...and he's not smart."

"I'm going to call Greyson and update him on our situation here. Here's Rawlins' business card. Do yourself a favor and call him. Who knows what's he's hiding under that frosty demeanor."

JORDON SELLERS

When Horace barged into Zinnie's East, he spotted Jordon Sellers immediately. He was the only one wearing a thousand-dollar suit.

"I don't appreciate being threatened," said Sellers in greeting. "I've talked to one of the partners, and we're going to sue your ass, if I'm mentioned in Julia Levitt's murder. Is that understood?"

"Perfectly," said Horace, smiling at the aggrieved man. "Would you care for anything to eat or drink? I've heard the Reubens are great."

"Fuck you, let's get this over with."

"Suit yourself," said the retired detective as they sat down, and he pushed a manila folder across the table. "These are the pictures I told you about on the phone."

Sellers hands were unsteady as he took one photo at a time from the package. When he looked at the last one, he looked up and said, "What do you want?"

"Tell me about Julia Levitt and how this works."

"I don't know where to start," he began. "I knew Julia when she was just another attorney, before she was named to the bench. She was married then, and I always thought she was bright and attractive. Suddenly her husband kills himself and my wife passes away a few months later. I hated being alone, I was miserable. Fast forward six months, and Julia happened to be the guest speaker at a conference I attended in Cincinnati. I met her for drinks after her presentation, and she asked how I was doing. I told her the truth. We talked for a while, and then she got up to leave. Before Julia walked away, she kissed me on the cheek and said she'd call me after we got home. For the first time in months, I was excited. But it wasn't what I expected."

"What do you mean?" asked Horace.

"I thought she was open to a relationship. She wasn't. Instead, Julia told me about a group she was a part of that consisted of people who met for dinner and had sexual intercourse with no strings attached. She called it the Society of Kamadeva. There was a yearly fee, which opened access to other like-minded individuals. If you connected with someone online, you'd meet for dinner and take it to the next level if there was a mutual attraction. Julia made it clear from the beginning that she didn't do long-term relationships, and at first I was skeptical. I thought she just needed to meet the right person, and later I convinced myself I could change her mind. Membership in the group was by recommendation, and she'd recommended me. I thought that meant something."

"How does the Society of Kamadeva work?" asked Horace.

"There's a background check, of course, and a vote of acceptance by the board. If you're accepted into the society, you receive an information package in a few weeks. That explains everything."

"The pictures I handed you suggest you were intimate with Julia," stated Horace.

"And I was, but it was the oddest thing," commented the attorney. "After the conference in Cincinnati, I became infatuated and kept pursuing her. Finally, we met for drinks to discuss my advances. She was blunt and explained she'd sleep with me but only once. After that our relationship would change. I laughed, but Julia was serious. We had one intimate night together, after that, she wouldn't return my calls or see me outside of work."

"We found some cards in the judge's house that we haven't been able to identify," Horace said, sliding an evidence photo toward Sellers. "What can you tell me about them?"

"The snake is supposed to represent virility, and the orchid femineity and lust. I don't know who came up with the design, but I think the cards are for out-of-town hook-ups. I've never used one, and I could be wrong about that."

"Tell me about the society," said Horace.

"The Society of Kamadeva is in every state in the country and in parts of Canada. It operates using a secure server as a conduit for its members. If two people are interested in a date and they want to meet up, the card is used for identification and to match sexual preferences. I've heard some of these encounters are pretty kinky."

"Who sets up the logistics; the date, time, meeting location, and what happens if something goes wrong?"

"The initial meeting is booked by the Society, and it's always in a public place. Where the hook-up happens after that is up to the individuals. In Julia's case, I suggested she come to my house. I've never heard of problems, but they probably exist."

"I need to talk with someone at the society. How do I do that?" asked the retired detective.

"I don't know. The Society of Kamadeva is nothing like the adult dating service in the news a few years ago. You don't go online and sign-up, you have to be recommended by a member and pass a background check. Everything is tracked through the server, even hook-ups."

"Do me favor, Mr. Sellers. Go online and ask the system administrator to reach out and contact me," said Horace handing the attorney his business card. "Tell him or her I'm investigating the murder of a member, and it's in their best interest to reach out because I will find them."

"I'll do my best," said Sellers. "Do you need anything else from me?"

"Not for now," answered Horace standing to signal the meeting was over. "Mr. Sellers, I appreciate your cooperation. As of now, I see nothing you've done to break the law, and I'll do everything in my power to keep our conversation confidential."

COMMITTED/NOT COM-MITTED

Emilio's rehab clinic looked less like a healthcare facility and more like a five-star spa. What the hell, Greyson thought. He stood in the visitor's lounge waiting to meet Emilio's attending physician. He was beginning to suspect he'd been sent to the wrong room when an inner door opened and a diminutive man wearing thick black rimmed glasses and a full beard appeared.

"Are you Greyson?" he asked in a voice devoid of inflection.

"I am. Thanks for seeing me, doctor."

"You may not like what I'm going to tell you," replied the small man whose name was Dr. Alexi Romanoff. "Dr. Levitt is gone."

"What do you mean he's gone? When?"

"We did a bed check several nights ago, and he wasn't in his room. We've checked the hospital from top to bottom, and he's nowhere to be found."

"And no one thought to notify the police?" asked the aggravated cop.

"He wasn't under arrest officer," said Romanoff. "We were under no obligation to call the police. Dr. Levitt was here voluntarily."

"He assaulted a police officer with intent to do bodily harm, and it was noted in his paperwork. I know because I made sure it was included. There were also instructions to contact me if and when he was discharged."

"You can't hold me responsible when a patient leaves this facility. My god, man. This isn't a prison."

Greyson was hot under the collar; he wanted to slam Romanoff against the wall. Instead, he turned and walked away.

***

He called Vivian Gales from the car.

"What can I do for you, detective?" she asked.

"Have you seen your brother?"

"No, he's a patient at Saint Joseph's, but you know that. What's going on?"

"He apparently checked himself out, and didn't leave a forwarding address," Greyson said sarcastically. "I'm on my way to his house now. Is Murphy still there?"

"No, I told him I didn't need his services after Emilio checked himself into rehab."

"It's just a suggestion, but I'd rehire him if I were you."

"Why?"

"We didn't want to alarm you, but a black ski mask and skinning knife were found at your brother's house when he was taken into custody. I think it's a fair assumption he was the person you saw looking in your window."

"Oh my god!" exclaimed the now frightened woman. "Emilio swore to me he had nothing to do with that. I can't believe he lied to me."

"Either go home to Nashville or call Murphy," advised Greyson. "I'll let you know if I find your brother."

"Are you going to arrest him?"

"He tried to assault a police officer, so the answer is yes. If he contacts you call the police. It's for your safety and his."

***

The front door to Levitt's house was open when Greyson pulled into the driveway with a newly issued search warrant. Within minutes two backup police cruisers arrived.

"You two take the rear of the house I'm going in the front. Make sure your bodycams are on. Our suspect is Dr. Emilio Levitt, and he recently checked himself out of a rehab facility. Dr. Levitt is unstable, so do not engage if you make contact. Back out and give me a call. I don't want a dead body. Let's go!"

As the two officers disappeared from view, Greyson stepped into the foyer his gun drawn. He wasn't taking chances after Levitt had charged out his house holding a hammer the last time he was here.

"Emilio, I'm John Greyson with the Memphis Police Department," he called out. "I'm not here to hurt you. Can we talk?"

The only sound in the huge three-story home seemed to be coming from the next room as a large grandfather clock sounded the hour – bong, bong, bong. Greyson was tempted to check his watch but didn't. Inching forward, he could see someone had recently rummaged through the house. Drawers had been pulled from dressers and a wall safe was left open. Greyson found an empty gun holster on the floor in Emilio's mudroom.

"Our suspect may be armed," he whispered into his radio. "Exercise extreme caution." He got two quick clicks of acknowledgment in return. Two cars were in the garage off the mud room, their engines cold. There was space for a third, but it was empty. One thing Greyson noticed was that Levitt was a packrat. Odd collections of everything from golf balls to seashells, old running shoes to broken glasses were in boxes everywhere, including both bathrooms on the main floor. Clearing the house didn't take long, it was obvious that their suspect had come and gone.

"Check with the neighbors, and see when they last saw Levitt," said Greyson.

"Outside, the patrol officers hurried back to their cars. A middle-aged woman stood in their way, pushing a stroller. Inside, they spotted a small hairless dog.

"Excuse me, excuse me, are you looking for Emilio?" the woman asked. As the cops approached her, Greyson walked over and looked in the stroller. "My husband says I treat my dog better than I treat him, but the dog doesn't stay out all night drinking and chasing floozies. Do you know what I mean?"

"Yes, ma'am," replied Greyson drawing her attention. "Have you seen Dr. Levitt recently?"

"Emilio was here a couple of hours ago, and he looked terrible. Has he been in the hospital? I was on my way to the grocery store and honked when I drove by. My goodness, I thought I'd given him a heart attack. His hair was disheveled, and he was as pale as a corpse."

"What time was that, miss?"

"It's Mrs. Bruce, and I'd say around two. My husband was off with his friends supposedly playing golf, which means I'm not cooking to-night. If he wants something to eat, we can go out."

"What kind of car was he driving Mrs. Bruce?"

"He wasn't in a car. Emilio was on a motorcycle."

"Do you know where he went?" asked Greyson.

"Heavens no, I have trouble enough keeping up with Henry. That's my husband, he's a dentist. Is Emilio in trouble?"

Greyson didn't answer the question. Instead he handed her his business card.

"Mrs. Bruce please call me or 911 if Dr. Levitt returns home. It is of the upmost importance."

"Am I in danger?"

"I can only advise you to let the police interact with Dr. Levitt. It's for your benefit and his."

"You're scaring me," said the woman as her dog began to whine. "See, you've got Baby upset, too."

As she hurried away, one of the officers remarked, "I feel sorry for Henry."

"I do too," replied his partner, breaking into a big grin as if he'd won the lottery. "I almost married a woman like that, but luckily for me, I was sent to Iraq instead."

Greyson and the other officer burst into laughter.

***

Greyson called the DMV and talked to a supervisor. After explaining he needed information on Emilio's motorcycle, he discovered what most people know. The DMV is not your friend, and they don't know everything.

"He has two cars registered with the Department of Motor Vehicles, no motorcycles," said the supervisor at the DMV. "If it's his, and he's driving it on our streets, Mr. Levitt is breaking the law. Too many people ignore the law and drive without a license. It's a travesty."

"Yes, ma'am," answered Greyson not wanting to continue this discussion any longer than necessary. "I'll see what I can do about it."

"Good," stated the supervisor seemingly satisfied she'd made her point. "Have a good day."

Have a good day indeed, thought the detective. Hard to, though, with Levitt on the run and Barnett in hiding. Could they both be involved in this murder, he asked himself. It was a bizarre idea but not out of the realm of possibility, and Barnett did own a motorcycle shop. He needed to talk to Marcy and get more information on the body she'd found. She answered his call on the third ring.

"Where are you?" he asked.

"I just got out of the shower. I'm trying to wash the cadaver smell out of my hair."

"Grab Emily and meet me at the Windjammer."

"I'm not doing that to her again. She has a date with Todd tonight, and I don't want to fuck it up."

"Okay, how long will it take for you to get ready?"

"John, I'm meeting Murphy at the P&H in an hour. Grab Horace and we can talk there."

He didn't say anything for a beat, but finally replied, "No, go have fun, and I'll see you Monday morning."

TIME TO THINK

It didn't take a crack detective to conclude Blue was glad to see his owner. When Greyson opened the door, the dog was spinning in tight circles. Horace wouldn't be here this weekend. He was flying home to St Pete and wouldn't be back until Tuesday, so it was just the two of them.

"Okay, let me grab your leash and get something to drink," said Greyson, smiling as his dog zoomed from room to room. Greyson had always liked dogs, but his relationship with Blue was special. It embodied everything important to the detective: trust, loyalty, love, and companionship all wrapped in forty pounds of slobber and muddy paws. The house would be dead without him; he added to its character, not to mention its furnishings. Dog toys and blankets were scattered in every room.

"Let's go, Blue," was all he needed to say to get the ball rolling. The game was on, but today Greyson had a destination in mind. They were going to Julia Levitt's neighborhood and talk to Ginny Barnett. He had some questions about her ex-husband.

They entered the park at Cooper and Poplar Avenue, cut across the number seven fairway, and followed a cart path to the stone bridge that crossed Lick Creek. Greyson took Blue off his leash and let him run. He was in his element, ears laid back, tongue hanging out, sprinting as hard as he could go. Eventually, they made their way to the Abe Goodman Clubhouse and found the pro washing carts and putting them away for the day.

Walking up, Greyson asked, "How're you doing?"

"Does that dog bite?" asked the man, his eyes never leaving Blue. "He should be on a leash."

"Don't worry about him," said Greyson flashing his badge. "A few weeks ago a black Mercedes was dumped in your parking lot. Do you remember it?"

"Yeah, what about it?"

"Do you have any idea how it got here?"

"No, why should I?" came a defensive response.

"How late do you stay open?"

"I close the snack bar at six-thirty and try to lock up by seven-thirty."

"What time do you start each morning?"

"Between six and six-fifteen. There's not much to do other than open the clubhouse, get out a few carts, and make coffee. The first golfers show up around seven."

"What about security cameras?" asked Greyson.

"Just inside the clubhouse," said the pro. "There's a sign as you pull into the parking lot warning customers to lock their vehicles. We aren't responsible for break-ins. That's about it."

"Okay, thanks," said the detective. "Have a good day."

Cutting across the Greensward in the direction of Ginny Barnett's house, Greyson stopped to look at the work being done on the new Metal Museum. That's when he noticed a crane with a camera mounted near the top.

"Maybe, just maybe," he mumbled to himself as he hurried toward the construction site. Being Friday and late in the afternoon, he expected everyone might have gone home for the weekend. Instead, he managed to catch an unhappy-looking foreman, as he was climbing into his pickup.

"I don't care if you're the Prince of Persia," said the foreman after Greyson explained what he wanted. "You're going to have to wait until Monday to get access to our security videos."

"You do understand this is a murder investigation," Greyson responded calmly.

"Listen, I'd like to help you, but everyone is gone for the day. I build things or tear them down; I don't know shit about this stuff."

"Surely there's someone you can call," persisted the detective. "You may help us catch a killer."

***

Greyson had to wait almost an hour, but he finally reached the owner of the company, who promised to personally deliver the work site's security video to Greyson's office Monday morning. It wasn't ideal, but it was what he could get.

As the sun began to drop below the horizon, Greyson and his four-legged companion resumed their earlier journey to talk to Ginny Barnett. As they approached the house, every light appeared to be on, and a party was in progress. Cars lined the street, valets rushed to service new arriving guests, and he could hear music coming from the rear of the house.

"What do you think, Blue?" Greyson asked bending down to pat his dog's massive head. "Should we crash the party or not?"

MONDAY MORNING

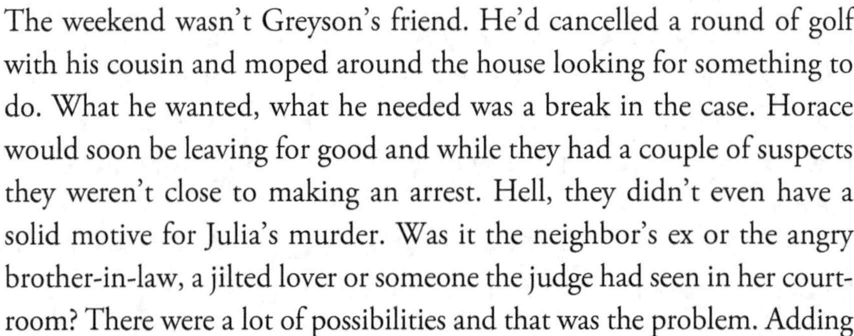

The weekend wasn't Greyson's friend. He'd cancelled a round of golf with his cousin and moped around the house looking for something to do. What he wanted, what he needed was a break in the case. Horace would soon be leaving for good and while they had a couple of suspects they weren't close to making an arrest. Hell, they didn't even have a solid motive for Julia's murder. Was it the neighbor's ex or the angry brother-in-law, a jilted lover or someone the judge had seen in her courtroom? There were a lot of possibilities and that was the problem. Adding to the drama was the fact that the mayor was pushing for an arrest. Greyson waited until Sunday to send a message to Emily and Marcy.

"How about breakfast at the Blue Plate in the morning? I'm buying."

A one-word reply from Marcy asked, "When?"

"How about seven? I'll get us a table."

The Blue Plate was an East Memphis favorite with probably the best sausage gravy and biscuits in town, and it opened at six a.m. Greyson wasn't the first person in line, but he was close.

"I'm meeting two people at seven and need a table where we can talk privately," he said showing the hostess his badge. "Anything you can do would be greatly appreciated."

"Not a problem," said the woman. "The Blue Plate used to be a house, so we have several out-of-the-way nooks that should work. What can I get you until your guests arrive?"

"Coffee for now," he said.

***

Marcy was the first to show up and looked ready to take on the world.

"I love this place," she said, "but I always forget it's here. How was your weekend, John?"

Emily showed up at exactly seven and looked like she'd been in a shoot-out. She had circles under her eyes, no make-up, and seemed to be in a foul mood.

"What happened to you?" asked Marcy, concerned.

"I broke up with Todd. Things weren't working out."

"What things?"

"For one, Todd's not twenty-seven, the bastard is twenty-two. God, I've been robbing the cradle."

"And you're not thirty-three, either," said Marcy laughing. "The last time I looked you were closer to forty."

"Whose side are you on anyway?" Emily snapped. "Another thing is Todd can't keep his mouth shut. He says the dumbest things, and it never stopped. He's gorgeous and the sex was to die for, but his non-stop gibberish was killing me."

"You do know I'm listening to this?" interjected Greyson. "We're here to talk about the case."

"I'm sorry, John," said Emily with a weak smile. "Last night we were in bed naked, and he was talking about pirates. That's not my idea of foreplay, if you know what I mean."

"Okay, I'm going to the restroom," said Greyson. "Get this out of your system before I return."

They both burst out laughing after he'd gone.

"You do know how to rattle him," said Marcy. "I thought he was going to stick his fingers in his ears."

"I love that man, but how in the world did his generation have children?"

"In the dark," came the reply which elicited more laughter.

***

They were still laughing when he returned to the table, but a gear had shifted. They were ready to go to work. Greyson began by recounting Horace's interview with Jordon Sellers.

"That is a crazy way to live your life," stated Emily. "You can sleep with someone, but only once and then you can't be friends. That's fucked up!"

"It's beginning to make sense after my conversation with Dr. Gales," responded Greyson. "I don't agree with it, but I can follow the logic. Julia Allen married a much older man, who'd become infatuated with her. I don't doubt he loved her or she him, but sex wasn't important to Gene. He'd devoted his life to his work and considered it a distraction. Knowing that a lack of physical intimacy could destroy a marriage, he or they came up with an unusual compromise."

"I agree with Emily," Marcy said frowning. "Whoever came up with this scheme had to be nuts."

"Be that as it may, it fits with what Vivian told us earlier about Gene and Julia's unconventional marriage covenant, and now it's confirmed by Jordon Sellers' narrative to Horace. I can see it and using the internet to arrange dates makes perfect sense, especially when the dating pool is controlled and vetted."

"What about the card in Judge Levitt's car?" asked Emily.

"That I'm not certain about. Hopefully, Horace can find an answer for us when he reaches someone at the dating site. Sellers indicated the cards may have been used as a means of identification for out-of-town hook ups."

"When will Horace be back?" asked Emily.

"In the morning. His plane arrives at six fifty-five. Do you want to pick him up?" he asked Emily.

"Yeah, I'll get him. He'd do the same for me."

"Two more things," said Greyson.

He explained that he wanted everyone to go back to the beginning, re-evaluate everything they'd done, and look for inconsistencies.

"We have two prime suspects, Levitt and Barnett," he said. "Look at everything again, see if anyone else needs to be added to the list: past lovers, co-workers, lawyers, defendants, neighbors…leave no one out.

One other thing," said Greyson who then explained seeing a camera on top of the crane at the Metal Museum. "It may be nothing, but the construction company owner is bringing us a copy of the security video on the night Julia died. He said his camera was top of the line, so keep your fingers crossed we get something."

FINALLY SOMETHING

When Greyson got to his office, a visitor sat patiently waiting for him. He was a short, wiry man wearing khakis and a light blue chambray shirt.

"Are you Greyson?" he asked when the detective approached.

"I am, and you're Mr. Dunavant. Thanks for coming in."

"I looked at my security feed over the weekend," said Dunavant. "You didn't mention it when we talked, but I figured you were investigating the murder of Judge Levitt. What we're doing to one another has to stop; I hope you catch this bastard."

"Me, too," said the detective, echoing Dunavant's sentiment.

"I found something, but I don't know if it'll help. A storm rolled in on the night of the murder, and my crane was moving around a bit."

"You're right about the weather," stated Greyson. "Judge Levitt was murdered on March 3, somewhere between ten p.m. and midnight. Trees were down all over the city the next morning."

Handing Greyson a thumb drive, the construction company owner remarked, "The images aren't the best, but maybe you can do something with them."

"Thank you, Mr. Dunavant. I'll get this to the crime lab and let them do their magic."

"Will you let me know if it helped? I have a daughter about Judge Levitt's age. I don't know what I'd do if something happened to Becky."

"Most certainly," said Greyson reaching to shake the man's hand. "Investigating a murder is like working a puzzle. Very seldom do we know what happened when we begin an investigation. It's the assembly of small pieces of evidence that directs us. When we're successful, we usually know who to hold responsible."

"Good luck," said Dunavant looking back as he walked away. "I'd hate your job, detective. I don't know how you sleep at night."

"Sometimes I don't," whispered Greyson to himself.

***

Marcy intercepted him on his way to the crime lab.

"Do you have a minute?" she asked.

"Walk with me," came the hurried response. "I want to get this to Isoke before he leaves for court," said Greyson, as he held up the thumb drive from Dunavant. "He's testifying in the MacDonald case this morning."

"The body we found at the fishing camp has been identified. It's definitely Barnett's girlfriend, Anna Leigh Styles."

"That was quick."

"Anna Leigh's fingerprints were on file; she'd been arrested four times for prostitution. Do you want to guess cause of death?"

Greyson stopped in his tracks.

"Strangulation?"

"That's right. The hyoid bone had been fractured," said Marcy. "Barnett has to be our killer."

"Maybe," said Greyson, "but we need more for an arrest."

"John, he lied to us about his whereabouts on the night Julia was murdered. He had motive, he made threats, and now he's disappeared. Add to that, we found his girlfriend murdered in a similar fashion as the judge. I've taken less to trial and won."

"With the right jury, he could walk."

"I'm issuing a warrant for his arrest," Marcy responded flatly. "I know you want a slam dunk but sometimes we take what we've got. I ran this by Director Edwards, and he agrees with me."

"It's your case, Marcy. Me, I'm going to keep chasing leads. At least until I'm convinced Barnett really killed Julia. Then I can stop," said Greyson, "but not a second before."

With that last comment, he turned and walked toward the crime lab.

"Shit, that went well," Marcy groaned once she was alone.. "I should have expected it. John wants more than a conviction; he wants absolute certainty that justice will prevail."

***

Greyson was angry. Angry that he hadn't found the killer, angry that people he respected were buckling under pressure from the mayor, and angry that his friend was gone. To say Greyson wanted revenge was an understatement. What was that old proverb about revenge, he asked himself? He who seeks revenge digs two graves. At the moment, that was okay with him.

Isoke was waiting when arrived.

"Did you say the construction company guy found something important?" Isoke asked as he plugged the thumb drive into his computer.

"I did," said Greyson. The video is cued to March 3. That's the night Judge Levitt was murdered."

"Okay, let's see what we've got," said Isoke as the video came to life apparently in the middle of a terrible windstorm. Intermittent rain pelted the lens in waves. A little more than a minute into the tape, a single beam of light appeared. It moved slowly approaching the Metal Museum's worksite.

"What is that?" asked Greyson pointing.

"I think it's the headlamp from a motorcycle," said the crime lab wonder boy. "It's too small for a car."

They watched as it moved closer to the crane and finally came to a stop. The rider got off the vehicle and looked around.

"What's he doing?" asked Greyson looking over the criminologist's shoulder.

Isoke remained quiet for several long seconds, staring at his computer screen before answering.

"He's looking for a place to hide his motorcycle, and he keeps looking in the direction of Judge Levitt's house."

"It has to be the killer. Who else would be out in a monsoon riding a motorcycle?" Greyson said. "Can you do anything to enhance the image?"

"Some," mumbled Isoke, his fingers flying over the keyboard. "Let me work on it, and I'll give you a call if I find anything."

***

Sol Hammersham was not a happy man. He'd gotten a heads-up from Sammy Hankins that the police were going to be all over him.

"You'll be lucky to stay out of jail, let alone keep your law license," Hankins had said almost gleefully.

The attorney hadn't respond.

"I gave the cops almost everything I had on Levitt. They're not happy with you; they know you lied to them."

"I didn't lie. How do you think they found you?"

"Did you tell them who hired you?"

"You know I did," came the response. "What are you getting at?"

'I have pictures of you and the real boogie man," said the private investigator.

"You're blowing smoke, Sammy," said the lawyer. "I have more important things to do than bullshit with you. I've gotta go."

"Fine with me," said Hankins enjoying the moment. "I guess you'd have no objections if I called that cop who pulled your ass downtown. Wasn't her name Emily something?"

"You can't intimidate me. You got squat, and you know it."

"I have photos of you in a meeting at Martyrs Park a week after the murder of your favorite judge. It's never a good idea to count your money in public, Sol. Someone is always watching."

"You're on dangerous ground," said the attorney barely keeping his anger in check.

"I've been there before," replied the private investigator. "I have a proposition for you, counselor. It's something you can't refuse."

WHAT THE HELL

Horace's flight was almost an hour late, which for Emily was a blessing in disguise. She'd overslept after staying up past midnight with Todd. Now she had time to get to the gate and eat breakfast before the plane arrived. Emily was going to miss her old partner when his time in Memphis ended, but maybe she could visit him in Florida. Hell, she might even bring her boyfriend, if she still had one by then. That would be a hoot, thought Emily smiling at the idea. She was scrolling on her phone when Horace walked into the lounge area and looked around. God, he was a big presence, she thought as she stood and waved to get his attention.

"Hey, Kiddo," he said, using one of his pet nicknames for Emily. "Thanks for picking me up."

"My pleasure. How was your weekend in St Pete?"

"Good I got some time on the water sailing to Pelican Bay. It's amazing how the stress falls away with blue water and a strong wind. Any breaks in the case?"

"As a matter of fact, yes. We found David Barnett's girlfriend. Her body was found at his fish camp outside Dover, Tennessee. Marcy is charging him with the murder of the judge."

"How does John feel about that?"

"He's not too happy about it. Marcy said he thinks it's premature."

"And she's doing it anyway?" asked the retired homicide detective, somewhat surprised.

"Apparently so. Marcy explained her rationale, but John wasn't buying it."

"I hope she can produce something definitive. Barnett could walk without hard evidence," said Horace. "I wouldn't ignore John's advice on something like this. He's right most of the time."

"Hey, it's her case, I'm just along for the ride. Let's get your luggage."

"Before we do that, let's grab a cup of coffee and talk," Horace said. "I want to run something by you."

"There's a new business lounge in Concourse B," said Emily. "It's private and the coffee is free."

***

Showing her badge, they were ushered into a conference room located between the rotunda and gate nine. The smell of newness was almost overwhelming. In a few hours this place would be packed with harried businessmen and women making connections in and out of the River City.

"Nobody is booked for the next hour, detective," said the attendant who was a retired Shelby County Sheriff's deputy. "Let me know if you need anything."

"Okay, what's on your mind, Horace?" asked Emily after they'd squirreled themselves away in a quiet corner.

"I think we've overlooked something in Judge Levitt's murder."

"John thinks the same. He wants us to revisit everything: go back over interviews, look at forensic reports again, and widen the prospective pool of suspects."

"Why do you think Julia's body was dumped at the cemetery?" Horace asked.

"The killer knew the area and thought no one would be around. To my mind, that's the most reasonable explanation."

"Then why bring Levitt's car back and leave it near her house? It's a twenty-mile drive from Overton Park to the cemetery."

"John may have an answer for you," said Emily. "He talked to the owner of a construction company doing work at the Metal Museum. A camera was mounted on top of a crane near the judge's house the night she died. It caught a motorcycle arrive at the work site a little after nine and leave again at twelve fifty-four in the morning. It appears the killer was coming back to get his bike and needed the car to dump the judge's body. That's another reason Marcy wants to arrest Barnett. He owned a motorcycle dealership."

"That makes sense," commented Horace. "I'm assuming the camera didn't get a picture of the killer's face?"

"No, but Isoke is trying to identify the model of the bike and anything unique to the rider: size, unusual features, clothing, anything identifiable."

"What if the location means something to the killer? That dumping the body was meant to send a message."

"What type of message?"

"That I don't know," said Horace. "I have names of the people buried near where Julia's body was found. Do you know anyone who has an Ancestry account?"

"No," came the response. "If I were you, I'd open my own account and put the charges on my expense report."

"I knew I kept you around for a reason," laughed Horace.

"Greyson wants us to rethink our approach to everything," commented Emily. "How much do we really know about the judge and the suicide of her husband?"

"What are you getting at?"

"Maybe we need to look at Gene's suicide again with fresh eyes."

"Interesting," replied Horace. "I've scanned the reports on Dr. Levitt's suicide, but I haven't dug any deeper than that."

"There has to be a reason Emilio thought Julia was responsible for Gene's death. It looks to me the investigation ended once the coroner ruled his death as a suicide."

"You mean a reason other than Emilio is nuts?" asked the retired detective.

"Maybe or maybe not," responded Emily.

"Okay, it's time to get to work. Looks like we've got other avenues to explore. Let's go get my luggage."

"You do your genealogy stuff, and I'll go back and look at Levitt's suicide," said Emily. "How about drinks after work to compare notes. It'll be like old times."

***

This was not good, thought Hammersham, as he paced with his phone pressed to his ear.

"It's me," said the attorney in a low voice. "We have a problem. The investigator I hired to get something on Judge Levitt may have pictures of us meeting at Martyrs Park." After listening for a minute, Hammersham continued, "No, I haven't seen them, but he knew about the payoff. I can try to bullshit my way out of it, but if you're in the picture handing me money. Well, that complicates matters for us both."

"How much does he want?"

"A hundred thousand dollars and then he goes away."

"Do you believe him?"

"No, Sammy is a bloodsucker," declared Hammersham with certainty.

"Then he has to go…permanently."

"There has to be another way."

"Squeamish? You didn't seem to have that problem with Levitt. What's the difference?"

"That fucking bitch deserved it. She busted my balls every time I walked into her courtroom. Plus, I wasn't the one to kill her."

"Didn't you? What would the police say about that, counselor? Don't worry I'll take care of it. It's what I do, something you should remember."

"I may look like a pushover," replied Hammersham, his voice cracking, "but if something happens to me, Greyson gets a letter. You remember him, don't you? The friend of that whore. You won't like what happens next."

"Another threat Hammersham?"

Even as a boy, being teased or made fun of drove Hammersham mad. It was the real reason he'd agreed to get rid of Levitt; she'd made fun of him. Laughed at his legal arguments, disparaged the way he dressed, and even ridiculed the way he talked. He was glad she was dead; in his book, she deserved it. Looking out his office window, Hammersham knew the voice was right. Hankins had crossed a line and had to be eliminated...permanently.

"You're right; I'll do it," said the attorney. "It'll be done by the end of the week."

A SLIGHT SHIFT IN DIRECTION

Greyson was looking over crime scene photos for probably the tenth time when Isoke called.

"Detective, can you come down to the lab?"

"You got something," Greyson said.

"I got something unusual, but I'll let you decide if it's important or not," replied the crime lab boss.

"I'm on my way."

Isoke was young and a bit eccentric, so Greyson wasn't surprised to see him sporting spiked hair, but the black shirt, skinny white tie, and red high-top Chuck Taylor All Stars put him in a different class of eccentric.

"Detective, over here," he said, waving to get Greyson's attention. The lab was buzzing with activity. "I think I've identified the motorcycle in your video, and it's a beauty. I'd love to have it."

"You ride bikes?"

"Every day, I have a 2021 Moto Guzzi V7. It runs like new."

"I used to ride, but I preferred Hondas."

"Then you might recognize this cycle," said Isoke. "I'm almost certain it's a 750 Honda. As for year, I'd say somewhere between 1969 and 1977. That's when it underwent a major redesign."

"I don't doubt your findings, MK, but give me the *Reader's Digest* version of how you came to that conclusion."

"Our mystery rider's face was covered, but he made a careless mistake. When he ditched his bike, he got too close to a streetlight, and I got an image of the bike's logo off his face shield. Throw in the dimensions and shape of the headlight, and it all fits. I sent my findings to Torrance, California, the home office for Honda in the U.S, and they believe it's a 1976 model. The design stayed much the same until 1977, so it could be a little newer than '76, but not by much."

"It's not a home run," said Greyson slapping the young criminologist on the back, "but it's definitely a base hit. There can't be that many fifty-year-old motorcycles still on the road today."

"Okay, I'm glad I could help."

"Anything on the jewelry box and cards I found in Julia's house?" Greyson asked.

"Unfortunately no," said Isoke. "The paper is expensive but in high demand and sold all over the country. As for Judge Levitt's jewelry box, it's a specialty product. Only a few dealers, like Barton's, carry it, and I've been monitoring their sales but nothing so far. I'm sorry, John."

"You tried and that's all I can ask," responded the detective.

Greyson hurried to his desk and called Vivian Gales. His call went to voicemail, and he left a message.

"Dr. Gales this is John Greyson. Can you give me a call? I wonder if you know the year and model of the motorcycle your brother owns. Please return my call as soon as possible, it's kind of important."

***

Horace was looking for obituaries online and to say he was frustrated would be an understatement. He'd started his search by checking the archives of area newspapers. That hadn't worked, so next he picked up the phone and dialed the funeral director at the Mt. Moriah Cemetery.

"Have you checked any of the genealogy websites?" the funeral director asked after Horace caught him up to speed.

"Not yet, I started with the local archives."

"The newspapers aren't easy," the director said. "I'll have to check, but I think we've been keeping obits for our guests since the 1970s. Anything earlier, I'd suggest you check with historical societies or maybe the main library. They keep an amazing amount of data."

"Huh, I hadn't thought of libraries," mused the retired detective. "That's an option. How hard would it be to get the obits from your company?"

"Not hard just time-consuming," came the reply. "I don't have a large staff, so we'd have to do it when there was a lull in business."

"Do you get many lulls?"

"Not really," said the funeral director. "Business is literally rolling through the doors as we speak."

"What if I came to your place and did the search myself?"

"Let me check with the owners and call you back. If they don't object, it's okay with me."

***

Greyson was at lunch at a walk-up diner three blocks from his office when she called back.

"Detective, this is Vivian Gales. Emilio got his motorcycle when he was a senior in high school, and I think it was new."

"What year did he graduate from high school?"

"He and Gene graduated from Central in 1977. Emilio wasn't as smart as his valedictorian brother. The motorcycle was a present from our mother for him being inducted into the Honor Society. She did things like that all the time for Emilio."

"Do you know the make and model?" Greyson asked anxiously.

"It was a Honda, that's all I know. Detective why is this important?"

"We believe the person who killed your sister-in-law was riding an older model motorcycle, probably a Honda."

"If Emilio killed Julia, he needs help not prison."

"That isn't for me to decide," responded Greyson. "My job is to arrest the person who committed the crime, and right now that's looking more and more like your brother. Have you seen or talked to him recently?"

"No or I would have called you."

"Do you have any idea where he may have gone?"

"It could be anywhere," said Gales. "Emilio has money, and he speaks several languages, including Spanish. He could be in Mexico."

"We're acting under the premise that your brother is still in the area. There's no record Emilio has gone through customs."

"It's possible, but I don't know where he's gone. If I did, I'd tell you."

"Did you rehire Murphy?" asked the cop.

"No, I think I overreacted last time. My brother is not going to hurt me; I'm convinced of it."

"I think that's a bad decision, Dr. Gales. But it's your decision to make."

"Anything else detective?"

"No, that's all," said Greyson.

***

On the way to his office, Greyson called Marcy, "Didn't Barnett have a Honda dealership?" he asked when she answered.

"No, it was Suzuki dealership. Why?"

Greyson recounted his meeting with the crime lab genius and the identification of the motorcycle on the security video."

"A 1976 Honda? You've got to be kidding me. That's almost twenty years before I was born."

"Guess who owns a Honda bike from that era. I'll give you a hint; it's not Barnett."

"Don't tell me," she replied.

"Emilio Levitt," announced Greyson. "His sister confirmed it was a gift from his mother."

"Shit, you tried to warn me I was jumping the gun charging Barnett. I'm sorry John."

"No, we need to find Barnett. I'm beginning to wonder if he's not dead, too."

"What do you mean?" asked Marcy.

"He's here one day and falls off the face of the earth the next. Then we find his girlfriend murdered at his fish camp. Either he's dead, too, or we may be looking at a scenario where Levitt and Barnett both had something to do with Julia's murder."

"Do you think that's possible?"

"I think anything's possible at the moment," replied Greyson.

THE SOCIETY OF KAMADEVA

The Society of Kamadeva was a phantom. It didn't have a social footprint, it didn't advertise, and it wasn't known to law enforcement anywhere. Horace had checked. He was tempted to call Jordon Sellers and pressure him to name his contact at the group, but that type of coercion could create problems. Maybe, enough problems to tempt the attorney to stop cooperating, and his testimony might be needed later. Horace had discovered that Kamadeva was a Hindu god of love, desire, and passion, which he thought seemed appropriate all things considered. He was considering his next move when his phone rang.

"It's O'Malley," said the officer on duty. "You have a guest."

"Who is it?" asked Horace.

"Her card says Madeline Patrick-Cook, legal counsel for the Society of Kamadeva."

"I'll be right down," said Horace.

Madeline Patrick-Cook greeted him with a warm smile, firm handshake, and simple request.

"Can we go somewhere else and talk? There's a nice coffee shop in the Peabody."

"Give me a minute to grab my jacket," came the reply.

"If you have no objections, I'll meet you there," said the attorney. "What do you take?"

"I beg your pardon?"

"To drink," said Patrick-Cook. "Tea or coffee?"

"Coffee…thanks."

Horace found Emily at her desk and handed her Partick-Cook's business card.

"I'm meeting this woman in a few minutes. Find out everything you can about her and call me. We'll be at the Peabody Hotel."

"Are you looking for anything in particular?" asked Emily.

"No," he said over his shoulder as he walked away. "Get the big picture on her bio and make it quick."

***

Madeline Patrick-Cook was a regal-looking Black woman, immaculately dressed, and seemingly at ease wherever she found herself. She sat sipping her tea and glancing down at her cell phone as Horace approached.

"Detective Mann or is it Mr. Mann?" asked the attorney in a slight East Coast accent.

"Horace will do," said the retired detective. "I see you've done your homework. I was asked to consult in the Julia Levitt homicide, but you know that."

"I'm afraid I do. You were selected by John Greyson, who is the primary investigator in Julia's murder."

"That's not quite right," answered Horace as he put two packets of sugar in his coffee. "Marcy Thomas is the primary investigator. Detective Greyson stepped aside due to his personal relationship with Judge Levitt."

"I see," mused the attorney. "So what do you know about the Society of Kamadeva?"

"Not much I'm afraid. Not even the FBI has heard of your organization. I have to confess - I'm surprised you're here today. I must have unnerved Jordon Sellers."

"I'm afraid Jordon has not taken the death of his wife very well; I've suggested he see a grief counselor. His date with Julia was his first as a widower, and I'm afraid he wasn't ready. What we offer is not for everyone."

"And what is that exactly? What do you offer?"

"A safe place for our members to connect with like-minded professionals who are not looking for long-term relationships. Applicants are thoroughly vetted based on their professional histories, educational accomplishments, criminal and financial backgrounds. I can assure you that only a small percentage of the people recommended become part of the Society of Kamadeva."

"How are you funded?" asked Horace.

"We began with a large endowment thanks to the founders of our society, and there is a yearly membership fee. Our expenses are minimal, with the lion's share of funds earmarked to maintain our servers. Our payroll consists of about a dozen people: researchers mainly, a few schedulers, and a general secretary."

"You didn't mention attorneys," remarked the retired detective.

"I was asked to represent the organization in this matter by the Board of Managers, and I agreed to do it. I'm a member, Horace. We are an organization of professionals who are willing to donate our time pro bono for the betterment and safety of the membership. In this matter we've broken no laws. We're willing to help you… within reason."

"I want the names of the people Julia Levitt met," stated Horace.

The smile on Patrick-Cook's face told him that was not going to happen without a fight. As he was about to speak again, his phone rang.

"Excuse me, I need to get this," he said as he got up and stepped away from the table. It was Emily.

"What do you have?" he asked.

"Madeline Patrick-Cook is a heavyweight. She graduated from Spelman College and got her law degree from Stanford. She comes from money and has made a bunch of her own. No children and her late husband Ted Cook passed away from cancer fifteen years ago. He owned a string of radio stations on the West Coast."

"Anything else?"

"No. On paper, she's a model citizen."

"Okay, I gotta go, but I'll talk to you later."

When Horace returned to their table, Patrick-Cook wore an identical smile to the one he'd left with.

"Did I get a passing grade?" asked the attorney.

"You passed with flying colors," said Horace. "If you're not willing to give me a list of names, what can you do for me?"

"I can be available to answer your questions, and I can identify two society members who went on dates with Julia who have no alibi for the night of her death. After our general secretary heard what happened, he immediately opened an investigation. Several of our members have worked at high levels in various law enforcement organizations, and they agreed to look into the matter. They cleared everyone except for two."

"How many people are we talking about?"

"There were fifteen in the past twelve months." At that point, Patrick-Cook took an envelope from her purse and slid it across the table toward Horace. "You have my number, detective. Call me if you think I can help. Julia's death has had a profound effect on every member in the Society. Frankly, it has caused us to reevaluate our organization's existence. Life today has become so unpredictable and violent that we must ask ourselves if what we are promoting is still safe. If not, we need to let the organization die. Just so you know, Julia and Gene Levitt were early members of our group and a dear friend of mine. I fervently hope you catch the person who did this."

"How did it go?" asked Emily when he returned to the office.

"We've got two more suspects," said Horace, holding up the envelope he'd gotten from Madeline Patrick-Cook. "Where's Greyson?"

"I don't think he's in the office. Why?"

"No reason, I'll talk to him later."

HAMMER TIME

Growing up Sol Hammersham had been a wimpy kid who his classmates loved to torment - that is until they discovered he was a vindictive little bastard. If you pissed him off or didn't show the proper amount of respect, he'd make your life a living hell. He'd once planted drugs in a teacher's car and called the Crime Stoppers hotline after getting a bad grade. The scheme failed after another student gave the bewildered woman a heads-up, but his *don't fuck with Sol* message had been received. After that, he was untouchable. The Hammer, as he liked to call himself, boasted that all his family members were the same – sonsofbitches, which wasn't too far from the truth. His father was a career criminal, and his mother would cut your throat just because she could. As the saying goes, he came by it naturally.

Now, Sol's lifelong training was kicking in again. A call to Sammy Hankins had set up a meeting that afternoon at the Kudzu, a once-badass blues bar near downtown. He'd promised to give the PI ten thousand dollars if he'd show him some of the pictures he'd taken at Martyrs Park. It would be considered a down payment, he'd said. Setting up the meeting had been relatively easy. He knew money, especially a large sum of money, would entice Sammy. He hoped it would also cause the private investigator to lower his guard. He didn't want to go one-on-one with Sammy Hankins; he'd lose that fight. But not if he fought dirty.

***

The bar was closed for renovations, but not to Hammersham. He owned the Kudzu. His name wasn't on the deed, but it was his, nevertheless. He had arrived early and had the music cranked up when Sammy appeared. The PI hesitated before stepping inside.

"Come on in!" yelled the attorney from behind the bar. "What are you drinking?"

"What's going on, Sol? Why are we the only ones here?"

"You didn't want an audience when I handed you a satchel full of money, did you? Somebody might be watching," said Hammersham laughing amiably. "I can cook something up in the kitchen if you're hungry."

At that moment, the attorney bent over, picked up a leather knapsack, and placed it on the bar.

"You get this when I see the pictures," he said, still smiling.

"No tricks, Sol. I'll beat the shit out of you. Do you understand me?"

"Hey, it's not my money, so I don't have a dog in the fight. I told my client you'd honor our agreement and explained we needed to stick with the plan."

"What plan?"

"Sorry, Sammy. That's above your pay grade. Just take your money and have a good life."

"Okay, let's do this," said Hankins as he placed an eight-by-ten envelope on the bar in front of the attorney.

Hammersham pushed the knapsack toward the private eye and began looking at the photos.

"I didn't know you were such an accomplished photographer, Sammy," he said admiringly. "You nailed it. So what's next?"

"When can I get the rest of my money?"

"I've got it now, just not with me. I have a question for you. How do I know you won't come back later looking for another payday?"

"I don't know. I guess you'll have to trust me," Hankins said, grinning like a fox in the henhouse. "You do trust me don't you, Hammer?"

"Not for a minute," came the attorney's reply, "but what choice do I have?"

"Exactly!" said the private investigator, enjoying the moment. "Let's finish this. I have other things to do."

"When and where?"

"Since you have my money, what's wrong with now?" said Hankins. "Get it and meet me at my office."

"Don't try to screw me on this Sammy. If I go down, you go down."

Instead on saying anything, Hankins crossed his heart with an index finger. It was then that the attorney knew that he'd be back. Maybe not next month or even six months from now, but when the money was gone, Hankins would try to blackmail him again. If the Hammer felt misgivings for what he planned to do, they were gone now.

"Let's have a drink to seal the deal," proposed Hammersham. "What's your poison?"

When Hankins came to, the private investigator found himself strapped in a large wooden chair that had been bolted to the floor. The first thing he noticed was the overpowering smell of mold, and the scurrying feet of rodents just out of sight moving around in the semi-darkness.

"You motherfucker! You drugged me," said Hankins. "When I get out of this chair, I'm going to beat the hell out of you, Sol. That's a fucking promise."

"You mean if you get out of that chair," corrected the attorney. "Sammy, I really like you, but you've put me in a difficult position. You have something that can hurt me and my client, and I want it…all of it. Here's what's going to happen. You're going to give me the alarm codes for your house and office and then tell me where you hid the pictures from Martyrs Park. If you lie to me, I'm going to cut off a finger. To show you I mean business, I'm going to start by cutting off the pinkie on your left hand. Since you're a righty, you'll never miss it on the golf course."

In one fluid motion Hammersham grabbed Hankins' hand and severed the finger in one fluid motion. Blood squirted onto the floor and began to pool, all while the private eye screamed in agony.

"Yell all you want, Sammy. No one is going to hear you. You're in the basement of a building that was built in 1927. They used real wood and brick then. And we're at least ten feet underground."

As Hankins struggled to get free, the attorney dialed a number and put the call on speaker. When a man's voice answered, he asked, "Are you there, yet?"

"In the parking lot outside his office."

"Okay, Sammy. Here's your chance to save another finger," smirked the Hammer.

"Keep the money, just let me go," begged Hankins. "I swear to god I'll give you the pictures and never say a word to anyone."

"Sammy, you've already demonstrated I can't trust you. Why would I let you go?"

Before the PI could respond, Hammersham severed another finger. He laughed uncontrollably as more blood flowed.

"Give me the alarm codes and do it now," came the icy demand from the attorney. "You can walk away from this, Sammy. I'll even let you keep the ten thousand dollars, but I want the pictures, camera and your laptop, and I want you out of town. Do you fucking understand me!"

"I understand," said Hankins. "The security code is 04191965. It's my birthday."

"What about your house?"

"All my passcodes are the same. It makes it easier to remember."

"Smart," replied the attorney sarcastically. "Now where are the pictures?"

"In my office safe. The camera is there, too. A key to the safe is in the left-hand drawer of my desk."

"Sammy, I hate to admit it, but I'm a little disappointed you caved so quickly. I've been looking forward to this."

"You're working with someone. They're going to check everything I tell you before you kill me. Why go through the pain if it won't change anything in the end. I'll give you a tip, Hammer. You're not going to get away with killing a criminal court judge, not with Horace Mann and Greyson driving the investigation. You're smart, smarter than I thought, but those guys are on a mission. They won't stop. One day they're going to take everything you own and lock you away in a four by eight-foot cell. You'll be alive but only just."

"Did you get that, the alarm codes?" Hammersham asked his co-conspirator, ignoring Hankins's comment.

"Yeah, I'm already in the office and headed toward the safe. Give me a minute." Later, Hammersham heard, "I got them, but I'll have to make a second trip for the computer. Get on with it."

"How do you want to go, Sammy?"

"No last drink or cigarette?" responded the private eye.

"Maybe in your next life," said Hammersham as he walked behind the restrained man and place a gun to the back of his head. "This will only hurt for a second." He laughed and pulled the trigger.

The sound wasn't as bad as he'd expected, in fact he was a little disappointed.

"Damn, that was fricking awesome," declared the attorney, stepping back to admire his handiwork. "I should have filmed it."

***

Hammersham had orchestrated every detail. An hour after the brain of Sammy Hankins had been scattered across the basement floor, two men showed up and moved a wooden crate out of the basement and loaded it into a rental truck. It would go to a terminal on Channel Avenue and be loaded on a barge headed to New Orleans. Somewhere between Vicksburg and Natchez, the private detective's body would slide unseen into the dark, muddy waters of Ol' Man River. Where it would end up was anybody's guess. Hammersham didn't care one way or the other; his only concern was ensuring Hankins' murder couldn't be blamed on him. With the building closed for renovation, he'd decided to use paint thinner as the accelerant of choice. It was cheap, easy to obtain, and used widely in building projects such as this. The fire marshal would more than likely rule it as arson, but that could be blamed on vagrants. There were no shortage of them hanging out and breaking into empty buildings in this crumbling neighborhood. In fact, two other properties nearby had burned to the ground recently. Hammersham felt good about his chances of success. He'd rid himself of a property that was no longer yielding a return on investment and destroy evidence of a murder at the same time. It was a stroke of genius, a win-win situation, he thought.

The attorney emptied a can of the flammable solvent on the stairs leading to the main floor. He'd start the inferno in the basement, let the flames race through the interior of the wooden structure, and collapse in on itself. After collecting a few mementos and putting them in his car, Hammersham torched the Kudzu and never looked back. Forty-five minutes later, the roof caved in and put an end to the historic blues bar.

***

Everyone knows the expression: *the best laid plans of mice and men often go astray.* The murder of Sammy Hankins worked to perfection. The disposal of his body? Not so much. A carjacking, a police chase, and a newsworthy car accident completely upended Hammersham's perfect scheme. The men who'd been hired to make Hankins' body disappear disappeared themselves as they fled the scene. Meanwhile, they'd left Hankins' body in the back of their U-Haul.

Hammersham had seen the crash on local TV and heard the description of his hired hands, now at large. He winced two hours later when an unfamiliar phone number appeared on the screen of his cell.

"I give you one thing to do, and you fuck it up!" screamed Hammersham, spittle flying as he yelled. "Why did you run? The cops would have filled out a report and let you go. Now, they have your fingerprints."

"We wore gloves. We are good," said a calm voice on the other line.

"That's not the fucking point!" yelled the attorney, not believing what he was hearing. "Where are you now?"

"On the boat. We figured the police will never look for us here. We leave tonight at ten."

"When will you get to New Orleans?"

"Three days, we're pushing fifteen barges this trip. It's usually more."

"You better hope I don't find you before the police," responded

Hammersham as the rage continued to build. "Tell that bitch who hired you to give me a call. This isn't over!"

***

Greyson got a call from the medical examiner's office a little after two in the morning.

"Greyson," he answered in a scratchy morning voice.

"Sir, this is Doctor Longly at the morgue. Doc Richards said I should give you a call."

"What's up Longly?"

"A male victim came in a few hours ago, and his fingerprints matched those of a former police officer."

"Who is it?" asked Greyson, now alert.

"Samuel Hankins. He's been shot at close range and from behind, and there are signs he'd been restrained and tortured prior to his murder."

"Give me the details."

"The carjacking of an Infinity QX55 on South Third led to a police chase that ended when the Infinity ran a red light and hit a U-Haul on E.H. Crump Boulevard. The suspects in the hijacking were apprehended, but the driver and another man in the box truck took off running and disappeared. When the police searched the truck, Mr. Hankins' body was found in a wooden crate. Since he was a former police officer, I contacted Doc Richards, who in turn told me to call you."

"Thanks for the call Doctor Longly. I'll be down there as soon as I can get dressed."

He found Horace in the kitchen making a pot of coffee.

"The phone wake you up?"

"It's an old cop affliction," laughed the retired detective. "A phone rings in the middle of the night, and I'm wide awake. It drives Barb nuts. What's up?"

"Your old buddy, Sammy Hankins, is dead. His body was found a few hours ago in the back of a U-Haul."

"What happened?"

Greyson repeated what Longly had told him and ended with, "Sammy was shot in the back of the head."

"He always said he wanted to go quick," remarked Horace. "I guess he got his wish."

"How do you know so much about Hankins?"

"I recommended his termination. He'd gotten into some minor scrapes and was assigned to ride with someone more senior than his trainer. That was me. Sammy had all the ingredients to be a great cop, but the measurements were off. He was too aggressive on some things and not aggressive enough on others. Sammy would look the other way for people he knew, and then body slam a drunk driver. I liked Sammy, but he didn't have the right stuff to protect and serve. Get dressed, we can drive through a McDonald's. I want to look at the truck and talk with the medical examiner."

"Are you going to be okay?" asked Greyson, now concerned. "You don't look good."

"We'll see," came the response.

***

Instead of going to McDonald's, the two friends picked up coffee and donuts at a drive thru Dunkin Donuts on Union. The West Tennessee Forensic Center was less than ten minutes away. Greyson had called ahead, and Longly was waiting when they arrived.

"I pulled Mr. Hankins' body from the cooler for your examination," he said. "Toxicology reports will take a few days."

"Have you been able to determine the caliber of gun used to kill Sammy?" asked Horace.

"It was probably a 9mm, possibly a 45. There was a contact burn at the base of the skull with the trajectory of the bullet angled upward and exiting the right eye. My guess is the shooter was left-handed."

"What about personal items?" asked Greyson.

"None were on the body," Longly said.

"Any other injuries?" asked Horace.

"Two fingers on Mr. Hankins' left hand were severed. I recovered a few metal fragments in the wounds, which I sent to the lab for analysis," said the doctor.

"Someone wanted him to talk, and he did," remarked Horace, more to himself than Greyson or Longly. "Sammy was a big guy; he wouldn't have gone down without a fight. Check for something that would have incapacitated him, doc."

"I'll let you know when the toxicology report comes in."

"Greyson said the body was found in a wooden box. Is it here or have you sent it to the crime lab?"

"It's going out in the morning. Would you like to see it?"

"Absolutely," said the two lawmen in unison. "Lead the way."

Longly led them through a maze of rooms filled with stainless steel tables, monitors, saws, and various medical instruments used on the dead. Their journey ended in front of a locked steel door.

"Gentlemen, during an autopsy we inventory the deceased's personal items, photograph them, and store them in this room. It's locked at all times with a security camera in place to record anyone entering or leaving. This guarantees a positive chain of custody."

The crate was placed on two sawhorses positioned in front of a large overhead door; a plastic tag embedded with an RFID chip was stapled to its side.

"Is that an address?" asked Greyson, bending over and looking closer at the crate.

"It looks like a stamp of some kind," responded Longly. "We were going to let the lab guys figure it out."

Horace got down on his knees and studied the mark for several seconds before standing again.

"The address is smudged, but I can make it out. I'm pretty sure it says Port of New Orleans. How far is the shipping marina from where the accident happened?"

"You think someone planned to load Sammy Hankins' body on a barge?" asked Greyson. "That's nuts."

"What's that saying from Sherlock Holmes in *The Sign of Four?*" asked Horace, smiling at his friend. "*When you have eliminated the impossible, whatever remains, however improbable, must be the truth.* It's really genius. Get somewhere downriver from Memphis and on a dark, moonless night, drop the body in the water. It could surface anywhere from Tunica to Baton Rouge or not at all. We got lucky."

"Are you suggesting our missing U-Haul drivers could be crew hands on a barge?"

"It's possible. Why don't you work the barge angle, and I'll check the body," suggested Horace. "I can get a ride to work."

"Are you sure you're going to be okay?" asked Greyson again.

"Go, go, we got stuff to do," came the response from Horace. "Stop being a mother hen. It's not a good look for you."

CHECK TWO OFF THE LIST

It was Emily's job to investigate two members from the Society of Kamadeva who had no alibis the night Judge Levitt was murdered. One was a doctor from Atlanta, the other an airline pilot from Germantown. Emily started with the pilot since he was closer. His name was Mel Young, and he was forty-seven years old, divorced twice with two kids from his first marriage. She found him settling bets after a round of golf at his country club.

"Did you win?" asked Emily.

"I lost a little. Do you play?"

"I carry an eight handicap at Wedgewood."

"Impressive," said the pilot. "Do you have your clubs with you?"

"In the trunk of my car, but I'm not a member."

"You can be my guest. Let me talk to the starter and see if he can squeeze us in for nine. My name is Mel Young."

"I'm Sergeant Emily Morgan with the Memphis Police Department," said the woman detective handing Young her business card.

He frowned at first and then asked, "What's this about?"

"Can we go somewhere and talk? I'm investigating the murder of Judge Julia Levitt."

"Sure, let's step into the banquet hall. I was wondering when someone from the police would show up.

The banquet hall wasn't huge, but it was opulent; thick crimson carpeting, hanging chandeliers, and an array of accordion doors leading out onto a covered patio with breathtaking views of the course. This would be a perfect venue for a wedding reception, thought the detective.

"I suppose you got my name for someone at the society?" Mel said.

"I did," responded Emily. "Let's begin with how you met Judge Levitt."

"I saw Julia's profile on the society's website, liked it, and sent her a note to see if she'd be interested in meeting for drinks. She accepted my invitation."

"Where did you meet?"

"At Catherine and Mary's on the corner of Main and Linden. We engaged in small talk for a while then got down to business. A week later, we had dinner at the Rivermont, and she spent the night at my house the next evening."

"What do you mean 'got down to business'?"

"This is a little embarrassing," said the pilot.

"There's not much I haven't seen or heard, Mr. Young. I don't think anything you say will shock me."

"Some of us have certain fetishes, and it's best to clarify expectations before deciding to have an enjoyable evening."

"I'm assuming Judge Levitt was agreeable to your sexual predilections since she spent the night with you."

"She was. I enjoyed myself immensely, and I thought she did too, but the next morning her mood had changed. She was polite but informed me not to contact her again. I got a kiss on the cheek, and she left."

"Did that make you mad?"

"No, but I was certainly confused by it all. She was into everything we did, no objections at all."

"Where were you on the night Judge Levitt was murdered?"

"I have a house on Greers Ferry Lake in Arkansas. I was there, and I was alone."

"Did you see or speak to anyone who can provide you with an alibi?"

"I met two women in a canoe, but I didn't get their names. They were young, said they were from Memphis. One of them was a redhead. I thought they were college students or maybe just out of school. Other than that, I have nothing."

"You didn't buy gas or food while you were on the lake?" Emily asked.

"No, I came prepared. Unfortunately for me, it seems."

"Okay, thanks for your time. I'll be in touch."

"Let's hit the links next time," he said smiling. "We can talk as we go."

***

An hour after getting back to the office, Emily began contacting outfitters around Greers Ferry Lake. On her third call, she hit paydirt. A canoe rental shop gave her two names and phone numbers. One call later and Mel Young was no longer a suspect. The next person on her list was a cardiac surgeon in Atlanta named Dr. Asher Holiday. Luckily for her, he was not in surgery.

"Do I need to conference in my attorney?" he'd asked after Emily explained the reason for her call.

"That's your right, doctor," she explained, "but I'm trying to clear you as a suspect in a homicide. That's all."

"Okay, what do you want to know?"

"Tell me how you met Julia Levitt?"

His story was similar to that of Mel Young, except he'd flown to Memphis to meet the judge.

"We had dinner at a nice restaurant downtown; I don't remember the name, but Julia told me it used to be an old movie theater. I got a suite at the Peabody, and the next night Julia joined me. We had a wonderful time, and then I flew home."

"Did you see or talk to her again?"

"No, but not because I didn't want to. She had some odd rule about long-term relationships. She told me it was the reason she and her husband had joined the Society of Kamadeva, to provide a safe outlet for her fetish. Her word, not mine."

"Where were you on the night Julia Levitt was murdered?" asked Emily.

"I was home alone. I'd had a bad week, which is never good for a cardiac surgeon. It means you've lost a patient, and this one was twenty-two years old who'd been expected to recover."

"Did you talk to anyone, order take-out, or see a neighbor?"

"I got drunk. You see I'm an alcoholic, and I fell off the wagon. It wasn't the first time."

"Can anyone verify your story?" asked Emily.

"My sponsor at A.A.," Holley said. "He came to my house after I called him crying."

"Thank you, doctor," said Emily, writing down the contact information. "I'll be in touch."

Thirty minutes later Emily eliminated Dr. Asher Holiday from their list of suspects.

***

"Sammy Hankins is dead?" Emily asked in surprise after checking in with her old partner. "How?"

"Shot in the head execution style."

"Sammy was a big guy. I wouldn't want to tackle him alone," replied Emily, remembering her visit to his office with Horace.

"I believe he was drugged. I want you and Greyson to check the marinas that handle barges and concentrate on boats headed toward New Orleans."

"Why, what are you looking for?"

"Call Greyson, and he'll tell you everything."

A PHONE CALL

Date night at the Bombay Bicycle Club was long overdue. Marcy and Murphy's on-again, off-again relationship was drifting in the wrong direction. Whatever the reason - the crowd, the band, their bodies working up a sweat on the dance floor – everything seemed perfect to her tonight. The evening ended with them naked and ensnared in a lover's embrace at Murphy's house. It wasn't until the next morning when she looked at her phone that Marcy saw multiple messages from the same number. That had her looking for her clothes.

"Where's my fucking bra?"

"I think it's on the stairs with most of your other clothes," Murphy said smiling. "You couldn't wait to get me in bed."

"I've got to go," said Marcy, pulling on one on Murphy's T-shirts and hustling out of the room. "See you later, cowboy. Work on your foreplay while I'm gone."

"Hey, that hurts!" he yelled from the top of the stairs as she disappeared out the door her bra in one hand. She called Ginny Barnett as soon as she backed out of Murphy's driveway. No answer. She called again, but still no luck.

"Damn it, where are you, Ginny?" she said softly to herself.

Ginny's car was in the driveway, and everything looked normal until she reached the rear of the house. The back door had been kicked in, and a trail of blood led up the stairs to a bedroom. Inside, she found Ginny tied to the bed frame, her lip split and one eye partially swollen shut. A rag had been stuffed in her mouth and taped in place using duct tape.

"Dispatch, this is Detective Marcy Thomas. I need an ambulance and a squad car at 1951 Overton Park Avenue, female assault victim."

"Roger, detective," came the response. "ETA fifteen minutes."

Marcy quickly untied the bound woman and carefully removed the gag.

"Who did this to you?" she asked.

"David," said Barnett in a hoarse whisper. "He said he'd kill me if I called the police. He's coming back."

"Don't move I have an ambulance and backup on the way."

"Don't leave me!" cried Barnett, grabbing Marcy's hand.

"I'm not going anywhere, Ginny. I'll be here until an ambulance arrives. Where did David go?"

"To the bank. He needs money."

"What bank?"

"He always uses Union Planters, the one on Union near Crump Stadium."

"Okay, we're going to get him so he can't do this to you again. I have to make a call, but I'm not leaving the room. Do you understand?"

Barnett nodded but her eyes followed Marcy's every move. She was trembling when she returned.

"I issued an all-points bulletin for David, and we're going to catch him. Ginny, an ambulance is on its way, and they'll take good care of you."

"You're not going with me to the hospital?" sobbed the injured woman.

"No, I have to stay here to catch David, but there'll be an officer with you at all times. You're going to be safe, and I'll see you as soon as I can."

***

Emily beat Greyson to Ginny Barnett's house.

Pulling Marcy into a second bedroom, she asked, "Where's your fucking bra? The girls are putting on quite the show."

"I was at Murphy's when I saw Ginny's call, and I came directly here."

"And you didn't have time to dress? Come-on, we have enough trouble being taken seriously as it is."

"I left my bra in the car. Can you get it for me?"

"It's either that or I take off mine," said Emily smiling briefly. "I'll be right back and for your information Greyson is right behind me."

"Shit! Hurry up, Emily. I don't want John to catch me like this."

While she was gone, dispatch notified Marcy that David Barnett had been apprehended and was being taken to 170 N. Main to be held for interrogation. She couldn't wait to rip him to a new one.

"Hurry up and put this on," said Emily. "Greyson is downstairs talking to a crime scene tech."

"Turn around," replied Marcy, nodding toward the door.

"I don't think so," came the reply. "If Murphy can see them so can I."

"Suit yourself," laughed Marcy as she yanked off a Grateful Dead T-shirt and slipped on her bra. That's the scene Greyson found when he opened the bedroom door.

"I, ah, well, huh," he sputtered backing up. "Marcy, I'll be outside when you get dressed. Come see me."

When he closed the door, they both burst out laughing.

***

The first words out of David Barnett's mouth were, "I want a lawyer."

"Fine with me," said Marcy with a smirk. "Tell him you're being charged for the assault and battery of your ex-wife, robbery, and the murder of Judge Julia Levitt and Anna Leigh Styles. She was your girl-friend, wasn't she? Man, you should see what those blowflies did to Anna Leigh's body. I've got pictures if you want to see them."

"Fuck you, bitch. I didn't kill Levitt or Anna Leigh, and you can't prove it."

"Barnett, I'm going to be there when they stick a needle in your arm, give you a minute to say something stupid, and then watch you go to hell. I've heard the new drugs they use are really bad. They make the condemned man feel like he's on fire. Of course, that's only what I've heard, but it took over twenty minutes for that guy in Florida to stop breathing. Did you know they make you wear a diaper?"

When he charged her, his hands balled into fists, Marcy welcomed it. She stepped forward and drove the palm of her hand upward into Barnett's chin. He dropped like a sack of wet sand.

"Bad idea, asshole. Now you have an additional charge of assault on a police officer. What the hell did Ginny see in a dirtbag like you?"

"I didn't kill anyone, I swear to god!" cried Barnett. "Anna Leigh was supposed to meet me at the fish camp after getting money from MacKinzie Owens. We were going to Mexico to get away from this crap and start over. When I got there, she was dead and the money gone. My car was a piece of crap, so I took Anna Leigh's."

"Then you just happened to beat the hell out of your ex-wife for the fun of it?" countered Marcy.

"Ginny owed me. I was living the high life until the divorce, and it was all Levitt's fault. She should have kept her fucking nose out of my business."

"And that's why you killed her. You just admitted to having a motive and we now know the killer rode a motorcycle. You owned a motorcycle shop didn't you, asshole? It's called means, motive, and opportunity. You're screwed Barnett. Tell me what happened, and you might avoid the death penalty."

"I'm done talking," he said, beginning to sulk. "I want an attorney."

"What do you think?" she asked Greyson outside in the hallway.

"It's circumstantial, but we've won cases with less. Let Barnett cool his heels for now and hold off on charging him with murder. We can add it later."

"Okay, I'm headed to the hospital to get a statement from Ginny. Call me if anything new develops."

***

Things were moving fast. Greyson called Emily and told her to check the barge terminal on President's Island. He was on his way to the marina on Channel. They'd gotten lucky and had a name. The cab of the

U-Haul had been wiped clean, but a single thumbprint had been found under the liftgate. It belonged to Alton Smith, a career criminal who'd spent more time in prison than out. Horace and Greyson were both convinced that Smith was on one of the barges moving south headed toward NOLA. Once they had a crew manifest, they could call downriver and have the New Orleans Harbor Police waiting.

Horace decided to stay at the morgue; he had unfinished business. His history with the disgraced police officer was more complicated than he'd divulged to the team, and he had one final act to perform. As everyone rushed in different directions, Greyson's instincts told him that finally they had something solid, and he was determined to hold on for dear life.

TIME TO GO HOME

Horace sat in the morgue filled with remorse and not wanting to move. He was transported back to decisions he'd made more than two decades ago. Could he have done more, said something different, looked the other way one more time? Sammy Hankins had been his responsibility. Times were different then, the rules were less transparent, and Horace had been a hard-ass. He'd played it by the book. Sammy had begged him for one more chance, promised to change, to be a good cop.

"Give me one more chance, Horace. I swear to God I won't let you down."

The words echoed in his brain. He could hear them like they'd been said yesterday, but it hadn't mattered. Horace made sure Sammy Hankins had been fired. Oh, he'd helped him afterwards and kept an eye on him for a while, but it still hurt. He had so much potential, thought the retired cop.

"God, Sammy, I'm so sorry," he muttered, looking at the shrouded body lying on a cold stainless-steel slab. "If you'd only listened," he said as the words trailed off. Dr. Longly checked on him several times and finally sat down and asked if he wanted to say a prayer. Horace nodded and they joined hands.

***

Horace got a ride to the office and tried to work, but his mind was elsewhere and in another time. At three he got up from his borrowed desk, closed his laptop, and sent Greyson a message.

"I'm going to your house and walk Blue. We need to talk this afternoon."

"Are you okay?" came the return message.

"Not really, but there's nothing you can do, so don't try."

"I'm leaving early; give me an hour. I think we have a lead on Sammy's murderer," came the return message.

Horace didn't reply and turned off his phone. There was nothing Greyson could say to make him feel better. He didn't think he deserved it. He'd known Sammy's father, a big tough Irishman who would rather fight than make love to a good-looking woman, and he'd been hard on his son. He'd also been a cop and had asked Horace to get his offspring onto the force, which he'd done. Samuel Allen Hankins had graduated first in his class at the police academy, but trouble started soon after he'd earned his badge. Like father like son, Sammy was tough, but he was also immature. That's a bad mix for a police officer.

"You brought him on," the captain had said to Horace. "Set him straight or get rid of him. This is on you, Horace."

It hadn't worked out, and his death wasn't Horace's fault, but the boy deserved better. Horace was only three years older than Greyson, but he felt ancient. It's why he'd retired when he did and moved away. The shadowy faces of the dead never really went away. Through the haze of restless nights or hiding in the fringes of wakefulness, they revisited time and time again. Suddenly he knew what he had to do.

***

"Let's go to Dino's," Horace said. "I walked Blue, and I'm starving."

"Are you okay?" Greyson asked.

"I think so, but I've got to go home, John. I'm sorry but the daily grind is too much."

"The ghosts are back?" asked Greyson.

Horace shook his head no before saying, "Not yet, but I can hear their footsteps."

"You've done enough," said Greyson hugging his longtime friend in a bearhug. "When?"

"I fly out at eight-thirty in the morning," Horace said.

"Let's make it a going-away affair, and I'll call Emily and Marcy."

"No, just us," stated Horace with a smile. "Two old friends rehashing the good ole days."

"They were good," responded Greyson. "My god Horace. Where did the time go?"

The two old friends didn't discuss the case until the ride home from Dino's. Greyson explained the dragnet he'd set up to capture Alton Smith, one of the men in the U-Haul with Sammy Hankins' body.

"He's on one of two towboats sailing for New Orleans," Greyson said. "The local cops are waiting and will detain the crew until fingerprints are gathered. Then it's just a matter of identifying and arresting Smith."

"And you think Smith can tell you who killed Sammy?" Horace asked.

"I'm betting on it, and I think I know who he'll finger."

"The attorney, Hammersham," said the retired detective.

"That's right, and I think he's working with someone," added Greyson.

"Someone? Hammersham told us his client was Emilio Levitt. Don't you think that's who's behind this?" asked Horace.

"I don't know, but I have my doubts."

"You found something," said Horace.

"Maybe," came Greyson reply. "I'll let you know when I put some meat on the bones."

"You got one of your famous hunches," declared Horace.

"A few days ago at City Coffee," Greyson said. "That old coffee bar has magic in it."

"Come on…share," said Horace.

"Think smoke and mirrors," replied Greyson. "What if someone not in the picture is pulling the strings? They're close enough to know what we're doing, but far enough away to avoid suspicion."

"Like Ginny Barnett?"

"Someone like her, yeah. Somebody we all know but haven't vetted yet."

"Okay, I give up," laughed Horace. "I guess I'll have to wait for the movie to come out. What are the chances we didn't finish that bottle of bourbon I brought with me?"

THE CASE CONTINUES

Marcy was told that Ginny Barnett had been admitted to Method University Hospital for observation. When she walked into her hospital room, Ginny looked better than when Marcy had found her, but her ex had done a job on her. Her left eye was turning black and almost shut, there were bruises on both exposed arms, and she now had stiches in her lip.

"How are you feeling, Ginny?" asked Marcy, keeping her voice low.

"Where the hell were you? You said you'd be there if I needed help," snapped the young woman. "He could have killed me."

"But he didn't and why didn't you call 911?"

Barnett looked away as tears rolled down her cheeks. She looked small in the hospital bed.

"David called and said he needed money, that someone was trying to kill him. I told him to go to hell. I thought that would be the end of it, but he showed up and kicked in my back door. That's when I tried to call you, when I saw him walking up my driveway."

"Did he say who was after him?"

"No, just that he needed money to get out of the country. He said I owed him."

"What happened to his motorcycle shop?"

"David was behind in payments, so the bank foreclosed on his loan. Why is that important?"

"It might indicate who he was running from."

"I don't see how," Ginny replied. "I was a co-signer on David's loan. The bank will come after me to make good on his outstanding payments - not dispatch someone to kill him."

"Did you know Anna Leigh Styles?" asked Marcy, changing the subject.

"No, but she sat in the car one time when David stopped by to pick up some of his stuff. We never spoke."

"We found her body at David's fish camp," Marcy said. "She'd been strangled and dead for several days."

"Oh my god, what a horrible way to die. I can't believe David would do something like that."

"Look what he did to you," countered Marcy. "What else did David tell you?"

"That he was being set up, and he didn't kill Julia," replied Ginny.

"Do you have any idea who he thought would do that?"

"No.," Ginny said. "David sounded scared on the telephone, and it takes a lot to scare him."

"What did your ex steal from you?" Marcy asked.

"I had two hundred dollars in my purse, some jewelry, and David took my debit card and checkbook."

"Anything else?" asked the detective.

"Not that I can think of," Ginny replied, "but I need to go back to the house to make sure. I was stunned, detective. I've never been hit like that before."

"I assume you're going to press charges?"

"You can bet on it," said Ginny. "I want that motherfucker behind bars."

***

Emily had identified two towboats, the *Patricia Ann* and *River's Folly* headed toward the Cresent City and Alton Smith was on one of them. She was sure of it, and she'd driven like a bat out of hell to be in New Orleans when the boats docked. After handing out photographs to the harbor police, they'd notified the towboat captains that their vessels would be boarded, and the crews held temporarily once they arrived in port. Now it was only a matter of waiting. Emily was in a place called the Harbor Grill eating their self-proclaimed world's famous shrimp po' boys when her phone rang.

"The captain of the *Patricia Ann* just reported a man overboard," said Lieutenant Avery Scott, the commanding officer of a fifteen-meter Dauntless patrol boat. "We're launching our search and rescue boat in thirty minutes. You're welcome to join us, if you'd like."

"I don't know the city. Can you pick me up?"

"Where are you?"

"The Harbor Grill," said Emily.

"Order eight po' boys to-go, and I'll be there in ten minutes," Scott replied. "Make sure you get extra remoulade."

"Did the captain tell his crew the harbor police were stopping his boat?" asked Emily.

"Apparently," said Scott.

"I need Alton Smith alive!"

"Didn't you say two people ran from the U-Haul?"

"That's what was reported: two suspects, dark clothing, and no descriptions," said Emily. "After the accident, they simply vanished."

"You still have one man left if it was Smith overboard, and he's probably on the same boat."

"You mean if they didn't split up after the accident," countered Emily. She called Greyson and updated him on the situation while waiting for her ride.

"What can I do?" asked Greyson.

"Call the barge company and see if another man was hired at the same time as Smith. If you find someone, send me that information as soon as possible."

"I'm on it."

***

The patrol boat was bigger than Emily imagined and capable of 30 knots an hour. They reached the *Patricia Ann* in forty minutes and prepared to begin a search and rescue mission. Emily and Lieutenant Scott boarded the towboat to interview the captain.

"Sir, why did you notify your crew the harbor police planned to stop your boat?" asked Scott.

"I'm open with my men. I told them that criminals had no business on the *Patricia Ann* and to expect no protection from me if any of them were wanted by the authorities."

"And Smith jumped overboard? You saw it?" asked Scott.

"No, a crew member saw him slip and fall in the water," responded the boat captain. He shouted man overboard, and I immediately stopped my vessel. The pilot assigned a spotter even though it did no good, and I hit the man overboard button on the ship's GPS. We put out a distress call and I contacted the ship's owners. Then you showed up."

"Did anyone see Smith in the water?" asked Emily.

"No," replied the captain. "He could have been sucked under one of the barges. If that's the case, his body will float to the surface in a few days."

"That sounds incredibly callous," responded Emily.

"The river is a cruel bitch," came the response. "Every man who works the Mississippi knows she's out to kill him. One mistake and she'll take another soul."

"We're in search and rescue mode," said Scott. "When you dock in New Orleans, no man leaves your boat. Do you understand."

"I do, but I'm not doing your job for you. This ain't no prison."

"I'll go back with them," offered Emily. "It'll give me the chance to interview the crew and look at their cargo manifest."

"Okay, I'll leave an armed man with you," said Scott. "Good luck."

***

Nine people were working on the *Patricia Ann*: a captain, pilot, engineer, cook and five deck hands. Emily hadn't heard from Greyson and decided to postpone interviewing the crew until they reached port. She'd started her search of the vessel when a call from Scott changed everything.

"We found Smith. His body was in a side chute of the river where the channel narrows. It looks like he's been murdered."

It was then that shots rang out from somewhere near the wheel-house. Emily pulled her weapon and moved toward the disturbance knowing she was at a disadvantage. The shooter knew the boat's layout, and she didn't. She passed several crew members running the other way with one screaming hysterically,

"Terry shot the harbor cop and the captain!" screamed one of them. "I think they're dead."

Emily grabbed him and shouted, "Is there another way off this boat?"

"No, I don't think so," he responded before pulling away to rejoin his fleeing shipmates.

She stayed low, moving slowly but inching steadily forward, her gun leading the way. Her destination was the ship's wheelhouse. Emily would be in the open most of the time, so being hypervigilant could mean the difference in life and death. A miscalculation now and she could end up sharing the same fate as Alton Smith. As her foot touched the stairs leading to the next deck, movement inside the crew's quarters caught her attention. She dropped to the ground as glass exploded around her. Angling her body slightly Emily was in the perfect position when the shooter burst through the door, an automatic rifle in his hands. She fired three times, hitting him center mass; he was dead before his body hit the deck. As she rose to her knees, blood began to trickle down her face and puddle on the deck.

"Stay down, miss," said the ship's cook who had moved closer during the skirmish. "I think you got cut by flying glass. Let me help."

***

When the patrol boat arrived, Emily had the situation under control. She'd covered the dead with sheets gathered from a storage locker and collected their personal effects. The cook had bandaged her head, though she said Emily would likely need stiches. Meanwhile, the pilot had assumed control of the boat.

Greyson called Emily and told her what he'd learned from the barge company. Alton Smith had been hired in St Louis as a deckhand, along with his brother, Terrance. Both were two-time losers and another felony conviction would land them in jail for the rest of their lives. That explained the desperation, thought Emily. As Scott boarded the *Patricia Ann*, Emily pulled him aside.

"I'm sorry your officer didn't make it. Smith brought coffee to the wheelhouse and killed your officer and the captain when their backs were turned. They never had a chance."

"How could it be Smith?" asked Scott unsure of what he was hearing. "We pulled him from the river."

"The shooter was Alton Smith's brother, Terrance. He was hired with his younger brother in St Louis."

"I hate my job sometimes," commented Scott, looking up into a crystal-clear sky that promised fair weather. "How do you tell a wife that her husband isn't coming home? They've been married for less than a year."

Emily had been there, but she had no words to offer.

"Are you okay?" asked Scott, suddenly aware Emily had been hurt.

"I'll need a few stiches," came her reply.

"It's going to be a madhouse when we get back to shore," Scott said. "I'd suggest you start putting together a report of what happened. I'll do the same. Let's get off this heap."

"I wonder why Terrance killed his brother?" Emily mused, a puzzled look on her face. "We didn't have his fingerprints or a photo, so how could we identify him?"

"Is it important?" asked Scott.

"It is if another person onboard is involved," she answered. "We need to interview the crew."

"Can't this wait? We're moving again, and I don't want to block the channel any longer than I have to."

"Okay, but we need to start asking questions when we reach port," responded Emily her thoughts in hyperdrive. "A third person makes sense, someone calling the shots. Maybe, Alton and his brother were hired help."

***

Greyson's call to Mercury Barge and Transfer had been less than successful. He'd been transferred from person to person with each successive individual less helpful than the last.

"These sonsabitches are doing this on purpose," grumbled Greyson.

He'd explained he was calling on a matter of life and death. He'd asked to speak to someone in charge. He'd suggested forwarding his call to the company's legal counsel. Then, he'd practically begged to talk to the general manager. Nothing worked, and now he was through being nice.

"Listen to me!" he shouted at a woman who identified herself as Camille. "My name is Detective John Greyson and unless you want to be arrested as an accessory to murder, the next person I talk to better be your supervisor. If you hang up on me, I'll find your ass and drag you out of the hellhole you call a job. Do you understand me?"

Camille's response was exactly what he wanted.

"Yes, sir, one moment please," she replied.

From that moment forward, everything moved at warp speed, and he had the crew manifest in minutes…but not in time to prevent the murders aboard the *Patricia Ann*. His call to Chief Marie Montross in New Orleans was a sad but necessary task. She answered in a strong, resolute tone of voice.

"Montross, what can I do for you Greyson?"

"Chief, I wanted to convey my sympathies to the family of your slain officer and to you and your team on the loss of your man. I understand from my detective he was recently married."

"Yes, less than a year. I'm sure you've lost comrades in arms and know what it does to people. We're a small unit, each man and woman individually selected. They will grieve, and we'll take care of the young bride, but then we'll move on. It's what we do in law enforcement. Anything else?"

"My detective, Emily Morgan, is interviewing the remaining crew. She's convinced there's a third person involved in this shitshow. What do you know about the barge company, Mercury Barge and Transfer?"

"Not as much as I'll know in a few hours. I have people looking at the company now. Your detective showed incredible bravery. I hope her actions are recognized when she returns home. We'll have to keep her down here for a few days to complete our investigation on the shooting. I'll have Lieutenant Scott show her around."

"Thank you, Chief Montross. Again, I'm sorry for your loss. Please let me know if there's any way we can assist."

A SIGHTING

Vivian Gales was putting away her groceries when she looked into the backyard and saw her brother. Emilio looked almost feral. His clothes were filthy, and he wore a dirty red hat that covered his oversized head. He didn't see her as he went inside the weathered storage shed that had been there for as long as she could remember. The front tire of his motorcycle was barely visible from where she stood. That's how he's getting around, she thought to herself. As she watched, she had an idea.

"Maybe it's time," she said aloud. "I won't get a better opportunity, and the police are convinced he murdered Julia, especially after I convinced them that he'd threatened me. I could probably get away with it."

Vivian was never impulsive; she always looked before leaping into the deep end of the pool. The twins were the opposite. They'd staggered from one emergency to another and had been like that their entire adult lives. How many times had she dropped everything and rushed to keep them out of trouble, especially Gene? Thankfully, that painful experience had changed him.

Emilio was still a lost cause and always would be. Now he was hiding in the same shed he'd played in as a child. She'd be doing him a favor by ending his miserable life. Vivian felt an idea taking root. As she watched, he disappeared from sight and shut himself into what she could only imagine as utter darkness.

Vivian put away the last of the groceries before sliding into sandals and walking nonchalantly to the shed. If her neighbors hadn't sounded an alarm about an intruder, then she wasn't worried about raising suspicion for what she had planned.

"Emilio, it's Viv," she coaxed in a gentle voice. "Come into the house and get something to eat, honey. I know you're scared. Just let me help."

"Go away! You're like everyone else," he cried. "You don't care about me. First Gene dies, then that bitch steals our house, and now the police are trying to put me in jail. I just want to be left alone."

"Emilio, are you taking the medications I sent you? You know what happens when you forget to take them."

"Go away, Vivian. I don't need anything."

"I'm going to fix you a nice sandwich and leave it on the picnic table with a Dr Pepper. It's your favorite. Come into the house and get cleaned up. I think some of Gene's clothes are still here. You look like a vagrant, and you know how mad mother would get mad when we didn't look our best."

"She's dead, too," said Emilio through the closed door. "They put her in an asylum like they tried to do to me."

"That wasn't an asylum, honey. It was a behavioral treatment center. One of the best in the area."

"Go back inside, Vivian. I don't want to hurt you, but I will if you don't go away."

This was not what she'd expected. Emilio had always been like putty in her hands, unlike his twin brother. She could call the cops and let them deal with him, but what were the consequences for doing that? He could put everything at risk, and she couldn't allow that to happen. When she returned with his sandwich and drink, the motorcycle was gone and the shed locked.

"Damnit!" uttered Gales angrily. If she'd gotten him inside the house, she'd decided he wouldn't leave again, not under his own power. Her thirty-eight-caliber revolver was loaded, and in her pocket. It was definitely a missed opportunity but there was nothing she could do about it now. She called an unlisted number and waited.

"He was here," she said in a low, conspiratorial voice as if someone were listening. "The asshole has been hiding in our shed, and he's still on that goddamned motorcycle mother bought for him in high school. You need to find him and kill him."

"Why not let the police catch him? You said they think he killed the judge."

"If they catch him, they'll medicate him. If they medicate him, he might figure out what I've done. Why do you think I convinced him to leave the hospital? He was beginning to put two and two together."

"Do you want the body found?"

"Yes. Make it look like a suicide but be careful. Emilio is crazy as fuck, but don't underestimate him."

"Any idea where he may have gone?"

"I'd look at his office on Madison. If he's not there, your guess is as good as mine."

"Call me if he comes back," said the voice.

"I will," Gales said. "Emilio spooks the hell out of me."

"Why? He doesn't know anything. You're in the clear."

"I'm not so sure," replied Gales. "Emilio is one of those people who sees things others miss. He and Gene were the same in that regard."

"Don't worry about it. I'll take care of your brother. I might even keep his motorcycle. It purred like a kitten the night I borrowed it to kill your sister-in-law. I hated to take it back."

After the call, Vivian went inside to find a hammer. She had to know what her shit-for-brains brother had carefully locked away. He did scare her, regardless of what her partner had to say. When he was medicated, not many people were as perceptive as Emilio. If anyone could figure out what she'd done, it was him.

***

McKinzie Owens was in her office and if possible looked sexier to Marcy than she had the first time they'd met.

"Detective Thomas or can I call you Marcy?" Mac began with an alluring smile. "What a pleasure to see you so soon. I knew you'd be back."

"Oh, why is that?"

"It was just a feeling," said the owner of Danny's. "Did you check me out with Stu Ketchum and Father Pat?"

"I did and I did some checking on my own," said the detective. "And yes, you can call me Marcy."

"Are you on the clock or can you join me for a glass of wine?" asked Owens.

"Wine would be good; I've had a terrible day. Did you know David Barnett beat the hell out of his ex-wife?"

"No, but it doesn't surprise me," replied McKinzie as she poured Louis Roederer champagne into two Waterford flutes. "David is a loose cannon, and it was only a matter of time until he hurt someone."

She handed Marcy her glass.

"There, you look more comfortable with a drink in your hand. Marcy, you're a gorgeous woman – if I may be so bold. Why try to hide it?"

"Even when I'm this tired?" she said, half laughing. "It's tough being a woman and a cop. I'm lucky I work for John Greyson. A great guy who is nothing but supportive. I've learned a lot from him, and he's been my biggest fan. That doesn't always happen for women in militaristic organizations."

"You said you've done some investigation on your own. What did you learn about me?" said Mac changing the conversation.

"You were born in New Orleans and didn't know your father," Marcy said.

"That's not true," MacKinzie interjected. "Mom was always bringing some stranger home and introducing them as my long-lost father who'd had come back to take care of us. Instead, each one would stay a few days or weeks screwing my mother until they couldn't stand it anymore. Then they couldn't get out of there quick enough."

"You ran away from home at fourteen and ended up in child protective services," continue Marcy. "Your mother was killed by her boyfriend a month after you'd left."

"What a nightmare that was," laughed Owens bitterly before

sipping her champagne. "To become an orphan while I was a ward of the state. Fifteen dollars a day from the state for anyone willing to care for the poor indigents dumped on society. Child Protective Services did teach me one thing, Marcy. If you want to get ahead, the only person you can depend on is the one gazing back at you in a mirror. Fuck everyone else."

"You ran away again at fifteen and disappeared for three years. You got your driver's license in Jackson, Mississippi and listed your occupation as hostess on your tax returns."

"In Jackson I was working in a strip joint. I made more money than I thought possible," said McKinzie, refilling her wine glass. "An old man helped me with a fake ID, and I went to work in his club. He took me under his wing, kept me off the hard stuff, and made me put away money for emergencies. His name was Kelly Rawlins, and he was the only man who made me feel like I was worth something. He encouraged me to get my GED and taught me how to do the books for his club. I liked learning new things, got my GED, enrolled in community college and ended up with a four-year degree."

"What happened to Kelly Rawlings?" asked Marcy, now interested in this rags to riches story.

"Heart attack in his club. He left everything to me and that's how I got my start in this business. It's also why I try to help as many girls as I can. I was one of them. Hey, your glass is empty," said McKinzie, moving close to refill Marcy's glass. When it was full, she didn't step away. Instead, she leaned in and lightly kissed the detective on the lips.

"I think you're trying to seduce me," said Marcy with a smile of her own.

"Is that a bad thing? Have you ever been with another woman?"

"Kinda," Marcy said. "If college experimentation counts."

"Have you ever talked about it?" asked McKinzie.

"No, I think it was two young women trying things out, and we both felt awkward afterward. Listen, I'm flattered, and I find you extremely attractive, but I'm involved with someone at the moment...a man."

"Jack Murphy, I know," said McKinzie, "and I don't blame you. I applied all my feminine wiles to seduce him, but he wasn't interested. He said he was committed to a homicide cop, and I looked you up. That's why I was surprised when you walked into my office the first time. It's like something that was meant to be."

"How do you know Jack?"

"I hired him about a year ago when someone was stealing from the business. He and Cadera worked undercover as bouncers and found out my head cashier and accountant were skimming off some of my profits. They took about twenty thousand dollars before Murphy caught them."

"I didn't know," said Marcy. She was surprised but not surprised. Her boyfriend stayed busy and didn't often discuss his clients.

"No reason you should," stated McKinzie with a devilish smile. "I propositioned Murphy, and he politely refused…end of story."

"Let's get back to the reason I'm here," said Marcy, putting down her wine glass. "Did you know Anna Leigh was dead?"

"I did. One of the girls who works here was friends with Anna Leigh. She told me."

"According to David Barnett, Anna Leigh was coming to you for money, and they were running away to Mexico. What do you know about that?"

"I gave Anna Leigh five thousand dollars. She asked for ten. It was a loan, but I didn't expect to be repaid. I thought she should get out of town and start over. She was using again and coming apart at the seams. I didn't like it that David was going with her, but that was her decision."

"What else can you tell me?"

"Anna Leigh said David was scared and that he'd seen something he shouldn't have."

"Did she mention what?"

"No, but I got the impression it was something bad. Barnett's big and tough. It would take a lot to scare him."

"Do you think it had anything to do with the murder of Judge Levitt?" asked Marcy.

"Maybe, you do know he was sneaking by to see Ginny after the divorce. Apparently, he's good in bed and the girl has needs."

"What?"

"David bragged about it, and Anna Leigh confirmed it. He'd go by, fuck her, and she'd give him money."

"Goddamnit, I knew something was wrong with that woman!" exclaimed the detective slamming her hand on Owens' desk.

"I don't blame Ginny," declared Owens. "She was in charge for a change; cut her some slack."

"Anything else you can tell me?" asked Marcy.

"Not about the Barnetts or Anna Leigh. I can tell you something about Murphy if you'd like."

"Go for it," said Marcy.

"You can't domesticate him, no woman can. He's like Peter Pan. Have your fun, but don't count on a lifelong commitment."

"Says the woman who couldn't seduce him away from me?"

McKinzie chuckled. "I just see some of me in Murphy. Only I'm better, I promise. Think about it. I'll show you the time of your life."

"Thanks for your help, McKinzie," replied Marcy, ignoring the proposition.

***

Scott drove Emily to the emergency room for stiches and helped her find a hotel room in the French Quarter.

"If you're going to visit New Orleans, you have to experience the Quarter," he'd said proudly. Scott was a tall Black man with a slight Cajun English accent that he'd worked hard to lose. He'd stunned everyone in his family when he applied to be a cop instead of going to law school.

"What's the name of this place we're going?" asked Emily.

"The Le Richelieu," Scott said breaking the name down into its syllables. "It's not as famous as the Monteleone, but you're going to love the bar and pool, and the service is fantastic."

"Is it expensive?"

"You're our guest. Send your expense report to Chief Marie Montross," laughed the harbor cop. Changing the subject, he asked, "Do you want to begin interviews in the morning?"

"Yes, first thing, and not on the boat," replied Emily. "Where is crew tonight?"

"On the *Patricia Ann*," Scott said. "Since this is a murder investigation and none of the crew live in New Orleans, they're being held as material witnesses."

"I want to take them out of their comfort zone," Emily said.

"I like the way you think, and I have the perfect place in mind. Let's get you checked into the hotel and decide on dinner. I'm starving."

She was not one for one-night stands, but what the hell, thought Emily. Scott was good-looking, there was a certain vibe going on between them, and they both needed a shower. Besides, they could always call down for room service…later. He was gone the next morning as Emily woke. She'd furrowed her way into the bed's cool sheets clutching satins pillows to her bare breast, a satiated smile on her lips. He'd left a note with a rose on the bedside table.

"Where the hell did Avery get a long-stemmed rose?" she murmured, laughing out loud. The note said: *Last night was incredible. I'll send a car to pick you up at eight so get your ass in gear.* There was also a sketch of Emily sleeping, one arm partially covering her breasts. If the Memphis homicide cop hadn't been interested in Avery Scott before, she was now. A call to her room broke the spell.

"We got her!" Scott said excitedly. "She tried to slip off the boat before sunrise, but I had people in place to make sure that didn't happen. We got her, Emily. You were right about a third person."

"Her? You mean the cook?"

"That's right, and she has a record. She could change her name but not her fingerprints. Your driver will be waiting for you in the lobby. Get dressed!"

***

Her driver was one of those people who likes to talk. By the time Emily arrived at the Orleans Parish Prison, she knew almost everything about him, his family, and the history of the place they were going. The building was smaller than the Shelby County Jail but no less intimidating. Scott met her in the lobby by the security kiosk.

"Her real name is Samantha Johnson, and she grew up in St. Louis. She's been arrested four times but never for anything violent."

"Give me some examples," said Emily.

"Dealing in stolen merchandise, grand theft, passing bad checks. And she was busted for running a chop shop with her boyfriend in Kansas City. The good news is she has a history of talking."

"Has she asked for a lawyer?"

"No, not yet."

"Okay, we go in soft but not too soft. Samantha knows how it works; she's been here before."

"She's going by the name of Sally Johns now," said Scott. "I have her in an interview room on the third floor."

The electricity between them was almost palpable. Emily was tempted to say something about last night or reach for his hand, but she resisted the urge. Sally Johns was handcuffed to the table when they entered the room.

"Officer, take those off," said the Memphis homicide cop taking charge. "Sally, I'm Detective Emily Morgan and I work for the Memphis Police Department. Do you know why I'm here?"

Johns nodded, but said nothing, a blank stare plastered across her face.

"I'm investigating the murder of Sammy Hankins. Do you know him?"

This time Johns shook her head.

"It doesn't matter," responded Emily in a disinterested tone. "After you're transported to Memphis, you'll be charged as an accessory in his murder. You can help yourself by helping me. I want to know who pulled the trigger."

Johns only replied with a small, satisfied smile.

"Suit yourself," said Emily standing. "I'll be here for the next twenty-four hours. So call me if you change your mind."

"That's it?" asked Johns. "No deals or threats…nothing? You're just going to walk out of here?"

"To be honest, I don't think you can help us," Emily said with a shrug. "You know how the system works, Sally. You're looking for a get-out-of-jail-free card, so you hold out pretending to know more than you do. You want to avoid jail time, but it isn't going to work this time. I know your game, and I know you'll lie your ass off and say anything to avoid going to prison. I don't need you to make my case."

"What do you mean you don't need me?"

"I have a witness who saw the whole execution-style killing. I just need to get home and nail down the details."

"You don't have shit," spat Johns angrily. "You can't con me, bitch."

"I know that Sol Hammersham was the killer," responded the homicide detective guessing. "You're going away for a long time on this one, Sally. And the prisons in Tennessee aren't known for their social activities. I'd wish you luck, but I could care less… bitch."

As she turned to leave, Johns yelled, "I didn't kill anyone, I swear to god! But I can tell you who did. I only agreed to get rid of the body."

"I told you who did it," responded Emily, looking at Johns as if she were speaking a foreign language.

"I can get you proof," said the now desperate woman. "What can you do for me?"

"What kind of proof?"

"I have a recording. Sol told me he had a body and needed to get rid of it."

"How does that help me?' asked Emily interested but trying not to show it. "Did he admit to killing Sammy Hankins?"

"You need to hear it - you won't be disappointed," responded Johns, clearly playing her last card.

"Okay, I'll make some calls," said Emily, "but if the recording doesn't help me get a conviction, the deal is off. I'm not playing games, Sally. You belong in jail, but I'll help you as long as it benefits me. Do we understand each other?"

"What's next?" asked Johns.

"I'll talk to the DA in Memphis, and you'll meet with your attorney here," said Emily. "I'll let him know if a deal is possible. You get one chance at this. If you screw it up, I walk."

***

They didn't meet again until the following week. Sally John's court-appointed attorney was over-scheduled and understaffed, which wasn't unusual for public defenders in New Orleans or anywhere else for that matter. He didn't see his client until two days after she'd met with the Memphis homicide cop. Emily's inquiry with Internal Affairs went well. Witness statements corroborated her version of the shooting on the *Patricia Ann*, and the panel seemed satisfied. She spent her days with Scott, exploring his city and taking in its unique blend of ethnicities, music, and history. Emily's nights were special, too. Great food, intimate bars, mingling in the Quarter with people determined to have fun, and hot, steamy sex. It was a magical time for her, she didn't know when she'd been happier, but all things come to an end. A call from Greyson put her back on the clock.

"The DA is willing to consider dropping the charges against Sally Johns if she can deliver the goods on Hankins' killer," Greyson said. "I'm out on a limb, Emily. I told him this was related to Julia Levitt's murder. I need you to make it happen."

"I got it, John," she said, not a hundred percent sure that she did. "I'll set up a meeting tomorrow and get back to you."

"You did a good job down there I'm proud of you," said her boss, his voice softening slightly. "But it's time to come home. We have Julia's killer to catch."

He was right, she thought. The last few days had been magical, but she had a job to do, and Internal Affairs had completed its investigation. Time to leave Sally Johns in someone else's care. A call to her attorney set up the meeting followed by notifying the hotel that she'd be checking out in the morning. Then she texted Scott, who called her almost immediately.

"Do you have to leave so soon?" he asked.

"I do, but this doesn't have to be the end of things," said the Memphis homicide cop. "I want to see you again."

"Memphis isn't that far. Maybe, we can make it sooner rather than later," replied Scott. "I've never met a woman like you, Emily."

"How about I plan a week of vacation after we close this cluster-fuck? I've worked with Greyson for a long time, and I know when he's closing in. He's figured out something everyone else has missed, and he's ready to pull the trigger. I can hear it in his voice.

"You talk about Greyson like he's the smartest man in the room."

"He usually is, but this case has hit close to home. The victim was not only a criminal court judge but also his friend. It's hit John hard."

"What time do we meet Sally and her attorney?" asked Scott.

"At two," came the reply. "She has a good deal on the table, so I don't expect the meeting to last long. I'll get a rental car and meet you there."

***

Emily was busy – packing to go home, talking to a paralegal in the district attorney's office in Memphis, and getting copies of the transfer paperwork for Sally Johns. At two she walked into an interview room at the Orleans Parish Prison with Avery Scott following. Will Buck, the public defender, didn't look old enough to be out of high school much less law school. He was thin as a rail with reddish-brown hair combed straight down over his forehead. He reminded her of Opie Taylor from the Andy Griffith Show. Emily had watched every episode with her aunt during her summer vacations on her uncle's farm. She could just make out a faint scattering of freckles laid out across his face and hands.

"I've talked to the district attorney," he began before Emily stopped him.

"Mr. Buck, I have the agreement with me, and I'll give you time to confer with your client. Please understand there are no additional offers on the table other than the one I present to you today. I'm the messenger and not the negotiator, and I'm going home to Memphis in the morning. The agreement simply states your client will not be charged for crimes related to the illegal disposal of a body if Ms. Johns provides evidence that identifies and leads to the conviction of Sammy Hankins' murderer. That means Ms. Johns must tell me what she knows, hand over any and all evidence that supports her statements, and that she must testify in court if necessary."

"What about the shooting on the *Patricia Ann*?" asked the attorney.

"Since it happened out of our jurisdiction, that decision falls to the local parish district attorney. Perhaps, Lieutenant Scott can answer your question," stated Emily.

"We're prepared to join in the agreement with the Memphis District Attorney's office," said Scott in an assertive tone. "No charges will be level against Ms. Johns unless additional criminal activity is discovered."

"Mr. Buck, we'll step out of the room and let you discuss our offer. Let us know when you're ready to talk."

They were motioned back into the room a half hour later.

"What do you want to know?" asked Sally Johns.

Emily and Scott asked questions for the next two hours, which Johns never hesitated to answer. They discovered that Sol Hammersham had contacted her a week prior to the murder of Hankins and said he had a job. He didn't mention exactly what the offer entailed only that it involved dumping something in the river.

"I didn't know someone would get killed," declared Johns trying hard to look innocent. "Sol said I'd need at least two others and that he'd give me the specifics in a few days. That's when I called Terrance and asked if he wanted in. He did, and he recruited his little brother."

"When were you told what the job entailed?" asked Scott.

"The day before we left port in St Louis."

"Who else was involved in this scheme?" asked Emily.

"No one other than Hammersham, me, and the Smith brothers. I coordinated things. Terrance and Alton were to pick up the body and load it onboard. I planned to dump Hankins' body in the river somewhere between Vicksburg and Natchez. The water moves fast in that span of the river, and the high bluffs keeps things private."

"Who rented the U-Haul?" asked Emily who took over the majority of the questioning from that point on.

"It had to be Hammersham," came the answer. "I know it wasn't me, Terrance, or Alton."

"You told me you recorded your conversations with Hammersham."

"I used a third-party app that adds a recording line to any call you want saved. The app allows for playback, downloading, or sharing. It even has a transcription service. I hid my phone on the towboat, but I can take you to it."

"Why did Terrance kill his brother?"

"He killed Alton to create a distraction," replied Johns as if the answer was self-evident. "When the captain announced we were to be held in port by the New Orleans Harbor Police, he panicked. Terrance swore he'd never go back to prison. I think he hoped his brother's body wouldn't be found for several days and he could slip off the *Patricia Ann* when it reached port. He didn't plan on the patrol boat leaving an armed officer onboard. Or you," replied Johns, nodding at Emily.

"I'm guessing Alton and Terrance weren't close," responded Emily.

"Same mother different fathers," said Johns.

"Did Hammersham say he killed Sammy Hankins?"

"In so many words."

"Have you ever done something like this before?" asked Scott.

"I'm going to advise my client not to answer that question," interjected her attorney.

"How were you paid?" asked Emily, looking for a money trail.

"There were three wire transfers, and money deposited into my account matches the amount agreed to on the call with Hammersham," said Johns, knowing what the detective was after.

"Did Hammersham tell you how he killed Hankins or where he put the weapon?"

"No, and I didn't ask. In my business knowing too much can be a liability," replied Johns.

"Go over the plan again. How was this supposed to work?"

For the next half hour, Sally Johns described the call she'd gotten from Hammersham, how she'd recruited Terrance and Alton Smith, and docking in Memphis to collect three container barges destined for New Orleans, plus one dead body. It had been the perfect plan until it wasn't. A police chase, a wreck, and suddenly everything was ruined, according to Johns. No remorse, no accepting responsibility, they'd been caught because of a freak accident.

Emily felt angry that Johns would slip through the system again, but this was how things worked. Hopefully, karma was a real thing. If so, Sally Johns was destined for a bad ending.

"Okay, I'm satisfied," said the woman cop standing to signal they were through. "I'm requesting Samatha Johnson, aka Sally Johns, be extradited to Memphis pending the arrest of Sol Hammersham. Do you have any questions?" asked Emily looking at Will Buck.

"Who will represent Ms. Johns in Tennessee?"

"More than likely an attorney from the public defender's office. Either way you'll be kept in the loop."

"So we're done?" he asked.

"Not yet," Emily replied. "We have to retrieve your client's phone from the *Patricia Ann*, and the calls from Sol Hammersham have to be verified. Other than that, I think we're finished here."

In the hallway, she called Greyson.

"I think we got him. If Sally Johns is telling the truth, The Hammer is in a world of trouble," said Emily. Greyson could hear the excitement in her voice. "I'm on my way home in the morning."

"Come straight into the office. The district attorney wants to review your case notes before he issues an arrest warrant for Hammersham. If all goes well, we'll have him in handcuffs by tomorrow afternoon."

Scott was leaning against her rental car as she weaved her way through a pot-holed parking lot.

"That was impressive," he said. "I wouldn't want to get on your bad side."

She kissed him hard pressing her body into his. Whispering in his ear, she said, "I thought you liked my bad side. Let's go retrieve a phone."

THINGS HEAT UP

Emilio was paranoid; he knew it and didn't care. Vivian appearing out of nowhere hadn't helped either. She should be home in Nashville, he thought as he began to pace. They'd never been close, and he suspected she'd always hated him and his brother. She'd hated Julia, too, especially after Gene left her the house in his will. Now, she was hanging around like she cared. Of course it was all bullshit. Vivian wanted something, and he knew what it was. He'd seen her with him, overheard enough to know they were up to no good. The last few months had been terrible, but now he had a plan.

"Greyson, Homicide, how can I help you?"

Emilio almost hung up, when he heard the detective's voice.

"Is anyone there?" asked Greyson.

"Detective Greyson, this is Emilio Levitt," he finally managed to say. "Don't trust Vivian. She's a bad woman."

"Dr. Levitt, what do you mean?"

"You can't trust her. She lies," came a barely audible reply. "She hated Julia, she hated us all. Talk to her ex-husband, Mark. He'll tell you."

"Was she involved in Julia's murder?" asked Greyson, goosebumps appearing as he listened to Levitt breathe into the phone. He hadn't really looked at Vivian Gales as a serious suspect and now he was sorry he hadn't.

"I wouldn't be surprised," commented the doctor. "She has someone on the side; someone she's working with."

"Who?" Greyson asked.

"I can't tell you, Detective. But I'll give you a hint: mistakes from the past often reveal themselves in the present. Look at my brother's past."

"Dr. Levitt, let me help you," implored Greyson. "We can work this out, but first, you need to turn yourself in."

"I don't trust you, Greyson. I don't trust anyone. I've got to go; I need to keep moving."

"Are you in danger?"

"We are all in danger, Greyson. Watch your back."

Before he could respond, the line went dead.

***

"Goddamnit! What was I thinking?" Greyson muttered, mad that he'd overlooked the sister as a suspect. He'd let his emotions overrule his common sense. After he calmed down, he called Marcy.

"We need to look at Gales," he said. "I screwed up."

"What do you mean?"

"Emilio called. He said his sister hated Julia, that she hated them all. I need you to find Gales' ex-husband and talk to him. I think his first name is Mark. Hopefully, he still lives in Nashville, if not find him."

"Okay, but remember who you're getting this information from. Emilio Levitt is unstable and lives in his own reality."

"I know, but it makes sense. Think about it, Marcy. Gales shows up for the burial and doesn't go home. Why?"

"She said her brother planned to take possession of the house, and she thought it was wrong."

"That wasn't her job. Archibald McCutchen is the executor of the estate. Vivian has no right to be in Julia's house, but no one challenged her when she moved in. Emilio also said something else. It was a riddle that involved his brother. He said mistakes from the past often reveal themselves in the present. This family has a lot of secrets, and we need to find out what they are."

"Okay, anything else?" asked Marcy.

"No, find Mark Gales and talk to him about his ex-wife. I'm going to call Horace and see if he's up for a little long-distance research."

"What about Hammersham?"

"He's going to be arrested this afternoon. Emily is on her way back from New Orleans and has proof he killed Sammy."

"And you think he's also connected to Judge Levitt's murder," said Marcy.

"I do. He hated her because she intimidated him."

"That's a hell of a reason to kill someone," Marcy said. "Damn, John, what a cluster. I'll call you after I track down Mark Gales."

***

When Greyson called Horace, he was on the ninth hole standing over a six-foot birdie putt.

"I just can't get away from you," said the retired detective after missing the shot.

"Sorry to bother you, but my spidey sense is tingling, and I need to bounce something off you."

Greyson went on to update his friend on the case's progress, including Hammersham's pending arrest. He also tossed out a new theory.

"You've been busy, John. I'm impressed," Horace replied. "Is Emily okay? This isn't her first officer involved shooting."

"I think so, but I'll keep an eye on her. Besides, she'll have to see the departmental shrink when she gets home. The doctor's fitness for duty report comes to me."

"Emily's good at hiding things. Do me a favor and talk to her. She's special."

"You got it," said Greyson. "What do you think about my theory?"

"That Vivian Gales is behind the murder of her sister-in-law? I think it's possible, but you're a long way from proving it. What do you need from me? I know you didn't call just to chat."

"The company you work for, the British company, they use AI and advanced analytics don't they?"

"Well, I didn't expect this," commented Horace laughing. "You want me to tap into their resources and research the family, don't you?"

"Is it too much to ask? This is coming from me; I haven't approached Director Edwards about it."

"Moving into the twenty-first century are we?" teased Horace. Greyson was well-known for his aversion to new technology. "I'll see what I can do."

"I hate to ask, but can you do it sooner rather than later? I think we're on the verge of busting this case wide open."

"Can I finish the back nine first?" laughed Horace in the big horse laugh he was known for.

"As long as you don't spend too much time at the nineteenth hole," countered Greyson. "We both know how that ends."

With that done, Greyson began to dig through the research Horace had complied before he'd left to go home. His friend had done a herculean job organizing a massive trove of data and putting it into a recognizable format. The first thing that grabbed his attention was the picture of a headstone with its epitaph circled in red. It read: *Alice Denise Talbot - born August 1, 1964 - died December 10, 1989.* A baby's handprint had been chiseled below a line that read: *Rest In Peace.* There had to be some significance, Greyson thought, but Horace had run into a dead-end. Greyson had an idea. It was a little out there, but so was this case. The twists and turns they'd encountered had turned into a veritable rat's nest. A judge killed in the middle of a storm, her body dumped in a cemetery, a club espousing a polyamorous lifestyle, pornographic notes left in a box in the victim's home, a mad brother-in-law, a sleezy lawyer who'd hired a crooked private eye to spy on the woman murdered. Add into the mix a suspicious sister-in-law and amorous neighbor, it had all the ingredients of a cheap mystery novel. The name of the cemetery director was in Horace's notes, Maurice Cavendar. The name fit the description of the man's specialty, thought Greyson. Cavendar was in and available to talk.

"Mr. Cavendar, my name is John Greyson, and I'm one of the homicide detectives working the murder investigation of the woman found in your cemetery. I have a question."

"What can I do for you, detective?"

"How far back do your records go on the dead buried in your cemetery?"

"Mt Moriah was opened in 1973 after our original cemetery in the city closed," explained Cavendar, his voice high and nasally. "It was countryside then, but obviously not now. How far back are you talking?"

"December 10,1989," responded Greyson.

"That was before my time. I'd have to check, but I don't think we've digitizing any records older than the nineties. What are you looking for exactly?"

"Your records on Alice Denise Talbot; her family, cause of death, who paid for the internment, everything you've got. I know she was born August 1, 1964, and died December 10, 1989."

"What about her social security number?" asked Cavendar as he wrote down the dates Greyson had given him.

"The only thing I have is her date of birth and the date she died," came the detective's response.

"It'll take time, and there are no guarantees," the cemetery director cautioned.

"I appreciate anything you can do, Mr. Cavendar. I wouldn't ask if it wasn't important."

"I'll get started on it this afternoon. I'll call if I find something."

***

Emily and Greyson found Sol Hammersham in court asking for a continuance on a case he couldn't win; his client was a pimple-faced teenager who'd tried to rob a convenience store. Not only had the clerk gone to school with the gunman and quickly recognized him, but he'd pulled off his mask while getting into a rusty Dodge Dart and had his picture taken by an outside camera. The police were waiting for him when he returned home. It was a slam-dunk case, and the prosecutor was salivating in anticipation of getting Hammersham in front of the judge. What neither of them knew was that a continuance had already been granted.

"Mr. Hammersham, his Honor would like to see you in his chambers," said the bailiff.

"Is there a problem?" asked the attorney warily.

"I can't say, sir. I was just told that Judge Parker wanted you in his chambers."

The first person Hammersham spied exiting the courtroom was Greyson. A thin line seemed to have replaced the space where his mouth should have been. Instead of turning toward the judge's chambers, the bailiff directed him to where the detective was standing.

"What's this about?" asked the confused counselor.

"Put your hands behind your back," said Emily, coming from the rear. "You're under arrest for the murder to Sammy Hankins."

She quickly handcuffed Hammersham and read him his rights.

His mind was racing but all he could think to say was, "This is fucking ridiculous! I didn't kill anyone."

"I'd advise you to keep quiet," said Greyson, leaning in so close the attorney could tell what he'd eaten for lunch. "What was the name of that woman in New Orleans, the one on the towboat, Emily?"

"You mean Sally Johns?"

"Yeah, that's the one. What can you tell me about Sally Johns?" probed the detective, crowding Hammersham even more.

"I, I, I don't know anyone by that name," stammered the attorney, his face turning white as a sheet.

"Really?" said Emily, feigning surprise. "I wonder how she recorded all those conversations with you about dumping Sammy's body in the Mississippi River. You didn't know she recorded your calls, did you?"

"Let's go," said Greyson, roughly grabbing the attorney's arm.

"What about my client?"

"You'll see him tonight in lock-up," said Emily cheerfully. "I'll make sure you get adjoining cells."

***

"Has he asked for an attorney?" asked Greyson.

"No, he's going to represent himself," responded Emily with a half-smile.

"Let's do this then."

He'd spent his first night in jail, and Hammersham looked rough shackled to a table in his county-issued orange jumpsuit.

"How'd you sleep last night, Sol?" asked Emily. "Me, I slept like a baby."

"Fuck you," growled the attorney. "I'm going to sue the city and every one of you sonsofbitches. You don't have shit on me, and you know it."

Greyson sat down and sipped his coffee. He watched the whole exchange between his detective and the attorney as if observing an important scientific experiment. Finally, the attorney's focus settled to him.

"What the hell are you looking at?"

"I'm looking at a man foolish enough to represent himself in a homicide case," Greyson said. "Mr. Hammersham, the district attorney is going to pursue the death penalty. You're being charged with first degree murder, and the evidence against you is overwhelming. I'd advise you to get good counsel and cooperate, but that's just me."

"Don't think I can handle it, Greyson?" asked Hammersham.

"Not for a minute, but I hope you try. We know the Kudzu belonged to you, and that's where you killed Sammy Hankins. You tried to be clever using a dummy corporation to hide your identity, but you weren't clever enough. When arson is suspected, the first thing we do is establish ownership of the damaged property. Our arson investigators had your name within twenty-four hours. From there, it was child's play putting the rest together: a witness reported a U-Haul outside the Kudzu minutes before the fire, the wooden box carrying Sammy's body had been stamped Port of New Orleans, and only two towboats out of Memphis were headed south at the time. A couple of calls to the barge companies, and we had the names of every crew member on both boats. Oh, and one of the men you hired to get rid of Sammy's body left his thumbprint in the truck. Were you trying to get caught, Sol?"

"Fuck you, Greyson. I know you're lying, that's what you do. It's not working this time."

"The biggest mistake you made was trusting Sally Johns,"

continued the detective, a smug smile etched onto his face. "She gave you up the minute we said - accessory to murder. Would you like to hear one of the conversations Sally Johns recorded?"

A look of concern crossed the attorney's face, but Greyson wasn't finished. He opened his laptop, tapped a few keys, and listened as Hammersham's voice played from the computer's small speakers.

"I have a job for you. When are you coming through Memphis?"

"In about a week," replied Sally Johns. "I'll check the schedule and send you the exact date. What's the job?"

"I need to dispose of something."

"Hum, interesting," she responded. "Dead or alive? Some things I don't do."

"Very much dead. Or will be."

"Okay, it's doable for the right price. We lose things in the river all the time."

"How long do you stopover in Memphis?" asked Hammershm.

"At least four hours, sometimes six," said Johns. "It depends on the number of barges we pick up."

"You'll need help, at least two men you can trust."

"That shouldn't be a problem. We're always losing crew and hiring replacements on the river. I'll talk to the captain."

"Perfect, how much?"

"Ten for me and five each for the others with half up front."

"I can do that. I'll get back to you in a few days. Don't call me, I'm using a burner."

Greyson ended the recording and closed his laptop. The color had drained from Hammersham's face.

"That could have been anyone," he managed to say feebly.

"That's your defense," roared Greyson laughing. "It could have been anyone? Oh my god, you're going to get the needle. That's rich even for you, Sol. A tech from the FBI will match your voice to this recording in about five seconds, and I have four others all cued up and ready to go. If push comes to shove, I can also have Sally Johns testify, too. Why did you kill Sammy?"

He could see the attorney struggling to decide on how he'd play this.

"Sol, we got you." Greyson continued. "Make this easy on yourself. We can help each other."

"What do you want, Greyson?" he asked, his hands shaking slightly.

"I don't want you. I want the person who killed Julia Levitt, and I know you have a name for me."

"I spied on her, that's all."

"Maybe, but you know more than you're telling, and you're guilty of cold-blooded murder."

"What's in it for me?"

"It depends on what you know, but Judge Levitt's case is high-profile. The brass wants it solved. No one cares about a washed-out PI, but a criminal court judge is another matter. Think about it. Sol, you can help yourself."

"Give me some time," said the attorney his voice strained. "I need to think."

Pushing a business card across the table, Greyson said, "Here's my number. Let me know when you want to talk." Looking at the guard, he said, "We're through here, you can take him back to his cell."

Emily met him outside in the hallway.

"Fuck, he knows who did it. I could see it on his face."

"Let's get something to drink. God, I'm drained, it's all I could do to keep from strangling that piece of shit."

"I'll call Marcy; we need to talk this out, John. You're close, I can feel it."

"It's a team effort, Emily. We need one or two more pieces to fall in place, and we'll have everything, including the person who killed Julia."

ON THE RUN

Emilio had seen him cruise the neighborhood pretending to be sight-seeing. His bike was a good one, either a Ducati or Moto Guzzi, and much better and faster than his old Honda. He'd also watched him sneak into the house after dark to conspire with Vivian. His sister wanted him dead. But it wasn't going to happen if he had anything to do with it. Emilio had a secret weapon. He'd overheard things, things Vivian had planned to do and didn't want anyone else to know. Maybe none of this would have happened if he'd been more receptive to his sister-in-law's pleas to give her a chance. But that ship had sailed. Now, he was going to use Greyson, use him to stop the madness. The cop was smart in an unassuming way and determined. He could use that to his advantage. The phone call had been the first step, his warning about Vivian. Now, all he had to do was figure out a way to eliminate the Reaper. That was the named he'd given to the pale-skinned, soulless being Vivian had summoned from their past.

***

The Reaper peered into the shed looking at the items left behind; an old Army rucksack with Emilio's name barely legible in faded ink, an assortment of clothes wadded up and tossed in a corner, an air mattress rolled in a Salvation Army blanket, and a cooler filled with bottles of warm water. There was nothing the Reaper could use, nothing that would point him to where Vivian's little brother was hiding, but that was okay. Emilio would show up again. The shed kind of reminded him of Emilio's office. Empty and abandoned with only a name stenciled on the door to indicated he'd been there. What a sad fucking life, the Reaper thought. Vivian had explained to him that her brother had no loved ones, no friends only acquaintances, which made finding him more difficult but useful too. That meant he had no one to turn to, no one who cared if he lived or died. Vivian had a preference. She wanted Emilio dead. She was truly one dimensional when it came to getting what she wanted, and Vivian wanted it all. How she'd found him he didn't know, but he was glad she had. Finally the Reaper knew why he'd been abandoned and why his life was a trainwreck. It all made sense now in a perverse way. He was thankful for answers to long sought questions about his birth, but it wasn't hard to see where his partnership with Vivian was headed. There would be a time when he was a liability. A time when she'd try to get rid of him like all the others. One of them would have to die. They were too much alike for any other outcome.

***

Marcy was late getting to Yosemite Sam's. Talking to Mark Gales had taken longer than she'd expected. He had a lot to say. Greyson and Emily were already upstairs in a corner when she arrived.

"There she is," said Emily, getting up to hug her peer. "We have nachos on the way."

"I don't think I ate lunch," replied Marcy as she dropped into a chair. "John, I found Vivian's ex. He moved out of state after the divorce. In his words, I couldn't live anywhere near that woman without killing her."

"Sounds like a bitter man," responded Emily, reaching over to fill Marcy's mug.

"If half of what he told me is true, he has a right to be bitter. According to him, Vivian is a psychopath, charming but without another redeeming feature. He warned me not to underestimate her, saying she's capable of anything if the reward outweighs the risk."

"That sounds a little dramatic," stated Greyson.

"I'll start at the beginning," said Marcy.

"Give us the highlights," suggested Emily.

"Okay, here goes. Vivian and Mark were married after they finished their residencies, and the marriage lasted almost five years. According to him, he knew it was a mistake almost immediately but tried to make it work. He couldn't and it didn't. He caught Vivian in a series of affairs and had the pictures to prove it. The straw that broke the camel's back was her having sex with an adolescent patient. Mark told me Vivian came at him with a kitchen knife when he confronted her about it. He moved out the next week and filed for divorce, which took two years to settle. He had family money, she wanted it, and there was no prenup."

"Did he report his wife to the authorities?" asked Emily.

"No, he said it was his word against hers and confessed that he was afraid of Vivian."

"Did he ever meet the twins?" asked Greyson, changing the subject.

"On a couple of occasions. He liked them, especially Emilio."

"What was his impression of Vivian's relationship with her brothers?"

"It was strained, according to Mark. Their mother had left Gene the house and the bulk of her inheritance, and Vivian thought it should have gone to her since she was the oldest. She also complained about having to clean up the twins' messes, even though he didn't know what that was about. He said it had to be before his time in hell."

"Did he meet Julia?"

"Twice. Once when Gene and his new bride visited them in Franklin, and again at a medical conference in Memphis. He liked her but said Vivian didn't."

"Huh, that's different from what she told us," mused Greyson.

"I wonder how she reacted when Gene committed suicide, and everything went to Julia?" asked Emily.

"Archibald McCutchen would probably know," Greyson replied.

"There's something else," added Marcy. "Mark believes Vivian is broke. A friend told him their house, the one she got in the divorce, is in foreclosure."

"That's why she's hanging around," declared Emily. "She has nowhere to go."

"Julia had a lot of antiques, I wonder if they're still there," said

Greyson, beginning to worry. "Excuse me for a minute while I make a call."

"Something we should know about?" asked Marcy.

"I want to know if the contents in Julia's house has been itemized and an appraisal completed."

"Why is it taking so long to finalize the will?" asked Emily.

"It's being challenged by Emilio, and no one can find him," stated Greyson. "I'll be right back. I need to talk with Julia's attorney."

While they were meeting, Vivan was frantically looking for her brother. She'd left notes asking him to come home. One was tacked to the shed behind the house, the other on his office door. She'd even resorted to going to the park and walking the trails, his favorite place to go when he was upset as a kid. She wanted him dead, but Vivan had accepted the idea that the police might find him first. She'd worked both sides against the middle by making sure he stayed off his meds while stoking his anger and manufacturing evidence implicating him in Julia's death. She still had one trick up her sleeve. Vivian had the garrote used to kill Julia, and at the right time she'd plant it, so it'd be traced back to him. Then she'd earn what she deserved.

***

Emilio had seen her; he'd even read the notes asking him to come home. She'd forgotten that he knew her better than she knew herself. He'd been staying in an empty duplex he and his brother had bought as an investment decades ago. It was around the corner from Speedway Baptist Church and had never made much money for them, but now it was irreplaceable. To take a page from his favorite superhero, it was his Fortress of Solitude. He'd covered the Honda with a tarp and pushed it inside a detached garage behind the house. From there his bike couldn't be seen from the street. His plan was to wait for Vivian to meet the Reaper again, follow him home, get his name from a neighbor or from the mail in his mailbox, and then call Greyson. The cops could then apprehend Julia's killer and stop looking for him. After that he didn't know. Emilio's ability to plan only went so far when he was like this. For a brief moment he thought maybe it was time to get back on his meds, but that idea quickly vanished. They made him feel hollow, and Vivian had told him what they were doing to his brain. He might think more rationally, but they made him feel like one of the walking dead.

"No, that won't work," he said louder than he'd intended causing people in the coffee shop to turn and look his way.

EVERYONE TALKING AT ONCE

"Emily, I got a note that Hammersham wants to talk," said Greyson. "It's your turn in the batter's box."

"Why me? You had him on the verge of a confession, John."

"I want to keep him off-balance. Just be yourself."

They were at Miss Kitty's, and Greyson was more intense than usual, like he knew something they didn't.

"Hammersham knows the killer," continued Greyson with certainty. They were sitting on the back porch as a cool breeze drifted from the direction of the river. "Maybe not by name, but he can identify him. What I don't know is if he can identify the person pulling the strings, the man or woman behind the curtain. My initial impression was Emilio killed Julia, but now I don't think so."

"I don't think David Barnett did it either," confessed Marcy. "He's an unscrupulous sonofabitch, but he's no murderer. I'm meeting him and his attorney in the morning."

"If Emilio or Barnett didn't kill Judge Levitt, who's left?" asked Emily.

"Someone who slipped under the radar," responded Greyson. "My guess would be Ginny Barnett or Vivian Gales."

"The Society of Kamadeva is a dead-end," added Emily. "They've circled the wagons; we'll get nothing from them without going to court."

"Marcy, I want you and Emily to focus your attention on Barrett and Sol Hammersham," replied Greyson. "Push them and make them talk. As a favor to me, Horace is doing a deep dive into each member of the Levitt family. Something from their past could be important."

"What about you, John?" asked Marcy.

I'm going back to the cemetery where Julia's body was found. I believe Horace is right. There's a reason the killer left Julia's body on top of Alice Talbot's grave. If I can find the why, I can find the person who killed my friend."

"John, you said something earlier about an unknown person pulling strings, and not for the first time. What did you mean?" asked Emily.

"What if someone we've not identified has been playing us?" asked Greyson. "Someone trying to implicate Emilio as the killer, for instance? From the start he was our prime suspect thanks to Vivian. And what about Ginny Barnett? Marcy you said it earlier. You didn't think she was could have murdered Julia, and I agree with you. And we know Sol Hammersham didn't kill the judge; he has an alibi. After a long pause, Greyson continued, "Someone else is in the game."

"Who's your best guess, John?" asked Marcy.

"I don't know."

"Okay, what's next?" Emily asked.

"We talk to Barnett and Hammersham. Find out what they know, why they did what they did, and look at who benefits. Greed is a big factor in Julia's murder, but I think hate is part of it, too. I'm leaning toward a suspect, but I need more data before I can act. Keep doing what you're doing and give me time."

"You know who did it?" said Emily suddenly.

"I think so, and I think I know why," responded Greyson with a weak smile as if his heart wasn't in it. "But until I have something concrete, I don't want my theory complicating your investigations. In the meantime, we have a killer to find; I think his next target is Emilio. Take off the gloves and find out if Hammersham and Barnett can identify the killer. And remember, I've got your backs."

***

An attorney named Claire Roberts had sent a note to Marcy saying Barnett wanted to talk. He'd been in lock-up for ten days and was ready to deal. As much as she wanted to let his ass rot in jail, Marcy needed to know what he had to say. That's why she sat inside a meeting room at 201 Poplar waiting for him and his attorney.

"Prisons in third-world countries are more sanitary than this dump," complained the attorney as she entered the room. She was dressed to the nines in four-inch heels and wearing a three-piece navy suit Marcy was certain came from Gucci. Her first thought was privileged white girl living on daddy's money.

"Take it up with someone who cares," said the detective with a wry smile. "Your client beat the hell out of his ex-wife and put her in the hospital. I don't have a lot of sympathy for him. This is where he belongs."

"I'm filing a complaint with your superiors," snapped Roberts. "Your attitude and conduct are totally unacceptable."

"Grow up sister, when you associate with scum, you become scum. I don't have time to hold your hand while you play social crusader. Let me know when you want to talk about something important." Marcy stood to leave.

"Wait!" yelled Barnett starting to panic. Apparently, he was not doing well in lock-up. "I saw something."

"Okay, you need to be a little more specific. "I don't think Legal Eagle Barbie likes me very much, and my feelings are hurt."

"I saw who killed Levitt."

"Go on. You have my attention."

"We need a deal if you want my client to keep talking," said Roberts, trying to reassert herself into the conversation.

"Shut up and sit down," replied Marcy, pointing to a chair. "You've got five minutes and then I walk out of here, Barnett. Make me want to stay."

"I'd been with Ginny that night," he confessed. "I know it sounds sick, but we were still having sex after the divorce. I'd come over, fuck her, and she'd give me a couple of hundred bucks. It was a regular thing with her."

"I think that's the definition of prostitution," said the detective.

"It was her idea," protested Barnett. "I was sitting in my car smoking a cigarette when I saw Levitt's car pull into her driveway. She got out and suddenly a man came out of nowhere and attacked her. They fell through the side door, so I waited. I wanted to see what happened."

"You didn't think to help her or call the police?" asked Marcy, not surprised by Barnett's indifference.

"No, why should I? She screwed up my marriage."

"You did a good job of that yourself, sport. Go on, so far you're telling me nothing I don't know."

"This dude was in the house like maybe thirty or forty minutes. When he came out again he's carrying a body. It freaked me the hell out."

Marcy waited silently for Barnett to continue.

"He put the body in the trunk of Levitt's car and backed down the drive. That's when he saw me. I thought I was going to shit my pants, but he smiled and put a finger up to his lips. I knew what that meant."

"Can you describe him to a police artist?"

"Oh, yeah," replied Barnett eagerly. "I was an art major in college, but I had to drop out before I finished my degree."

"Okay, if he sees our artist, I'll talk to the district attorney about a deal," said Marcy turning to look at Roberts.

"Do what you want, I don't care," replied the lawyer looking a little queasy. "Daddy warned me about the people I'd have to represent. This is my third case as a public defender and every one of my clients is like this asshole. You can't pay me enough to come back to this hellhole."

Turning to smile at Barnett, Marcy said, "I think you're going to need a new attorney. Too fucking bad."

***

Sol Hammersham wasn't a big man, but he appeared to have shrunken since she'd seen him last. The only feature that hadn't changed were his eye. They appeared almost feral, like a domesticated animal returned to the wild.

"Where's Greyson and why the hell are you here?"

"Greyson is busy, and in case you've forgotten, my name is Detective Emily Morgan. So, what do you want to talk about?"

"I'm not talking to you. Get Greyson in here," he spat.

"It doesn't work that way, Sol. You don't mind me calling you Sol, do you? It's me or no one…you decide."

"How much do you know?" asked Hammersham.

"I know you hired Sammy Hankins to spy on Julia Levitt, and that you killed him in your bar. After the fire department cleared away the debris and our forensic team got into the basement, they found blood and brain tissue. Guess who it matched? Greyson thinks you can lead us to the person who killed the judge. Me, I don't think you know crap. You're looking for a free pass."

"There's one way to find out," responded Hammersham in a confrontational tone. "Get me a deal and I'll tell you everything I know, and I know a lot."

"That's not how it works. You should know that since you're an attorney. But maybe you missed that online course. Where did you get your degree again?"

"Here's what I want," said Hammersham ignoring the insult. "If I help you find the person who killed Levitt, I'll surrender my law license and plead guilty to manslaughter with a commuted sentence. Don't say it's not been done I've seen it, honey."

"You're dreaming, Sol."

"Take my offer to Greyson. If what I say doesn't pan out, you've lost nothing but time, but if you close this case? That's another story."

"Okay, I'll talk to John, but don't get your hopes up. Take him back to his cell," she said to the guard. "We're through for now."

Emily called Greyson on the steps of the Shelby County Jail. She didn't think the district attorney would agree to no jail time for Hammersham, but she'd lied about finding blood or anything else in the basement of the Kudzu. The structure had gone up like a bale of hay. Their case against the shyster lawyer was good, but it wasn't perfect. Hammersham had never mentioned Sammy Hankins on the calls recorded by Sally Johns, only that he wanted to get rid of a body, and the money trail was no slam dunk either. He'd had been smart enough to send several wire transfers on multiple days to seal the deal. Even though the amounts equaled what was agreed to on the calls, a good attorney might create reasonable doubt with the right jury. It was a winnable case she decided, the question was how far the district attorney was willing to go to find the killer of a criminal court judge. They'd been investigating the Levitt homicide for almost six months with not much to show, and no one was happy with the results, including them. In cases such as this, there were always trade-offs. It came down to which outcome was more important, more expedient. She didn't like it, but it was what it was to coin a phrase. She couldn't change the system, and she doubted anyone could.

LOOKING FOR EMILIO

The Reaper's life had never been happy or easy. There'd been no gifts on his birthdays, no setting out milk and cookies for Santa on Christmas Eve. He'd known at an early age that his mother had died in childbirth, and that he was a ward of the court. Years later, he'd uncovered her name and found out that she'd been committed to an insane asylum. Alice Denise Talbot had been twenty-five years old when she died in a mental institution on the day of his birth…apparently alone. If she had a family, no one had come forward to adopt him. That had been thirty-six years ago, and now he wanted retribution for the mother he'd never known. Thanks to Vivian that retribution had begun - first with Julia Levitt and next with Emilio. But he had to find him his first, and that was proving more difficult than he'd imagined. A few dollars stuffed in people's pockets had put him on the scent.

"I think I saw him on my way to work," said a waitress in the Concourse after looking at a picture the Reaper had gotten from Vivian.

"That could be the guy I bumped into walking towards the barbecue place on Jackson," said another.

"He might be the guy I saw riding his bike on Bellevue near the Baptist church," said the gardener at a senior citizen center. "He was flying and almost hit one of our regulars."

He was getting close; the noose was tightening. And the Reaper was certain he was the right neighborhood. But Levitt was elusive. The psychiatrist knew he was in danger and took precautions: constantly changing his appearance, walking one day, taking a bus the next, riding a bicycle he'd bought from a homeless man for twenty dollars, or cruising the backstreets on his motorcycle. His psychosis was off the Richter scale, but it was keeping him alive, at least for now.

***

Emilio panicked for a moment; he'd caught the Reaper's reflection in the mirror of a pop-up vendor selling hats in the parking lot at the Concourse. Taking deep breaths to steady his nerves, he made a mad dash inside the building, taking the stairs two at a time to the second floor. He then doubled back and exited out the rear of the building near the Y. Thankfully, he blended into the crowd. The beard was gone - something he'd had for twenty years - and his hair was cut short, especially on the sides. He looked more like a college student than the professor he'd been at the university. But Emilio was tired and running out of money. He couldn't continue to live like this. His paranoia was feeding his insomnia, and he couldn't remember the last time he'd slept through the night. It was time to flip the script, he decided. He'd been the hunted now it was time to be the hunter. Time to find out where the Reaper lived, and a new idea had sprung to life on how to do that. Then, Emilio could call Greyson, give him the address, and hope he'd deal with his brother's bastard son. After that, it might be time to turn himself in. He was so tired, so scared.

PROGRESS…FINALLY

He had a lawyer with him this time, and Marcus Black was one of the best criminal defense attorneys in the city.

"It's not that I don't trust you specifically, Greyson. I don't trust anyone," laughed Hammersham.

"No offense taken, Sol. Did you talk to Jeff Ward from the district attorney's office?" Greyson asked Black.

"I did," he replied in a scratchy voice that indicated he'd caught a summer cold. "I think the state could do better, but Mr. Hammersham is anxious to get this over with. Ward agreed that anything said today would not be used against my client at trial. With that said how do you want to handle this, Greyson? I have another appointment in an hour."

"Sol tells us what he knows, and we listen. If his information is truthful and leads to the arrest of the person who killed Julia Levitt, he's got his deal provided he's not the judge's killer. It's pretty simple counselor."

"Okay," said Black looking at his watch and then his client. "Tell them what you know and let's get this over with."

Marcus Black didn't make his next meeting, mainly because Hammersham liked to hear himself talk. Hammersham adored being the center of attention. After thirty minutes, Black stopped the proceedings and stepped outside to make a call. When he returned, he sat down, crossed his legs, and listened as his client rambled about what he called his minor role in the murder of Judge Levitt.

"You have to understand, I hated Levitt," he said. "She went out of her way to embarrass me every time I was in her courtroom."

He'd used Sammy Hankins before on sensitive jobs and hired him to get something on the judge.

"It wasn't as easy as we thought," Hammersham said smiling. "But we got lucky. Hankins discovered that Levitt's court clerk needed money and was open to bribes. Sammy got into the judge's planner and work computer. From there it was easy to set up surveillance."

Everything changed, according to Hammersham, when his client began talking about murder.

"You have to believe me, I wanted no part of that shit," he declared trying hard to be convincing. "That's a step too far even for me. I told him we were through."

"How'd that go?" asked Emily.

"Not good," came the answer. "This guy was scary. Even Sammy was afraid of him, and Sammy was no pushover."

"So what happened?" asked Greyson probing for something definitive.

"He agreed to pay me ten thousand dollars plus expenses for one more thing and then we were done."

"To do what?" asked the detective.

"To hack the judge's personal cell phone."

"Why?" asked Emily.

"I didn't ask because I didn't want to know," responded Hammersham, placing his right hand over his heart, "and that's the god's honest truth."

"How did you do it?" asked Greyson.

"I don't know. Sammy handled it. He knew someone and paid them twenty-five hundred dollars. The judge's clerk passed him Levitt's phone while she was in court, and Sammy got what the client wanted."

"Why'd you kill Hankins?" asked Emily.

"He tried to blackmail me, and I knew it wouldn't stop. Sammy would always blow through money as fast as he got it. He took pictures of me and the client exchanging money at Martyrs Park and threatened to send the photos to you," he said, nodding toward Greyson. "I couldn't take the chance, so I drugged Sammy and forced him tell me where he'd hid the pictures. I found a camera, memory card and the photographs in his office safe. I took everything and firebombed the building to clean up after myself. You know the rest. I shot Sammy at the Kudzu and called Sally Johns to get rid of the body, that's it."

"It's a good story," commented Greyson, "but it doesn't identify Julia's killer."

"I've got a name for you, but first you get me out of here. Home confinement, an ankle bracelet, whatever restrictions you want, and then I fulfill my end of the bargain. Quid Pro Quo!"

"We're prepared to put up a substantial amount in collateral and cash for Mr. Hammersham's release," offered Black.

"This is a capital murder case, as you know counselor," stated Greyson in a skeptical tone. "Bail isn't usually granted."

"The prosecutor and I have a number, but it's contingent on your approval to release Mr. Hammersham. What do you say Greyson? Do we have a deal?"

"Sure," came the response. "If you give me a name, Sol."

"James Wesley Smith but he goes by the last name of Talbot. I believe Talbot was his mother's family name. James Wesley Smith grew up in the system as a ward of the court."

"How'd you get that information?" asked Emily.

"Sammy was an excellent investigator, as you probably suspected. Not only did he take pictures of Talbot and me exchanging money, but he also followed Talbot home and got his name from a neighbor. How he got the other information about James Wesley Smith's mother, I have no clue. As I said, Sammy was good at his job."

"What's the address?" asked Greyson.

"I didn't get that from Sammy," said Hammersham with a chuckle. "Getting excited Greyson? I think you are."

Instead of taking the bait, the detective stood and said, "Wait here I need to make a call."

He called Horace from the hallway and asked if he could use his sources to research James Wesley Smith, aka Talbot.

"John, I think the name on the tombstone where Julia's body was found had the last name Talbot. I'll go back and check, but I'm almost certain I'm right."

"Shit!" Greyson exclaimed. "We need to see if there's a link between the woman buried at Mt. Moriah and the Levitt family."

"I'll get on it," Horace answered. "Keep me updated, John."

Greyson's second call went to Maurice Cavendar, the cemetery director at Mt Moriah.

"I was going to call you later today, detective," explained Cavendar. "I've had my assistant in our central offices digging through old paper records. I think I found what you're looking for."

"Let me ask you something first," said Greyson. "Wasn't Judge Levitt's body found on top of Alice Denise Talbot's grave?"

"That's correct," said Cavendar.

"What did you find?" Greyson asked.

"Alice Denise Talbot died in childbirth and had been a patient at Western State Mental Hospital. A death certificate wasn't included in Ms. Talbot's paperwork, but from my experience heart disease and stroke usually play a role in maternal mortality. You might want to reach out to the hospital. They're still in operation."

"Can you tell me who paid for Denise Talbot's internment?" asked Greyson.

"My assistant found an invoice, but it didn't tell us much. It was a cash transaction. All we have on the invoice is the customer's initials, G. C. L which goes against company policy."

"Can you tell me why Ms. Talbot was in a mental institution?" Greyson asked.

"No, but at that time, I believe the patients sent to Western State were involuntarily committed there. That usually indicates the patient is a danger to themself or others."

"Can you send me what you've got? I need it for my records."

"Certainly, I hope it helps in your investigation," Cavendar replied.

"It does and thank you for your assistance," added Greyson as he quickly hung up. He needed Gene Levitt's middle name, and he knew where to get it.

Doc Richards was preparing for a budget meeting when Patty, his do-everything person, stuck her head in his office and said, "Greyson needs a minute."

"I don't have a minute. See if you can help him. It probably has something to do with Julia Levitt's murder, and you have access to everything that I have."

"John, he's busy and grumpier than usual," explained Richard's assistant when she returned. "He's asking for more money from the county. What can I help you with? Does it involved Julia Levitt?"

"Yes, indirectly," answered Greyson. "Julia's husband committed suicide a few years ago, and Doc did his autopsy. I need the deceased's middle name."

"Okay, let me look…hang on."

He could hear computer keys clacking as he waited.

"Okay, it was almost three years ago this Christmas, and Gene Levitt's middle name was Cash. Is that what you were looking for?"

Instead of answering the question, she heard him shout, "I'll be damned," and then the line went dead. Just like Greyson, she thought. He was like a bloodhound with his nose to the ground. Until he ran down his prey, he was oblivious to the world.

THE HUNT IS ON

They had a name…finally. Greyson pulled everyone together; he wanted to make sure they were working from the same playbook. This was Marcy's investigation, but in name only now. Greyson could smell blood in the water and was moving quickly to make an arrest. As he updated his murder board, Horace called.

"I wish you were here, my friend," Greyson told him, his excitement palpable. "It would be like old times."

"I'm sending you everything I have on the Levitt family and what I could find on James Wesley Smith. Something was going on in Gene's life around 1990. It appears he checked himself into a sanitarium in January of that year after supposedly suffering from stress and depression. The facility closed in 2000, so information is scarce. I'm looking for the insurance company that paid the bill. Call me back if you have questions."

The patriarch of the Levitt clan was what Greyson's father would have called a scoundrel. He came from money, lost it all by the time he turned thirty, and made a fortune stealing mineral rights from unsuspecting ranchers in West Texas and southeastern New Mexico. He seldom lost a lawsuit, even though there were a lot of them. All told, Albert Lee Levitt had been sued more than a hundred times and lost only twice…not a bad winning percentage, thought Greyson. A fatal plane crash outside Hobbs, New Mexico during a lightning storm changed everything.

A rumor started shortly after Levitt's death claimed more people celebrated him dying than those who grieved, and allegedly, his first wife threw a party that lasted five days. From what Greyson had read, it seemed possible. The second wife, Victoria Ann Bettis-Levitt, had been a socialite from the Mississippi Delta whose father sounded as bad as his future son-in-law. Most people thought the marriage was more a business transaction than a romance, but everyone got what they wanted. Victoria's father got a new business partner, Al Levitt got the beautiful woman he desired, and Vicky got away from her life in the Delta.

The newlyweds moved to Memphis. A stately home in the "it" part of town and the parties. Oh, the parties were the best with only the most wonderful people who seemed to hang on her every word. When her husband cheated on her, she returned the favor, and neither seemed to care. Life went on, at least until the next social event and the next lover. She was twenty-five when Vivian was born and thirty-five when the boys erupted into this world. Still a young woman in her prime and not wanting to be burdened by children, they were dutifully paraded out at holidays and on special occasions. But for the most part, the Levitt children were raised by a nanny until they were old enough to be shipped out off to boarding schools.

One photograph from Horace's report grabbed Greyson's attention. It illustrated a distraught mother dressed head to toe in black holding the hands of two bewildered little boys but no Vivian. He made a note to check if she'd attended her father's funeral. He remembered her account of her father sneaking into her bedroom and molesting her when she was a teenager. What a screwed-up family, thought Greyson. Vivian went on to finish her undergraduate degree and followed that by being accepted into medical school, where she met her future husband. The boys would follow her lead. The only other interesting note in Horace's attachment concerned Gene. He'd had several complaints filed with the Tennessee Board of Medical Examiners by patients citing unprofessional conduct. All were dismissed and the records sealed which made them all the more interesting.

Vicky Bettis-Levitt rebounded from her husband's death after a stint in an alcohol treatment program and began a long series of amorous scandals that both shocked and thrilled Memphis' social elite. She died of an undisclosed illness at sixty-nine and if the picture in her obituary was accurate, she remained strikingly beautiful until her dying day. The bulk of her estate she left to her oldest son, Gene.

James Wesley Smith's life couldn't have been more different than that of the Levitt children. While they lacked for nothing, he was sent to an orphanage. Newborns were usually adopted quickly, but not him. He was sickly, and most young couples looking for a baby didn't want or couldn't afford a child chronically ill all the time. As a result, he wasn't adopted at all. Instead he moved from one foster home to another. The result was an early introduction to the juvenal justice system. The photo Horace had sent showed a sullen sixteen-year-old James Wesley Smith with big brown eyes and dirty blond hair. He would have been handsome if not for his smile. Something about it seemed wrong. After turning eighteen, he appeared to have either straightened out his life or gotten better at hiding his crimes, because Horace found little else on the boy.

***

"Okay, come in and take a seat," said Greyson after Emily and Marcy stuck their heads in his office door. "Horace has been busy. Familiarize yourself with his report on the Levitt family and James Wesley Smith, who's now our prime suspect in the murder of Julia Levitt. Everything is on the table in front of you. Our suspect may have changed his last name to Talbot, which was his mother's surname, and there's an old photo of him included in the information packet. The last address Horace found on Smith was from 2005. He's probably moved, but we have to check it anyway. Emily, that's your job, and I want you to take a SWAT team with you. No arguments! This guy is a killer and has nothing to lose by doing it again. Move quick and control the situation. Marcy, I want you to shadow Gales until I tell you to stop. Take three or four people with you and set up a schedule, but make sure they're locked in...no mistakes. The two names circled in red on my case board are who we're focused on. First, we find James Wesley Smith and take him into custody, and then we build a case on Vivian Levitt-Gales for the murder of her sister-in-law. Any questions?"

"What about David Barnett?" asked Emily.

"Has he seen our police artist?" Greyson asked

"No, we're scheduled for ten in the morning."

"Okay, after he's finished, take Barnett's sketch and show it to Hammersham. If we're lucky, he'll confirm it's the same person who hired him to get dirt on the judge. Then check with the DMV. If Smith has a Tennessee driver's license, we might get a more recent address than the one Horace found."

"You think Barnett's telling the truth, that he saw the killer," stated Marcy as a matter of fact.

"I don't know, but we'll find out soon," replied Greyson smiling. "Let's get to it."

The address she'd been given for James Wesley Smith was on Agnes across the street from one of three recycling centers in the city. The homes were over a hundred years old, and well-tended. Most had either a Boston fern or pot of flowers decorating their front porch, adding to the appeal of the neighborhood. As she prepared her team for the breach, Emily had a bad feeling. Small children's toys were scattered across a wide front porch, and an old hound dog was curled up in the front yard sunning himself his eyes shut, head raised as if in prayer. As she looked for movement inside the residence, her headphone crackled,

"We're in position and move on your command," said the SWAT team leader his voice tense.

"Hold in place. Something's not right," ordered Emily. "I'm going to the house."

She heard, "That's a bad idea, but we got you covered."

Emily could hear children's music coming from inside the home moments before ringing the doorbell. She'd removed her lanyard and buttoned her jacket to hide her weapon.

"Just a minute!" yelled a woman's voice over the sounds of a crying baby. "I'm changing a diaper."

"Take your time," replied Emily peering through a window, her hand on the butt of her gun.

A few minutes later a young mother carrying a squirming red-headed boy in a blue jumper opened the door. She was young, in her early twenties by Emily's guess.

"Sorry, Jake is a handful this morning," she said, smiling. "What can I do for you?"

"My name is Emily Morgan, and I'm a homicide detective with the Memphis Police Department. Can we talk inside?"

"Do you have any identification?" asked the young mother pulling her baby into her chest and using the door like a shield.

After looking closely at Emily's badge, she stepped aside and opened the door to let the detective inside.

"What's this about?" she asked still unsure what was happening.

"Do you know a man named James Wesley Smith?" Emily asked.

"James? He was my mother's boyfriend, but I haven't seen or heard from him in years. What's he done?"

"Why would you ask that? Is James someone you'd expect to be in trouble with the police?"

She didn't immediately answer but finally said, "He scared me a little. There was something about James that bothered me. I can't explain it."

"Can I talk to your mother?" asked Emily.

"I wish," replied the young woman. "She died during the pandemic. It happened before the vaccines were widely available."

"When was the last time you saw James?"

"He was at mama's funeral, what there was of it. Not many people showed up because of restrictions on social distancing and masks. I didn't blame them for being careful, it was scary times."

"Did James live here with your mother?"

"No, why?"

"It's the last address we have for James," responded Emily. "Any idea where he lives?"

"James moved around, but at one time he lived in a boarding house on Poplar near Tech High School. I don't have the address, but the building had gargoyles on the roof. I thought they were pretty cool."

"I need to search your house," said Emily.

"You think I'm lying to you?" asked the young mother her cheeks turning red.

"No, but I have to make sure," came the response. "James is wanted in connection to the murder of a criminal court judge. There's a SWAT team outside waiting on me to tell them what to do. Please don't make this more difficult than it already is. I'm sorry."

"Go ahead, I'll wait on the porch."

The SWAT team quickly cleared the house. It was empty: no sign of Smith. Emily left her business card with a warning.

"James Wesley Smith may be responsible for several murders. He's a dangerous man so don't contact him after we leave. If you hear from him, please let me know."

Once in the car, she updated Greyson.

"Check the boarding house," he ordered. "There can't be many houses near Tech with gargoyles on the roof."

***

Marcy pulled five new detectives from easy-to-solve cases to shadow Vivian. Her instructions were simple, but she reviewed them in excruciating detail which caused one newbie to complain.

"I'm not an idiot, and this isn't my first fucking surveillance gig, Marcy. I got it!"

His comment made her smile; she'd made her point.

"Okay, I'll take the first watch," she said. "Roger, you're with me. Buddy and Cat take over at four, and Samantha, you and Harry are on at midnight. Everyone has a picture of James Wesley Smith. He was sixteen when that photo was taken, but the eyes and mouth don't change. Focus on them for an identification. Remember, this guy is dangerous, which means you don't approach him alone. Anything unusual happens or you see Smith, call me night or day. Let's get to it."

It didn't take long for Marcy to remember why she hated stakeouts. The boredom would drive a normal person insane, so what did that say about her? So far, all Vivian had done was stumbled down the driveway in a shabby housecoat and fuzzy pink slippers to pull her trash to the curb. From the street, they couldn't see inside the house; all the blinds were drawn. *It must look like a cave in there*, she thought. The last time she'd been in the grand drawing room, sunlight streamed through floor-to-ceiling windows; it had been magnificent.

They didn't see her as much as hear her coming, as Gales' big Buick Electra began backing down the drive.

"Okay, the game is on," said her partner. "It shouldn't be hard to follow that tank."

They didn't go far and had to be careful not to be seen as Vivian slowly cruised the neighborhood before turning left on North Parkway and heading toward downtown. At Cleveland, the big car turned left before turning right into the old Sears building, now converted to the Concourse.

"If she pulls into the parking garage, drop me off at the front entrance," said Marcy before undoing her seatbelt. "She doesn't know you, so stay close but not too close. I'll pick her up when she comes outside."

At first, Marcy thought Vivian might have pulled into the entrance one way and quickly exited onto a side street to lose their tail, but there was no way she'd seen them. Roger had been careful and stayed well back. After a long few minutes, she heard her earpiece come to life.

"Vivian is on the phone and man is she's pissed at something," whispered Roger. "What do you want me to do?"

"Wait where you are until Vivian gets out of her car. When she does, swap places with me at the main entrance, and I'll follow her into the Concourse. A dollar to ten she's meeting Smith or her brother."

As Marcy watched, Gales hurried out of the parking garage and disappeared into the building, wearing something that resembled a hijab with oversized sunglasses.

"Vivian is going inside the building and I'm following," said Marcy, talking fast into her lapel mic. "She should be easy to spot if she comes your way. She's wearing sunglasses and a long flowing black headscarf."

The woman psychiatrist never looked back; she knew where she was going. In the Central Atrium, Gales turned left and started up the stairs.

She had almost reached the top when he showed himself, a cruel smile chiseled across his face. They were six feet apart when she saw the gun and screamed. It made no difference. James Wesley Smith fired three times hitting his target with devastating accuracy. He watched as Gales' body tumbled down the stairs, savoring the sheer panic and fear he'd created for everyone but himself. That's when he saw Marcy, a woman who wasn't running or hiding like the others. In that flickering moment, he knew that she was a predator, and that she was hunting him. Smith had planned for this; the call, the meeting, the killing, and most importantly the escape. Now, it was simply a matter of following through.

He stepped into an elevator, just like he'd rehearsed. Once at his destination, Smith hit a button for every floor and walked away. He retrieved a change of clothes he'd stashed earlier in an electrical closet and discarded the wig and fake moustache he'd worn when he'd shot Gales. Now, he was weaving through the horde of bystanders buzzing around in sheer panic. Once he made it to his motorcycle, he would be home free.

***

Marcy felt like a fish swimming upstream, fighting against a swarm of people racing in the opposite direction. She could understand it, but it still pissed her off.

"Police!" she yelled at the top of her lungs as she pushed forward.

Smith had seemingly appeared out of nowhere, shot Gales, and then disappeared just as quickly. There was no way the woman could have survived both the fall and being shot three times, but as Marcy rushed up the stairs, a man and woman were attending to the psychiatrist's broken body. A quick glance told Marcy there was nothing they could do other than call a priest. Now her job was to apprehend Smith.

"Where are you, Marcy?" squawked her partner in her earpiece.

"It's Smith. He shot Gales, and I think she's dead," said the murder cop her breath ragged from adrenalin and exertion. "Hold your position and call for help."

"Greyson is thirty minutes out," came a rapid response. "I called him when I heard the shots."

"Roger that," said Marcy. "Keep your eyes open. There's a chance Smith will try to fake us out and come your way."

Marcy didn't know how right she was. As she worked her way toward the elevators, Smith was exiting the building. He'd joined a group of scared shoppers looking for shelter. He could hear sirens in the distance and knew they were only minutes away. He didn't see Marcy's partner until it was too late.

"Smith, stop where you are! You're under arrest!"

Instead of doing what he'd been told, James Wesley Smith did the opposite. He grabbed a young mother by the throat as she frantically clutched her baby, pulled her close, and came up firing. The first two rounds hit the detective's protective vest traveling at an upward angle from left to right. The third round shattered his ulna and nicked an artery, dropping Marcy's partner to the ground. It gave Smith time to get away. Five minutes later, Julia's killer was cutting down side streets and heading north to the interstate. She'd been close, but in a game where close didn't count, Marcy knew at least they'd been lucky. Smith had gotten away, and only Vivian Gales had been killed. It could have been so much worse if Smith had fired into the crowd. When Greyson arrived on the scene, a trauma surgeon was seen getting into a waiting ambulance with his wounded detective. The doctor had been having lunch with her husband and had dropped everything to treat the fallen cop.

"How's he doing?" asked Greyson, nodding at the departing ambulance.

"The doctor said he'd recover, barring something unexpected. We were lucky - Dr. Ascar works at The Med. That's where they're taking him now."

"What about Smith?"

"I'm afraid he slipped through our fingers. After he shot Roger, witnesses said he ran through the breezeway at the end of the building. A maintenance worker swears he heard a motorcycle engine start a few minutes later. It had to be him."

"And Vivian is dead?"

"I'm afraid so. She was meeting Smith when he shot and killed her. I saw it myself."

"This throws cold water on my theory," commented Greyson. "I was convinced Vivian was behind Julia's death."

"She still might be," came the reply from Marcy. "There's no honor among thieves and murderers."

"You may be right," said Greyson. "With Vivian dead, finding Emilio is more important than ever. He may be the only person left, other than Smith, who knows why Julia was murdered."

TIME TO REGROUP

After Vivian's body had been removed from the Concourse and security camera footage downloaded, the focus shifted to taking witness statements, and there was no shortage of them. All told, more than fifty people had seen James Wesley Smith kill Julia Levitt's sister-in-law or shoot Marcy's partner. It was a small consolation considering Smith had gotten away, but at least they now had a current photo of him. That's how Greyson ended up on the evening news asking for the public's help.

"If you see James Wesley Smith, please call 911 immediately," said Greyson seconds before Smith's picture flashed on screen. "He is considered armed and dangerous and should be avoided at all costs. Crime Stoppers is offering a fifty-thousand-dollar reward for his arrest and conviction."

The detective's news bulletin caught Emilio unprepared, and the idea of his sister's death put him in a state of panic. The notion she'd no longer be around seemed to violate some law of nature. She'd been like the wind or the rotation of the earth…a constant force in his life. It also meant Smith would reinforce his effort to find him and right a wrong that never should have happened. The question was what to do. The picture in Greyson's newscast wasn't the best, and Smith had been wearing a disguise. Hoping the police would come to his rescue was a pipe dream, and he realized taking matters into his own hands wouldn't work either.

Emilio didn't know how to use a weapon, and besides, he was a coward. Greyson seemed to be his best option. At least one positive had come out of the tragedy today: the police would be looking for Smith now and not him. In the end, he might end up in a sanitarium, but not a jail cell. God, it was all so sad and confusing. When Gene killed himself, he killed a little of them all. Maybe he and his siblings were like Willy Loman, the character in *Death of a Salesman.* They'd been lying to themselves for so long, searching for the American Dream - that dream where you could have everything, do anything without consequence, and your infidelities didn't matter. But they did. They did and always had. Emilio had never felt more alone. If only Gene were here, he thought miserably. His big brother could make it all go away. He always had.

***

Emily found the boarding house - the one with the gargoyles on the roof - and called Greyson.

"How do you want me to handle this?" she asked. "I count six mailboxes on the porch. If something goes wrong, the chance of civilians being hurt is high."

"What do you suggest?"

"Set up surveillance and have a SWAT team on standby," came the reply. "If we go in, we go in late at night or early in the morning, unless Smith forces our hand."

"Be careful. Smith has shot one of our officers today, and I don't want to give him the opportunity to shoot another one."

"You know me," laughed Emily.

"I do - that's why I said be to be careful. Seriously Emily, this guy plans to go down in a hail of bullets, and he wants to take as many of us with him as he can."

"Why do you think Smith killed Gales when he did? He could have done it anytime and in a more private setting."

"She did or said something he didn't like. I suspect she insisted on the meeting today and set it up where she thought she'd be safe."

"So you still think she's the mastermind?"

"It all points to her, Emily. I believe she misjudged the players and paid the price. Vivian thought her brother would fall apart at the first sign of trouble, like always, and she thought she could control Smith. She couldn't."

"Do you think we'll ever know the real story?" asked the woman murder cop.

"We already do, most of it anyway," responded Greyson. "If we find Emilio alive, we'll get enough to be satisfied. I gotta go. Be careful…that's an order."

She got lucky. The same letter carrier had been delivering mail to Smith's apartment building for almost six years, and he remembered him.

"Yeah, but he goes by the name of Talbot," he said, looking at the photo Emily handed him. "I haven't seen James in weeks, and his mailbox is full of junk mail. I got the impression he worked nights and slept during the day."

"Did he get any mail today?" asked the homicide cop.

Looking in his tote box, he pulled out a campaign flyer asking for money and an advertisement for replacement windows. That was it.

"What about personal correspondence?"

"James didn't get much, but I remember he got something from an attorney once. He showed me the envelope, and he was pretty excited about it."

"Do you remember the name of the firm?" asked Emily.

"Not the name but the return address was from Franklin, Tennessee. I remember because I've got a cousin who lives in Franklin, and according to her the grass is greener, the air is cleaner, everything is better," he replied laughing. "She's like that; her stuff is always the best."

"You said Smith was excited. Did he mention what the letter was about?"

"Something about an inheritance and an aunt, or maybe it was a cousin, but I didn't put much stock in what James was saying. He tended to make things bigger than they were, if you know what I mean."

"I do," Emily said nodding. "For your safety, I'm going to have a police officer deliver your mail today, at least to the addresses on Poplar. If you see Smith, you need to call me."

"What did James do?"

"He shot and killed a woman at the Concourse today, and we believe he murdered a criminal court judge six months ago," answered Emily handing the postman her business card. "If you see him, call me."

"Yes, ma'am, I sure will."

***

They breached the rooming house at two the next morning creating a chaotic scene for the boarders. Emily led the assault with Greyson and Marcy close behind. They'd gotten word from the out-of-state corporation who owned the building that James Wesley Talbot had paid his rent six months in advance and had three months remaining on the lease. The police hurriedly escorted five people out of the building while the homicide detectives tore through Smith's apartment, which was more like a studio. The small space was organized, and hospital-room clean. They could still smell the bleach Smith had used to clean the bathroom and kitchenette, and he'd been here recently. The milk's expiration date was good, and there were eggs and bagels in the apartment's tiny refrigerator.

"Do you think we jumped the gun, and he'll come back?" asked Emilio looking at her boss.

"No, he has to figure we'd find this place after today. His picture is all over the news. Smith is in the wind, but I think he's still around. He isn't finished, yet."

"And you think he's after Emilio," said Marcy.

"I do, and I believe I know most of the reasons why."

"Okay, spill the beans," commented Marcy as Emily listened nearby.

"I think Gene impregnated a patient who'd come to him for help. When she told him she was carrying his baby, he and his siblings had her committed, and she died in childbirth. That woman was James Wesley Smith's mother, Alice Denise Talbot."

"My god!" gasped Marcy. "Where did this come from?"

"Some of it from Horace's program, and the rest from information we've gathered," Greyson responded. "We know complaints filed with the Board of Medical Examiners had been lodged against Gene Levitt citing unprofessional behavior. Horace tracked down two women who had filed grievances against him. Their stories were the same. Gene Levitt seduced them into sleeping with him and refused to see them again after they demanded more from the relationship."

"Those complaints were dismissed and sealed," said Emily. "How did Horace find the witnesses?"

"Did you know that once a lawsuit has been filed there's a record of it?" replied Greyson. "Even if it's voluntarily dismissed, it still remains a matter of public record. The women Horace talked to filed lawsuits after the Board of Medical Examiners refused to act."

"Why didn't their lawsuits become a public scandal?" Marcy asked.

"Because Gene paid each of them a hundred thousand dollars to drop their legal action against him. A hundred thousand dollars was a lot of money in the 1970s. It's the equivalent of half-a-million dollars today."

"What else do you have for us, John?" asked Marcy.

"The date Alice Talbot began seeing Gene as a patient corresponds to the timeline when he was seeing the other women, and we know he paid for Alice's burial. Horace also dug up insurance records where Gene checked himself into a mental health facility six months after Alice Talbot died. I believe he felt guilty for what he'd done to one of his patients. It's circumstantial, but it fits. And it could explain Gene Levitt's disinterest in sex and his suicide."

"Why have Alice committed?" asked Emily.

"Malpractice comes to mind not to mention the scandal that would ensue after Gene's indiscretions became known. Remember, several complaints had already been filed against Dr. Levitt for engaging in improper conduct with some of his patients. If Alice wouldn't go away, another incident could have cost Gene his license."

"And you believe Smith is out to avenge his mother's death. But why kill Julia?" asked Marcy. "She had nothing to do with committing Alice to a mental facility."

"I think that's where Vivian comes into the story," explained

Greyson. "We might never know everything, but offhand, I can think of several scenarios Vivian might use to persuade Smith to kill Julia."

"Such as?" quizzed Emily.

"Julia was keeping him from his inheritance, or she'd also been dating Gene when he impregnated Smith's mother. In both cases, Julia had to die. And don't forget that Vivian was an accomplished liar. She fooled us. It was all bullshit, but we bought it hook, line, and sinker."

"Where does Emilio come into this horror story?" asked Marcy.

"He was attached to his brother, and from all accounts, would do anything to protect him. Horace discovered Emilio was one of three people who signed the commitment paperwork that sent Alice to Western State. The other two signatures were from Gene and Vivian. It was a cover-up, plain and simple. They needed to get rid of a problem, and this is how they planned to do it. Horace, with help from the district attorney's office, is trying to obtain all of Alice's medical records from the hospital. Hopefully, it'll tell us more and provide a cause of death."

"She was tossed out like a piece of garbage," commented Emily, now getting angry. "I wonder when Western State realized she was pregnant, and what they did about it?"

"It should be in her records," responded Greyson, bothered by the whole affair but trying not to show it. His team needed to be focused until Smith was behind bars.

"So we keep looking for Emilio and Smith," said Marcy stating the obvious.

"That's about it," came the response from her boss. "It's almost six in the morning; everyone go home and get some sleep. We've been running hard for the past twenty-four hours, and I want everyone to be sharp when we find Smith."

Greyson wasn't in a hurry to go home and stayed back going through the apartment again. He was walking to his car when a passing motorcyclist caught his attention. The driver slowed down and turned to stare before speeding away. Even though the incident took only seconds, the exchange rankled the detective. He called Emily. "Where are you?" he asked.

"On Poplar almost to East Parkway. Why?"

"I think Smith just passed the apartment building on a motorcycle. I can't be sure, but it felt like him."

"Stay where you are, I'll turn around and come back," Emily said. "Give me five minutes."

"Could we have missed something in the apartment?" asked Greyson going over the search in his head.

"I don't see how," responded Emily, "but it's possible."

***

Greyson was right. They found a key to what appeared to be a safe deposit box taped to the inside of a light switch. It had been missed in the initial search.

"Okay, I'm out of here," said Emily holding back a yawn. "What about you?"

"In a little while," replied Greyson. "I won't be long."

"I'm going to sleep for twenty-four hours straight," laughed the detective. "See you later, John."

Smith had doubled back and was watching them from the apartment complex across the street. He'd almost screwed up; he didn't think the cops would find his apartment this soon. The woman interested him. He'd seen her outside his girlfriend's house on Agnes. He sometimes rode by to remember the good times, and he's seen her on the front porch talking to Lola's daughter. She was attractive, and he needed to talk to someone, to explain it all. Why not her he decided in a flash of inspiration. Follow her home, create a diversion, and take her when her guard was down. It was a risky move, but the upside was titillating, and there was no better time than now when he could see she was exhausted.

***

Greyson was almost comatose as he dropped into his bed begging for sleep to sweep him away. Where? He didn't care as long as it wasn't here. An accumulation of stress, too much coffee, irregular hours, and junk food had taken its toll. He couldn't remember when he'd been this tired. When his phone began to vibrate, he ignored it. Whoever it was they could wait he rationalized. But the steady pounding wouldn't go away. In fact, it grew louder and louder and now he could hear a voice.

"John, get up, we have an emergency," screamed Marcy pounding on his front door.

Blue was in guard mode now, a low growl coming from somewhere deep in the past, a primordial warning to a threat directed at his master. Greyson staggered to his feet unbalanced and disoriented.

"Okay, give me a minute!" he yelled as he stumbled toward the noise, his service pistol in his right hand.

Marcy was standing on the porch when he opened the door, and she looked as bad as he felt.

"What the hell," Greyson began before Marcy cut him off.

"Smith grabbed Emily. A neighbor coming home from a business trip saw him put her body in the trunk of his car an hour ago. He called 911, but Smith was gone when the police arrived."

"What time is it?"

"Almost noon," replied Marcy. "The bastard took her when he knew no one would expect it."

"And you're sure it was Smith."

"Emily's neighbor was sure," responded Marcy. "He said he recognized Smith's picture from the front page of the morning paper."

"Get someone on the cameras around Emily's house," ordered Greyson. "We need the make and model of the car Smith was driving and the general direction he was traveling."

"That's being done as we speak," Marcy replied. "Get dressed - we've got to find Emily before Smith kills her. I have a bad feeling about this."

He had left his car running in case he needed to make a quick exit and moved businesslike to examine the lock on the front door. It was a piece of crap, which surprised him a little. A cop should know better, he thought. Smith was inside the house in under sixty seconds looking for the thermostat, which he found on a wall in the living room. Thankfully, the alarm system hadn't been activated. After turning down the air, he waited for the unit to kick on. Noise was his friend. The plan was simple, overpower his victim, inject her with ketamine, which he bought from a veterinary assistant he knew, then gag and secure her. Once she was immobile, Smith would put his captive in the trunk of his car and drive away. The most successful plans were the ones with the fewest moving parts he reasoned. The door leading into the master bedroom was open; he could see the outline of her body from the glow of a nightlight. The attack was quick, an injection in the upper shoulder followed by a pillow being pressed down over his victim's face to keep her from screaming. Then it was a waiting game. He'd been told it could take three to five minutes for the drug to take effect, but it seemed less probably due to the sudden rush of adrenaline he'd felt streaming though his body like an illegal drug. When she stopped moving, he rolled Emily onto her stomach and taped her hands behind her back and then her feet. The sash from her robe was used as a gag and taped into place. Everything was over in less than thirty minutes. The only hiccup came when someone a few houses down yelled as he closed the trunk of his car, but by then it was too late. Smith had what he wanted, and he was going to keep it.

***

As hard as she tried, Emily couldn't open her eyes. She was slowly waking up by degrees. Everything seemed fuzzy her body responding as if she'd been out on an all-night bender - something she hadn't done since college. It didn't take her long to realize the situation was serious. At first, her breathing was ragged and too fast, her heart felt like it might explode at any second.

"Get it together," she told herself over and over again. "If you're going to survive, you have to take control of the situation. You have to be smarter than him." She knew it was Smith, it couldn't be anyone else, but the burning question was why her. As far as she knew, they'd never met.

The sound outside the moving car changed, the road bumpier, as if they'd left a main throughfare and transferred onto one of Memphis's notoriously bad side streets. How long had she been unconscious, she wondered? She knew they'd traveled for at least forty-five minutes; she'd been awake for that long. Suddenly, the car stopped, and she heard the driver's side door open and a moment later shut. Emily tensed as the trunk opened, and then she was staring into the smiling face of James Wesley Smith.

"Good, you're awake," he said. "I thought you might be. I injected you with ketamine, so you'll feel like you woke up with a hangover, but it'll pass. Here's what we're going to do, and it's not open for debate. If you want to live, you'll do exactly what I tell you. Nod if you understand me."

When Emily signaled she understood, Smith pulled a hunting knife from its scabbard and cut the tape wrapped around her ankles.

"I'm going to help you out of the trunk; it would be a mistake to run he warned. Then we're going inside the cabin. Once inside, you'll be fitted with a collar that's attached to a chain bolted into the floor. Then, I'll remove your gag and cut the tape from around your wrist. There's a change of clothes inside."

***

Greyson felt a knot in the pit of his stomach. With each passing minute, the window for Emily's safe return was closing. The description on Smith's car fit the description of a thousand others on the streets of Memphis on any given day. An older white or light gray coupe, probably a Ford or Chevrolet, with tinted windows. Closed-caption cameras five miles from Emily's house had picked up a white Mercury Grand Marquis traveling east on Park Avenue until it was lost near the 240-loop. After that it disappeared into a jungle of side streets where there were no cameras.

"When did you say this happened?" asked Greyson, looking at his phone.

"The 911 call came in at ten thirty-one," she replied.

"Did you try to reach me around eight?" he asked looking at his recent calls screen.

"No, why?"

"Somebody did, and I don't recognize the number."

"Have the number traced," suggested Marcy, her lights flashing as she cut through traffic on the way to Cop Central.

MK Isoka answered on the first ring. He seemed to always know when Greyson would call.

"MK, I need a phone number traced," said the detective his voice tense.

"I'm ready," replied the crime scene supersleuth. "It should only take a minute."

Greyson called out the number and then waited for what seemed an insufferable amount of time. Finally, Isoke was back on the line.

"I'm sorry, John. It's a burner phone."

"Damn it to hell!" cursed Greyson angrily. "I need one fucking break and can't get it. Emily is in trouble."

"I heard. My guys are helping with the CCTV footage. If they get anything, I'll give you a call."

Director Edwards was in the Command Center when they arrived. He carried the look of a general on the battlefield, focused and in charge.

"Anything?" asked Greyson.

Instead of answering, Edwards shook his head no. Not the response he wanted.

"John, call the number on your phone," suggested Marcy. "It could be Smith."

Before Greyson could react, he felt his phone vibrating in his jacket pocket. He hadn't turned on the ringer, he realized.

"Greyson," he answered.

"Where the hell have you been?" scream a distraught Emilio Levitt. "I've been trying to reach you all morning."

ALONE WITH A KILLER

The chain bolted into the floor was about fifteen feet in length, which allowed her to lie down on a small cot pushed against the wall or sit at a small circular table nearby.

Smith had made her get down on her knees as he fitted a leather collar around her neck and secured it to the chain with a padlock. After that he removed the gag and cut the tape around her wrists.

"Why did you kidnap me?" asked Emily.

"I'm not sure," replied Smith, a puzzled look on his face. "I saw you talking to Lola's daughter, Riley. You were kind to her and held the baby for a moment while the two of you talked and the SWAT team searched the house."

"The house on Agnes," muttered Emily, remembering the scene.

"I loved Lola, and we'd planned to get married…that was before Covid. I got along with Riley, too. She was a teenager then, trying to exert her independence while her mother held on for dear life. It was fun to watch and the best time of my life. Then Lola died and everything fell apart."

As if hitting a switch, Smith changed the subject. "There's a pair of sweat pants and a long-sleeved T-shirt on the bed. Put them on."

Emily was in a sleep shirt and panties, which was not ideal for the circumstances she thought, but she didn't want to give her captor ideas.

"Turn around," she replied, hands on her hips.

The comment made him laugh. "I don't think so. Where else could

I get a free show at this time of day? Besides, if I wanted you, I'd take you."

"Not without a fight you wouldn't," snapped Emily, her eyes dancing with danger.

"I'm not a rapist," said Smith, looking away. "I'll step outside and smoke a cigarette. You have two minutes."

"Are you going to kill me, is that what this is about?" asked Emily. "If so I need to know."

"I haven't decided yet," said Smith after a pause. "I guess it depends on how I feel after we talk."

When she was alone, Emily quickly scanned the room, looking for something to use as a weapon. If anything was there, it wasn't obvious, and freeing herself from the dog collar or breaking the chain wasn't going to work either; she had already tried. Smith had done a good job making sure his captive couldn't escape.

When he returned, she was dressed and seated on the cot. "You said after we talk. What did you mean by that?" asked Emily.

"I want someone to know why I killed the judge and Vivian. Someone should know other than me."

"Smith, you have to know this isn't going to end well for you. If you want people to know why you murdered Julia Levitt and Vivian Gales, give up. Then you can tell your story in your own words."

He smiled before saying, "I don't think so, detective. My fate was sealed the minute Lola died and Vivian walked into my life. She rekindled the hate I'd spent a whole lifetime trying to bury."

"I don't understand," Emily said.

"I grew up a ward of the state, detective," said Smith. "I was passed around from family to family like a sack of potatoes until I turned eighteen and aged out of the system. To say my adolescence was a happy one would be an exaggeration. I was angry, and I did a lot of bad things to a lot of people. Then I met Lola. She was so kind and patient with me, and over time I changed. ..but it didn't last. Covid altered everything, and Lola died. That's when Vivian's attorney found me and said the magic words every foster kid prays to hear - you have family. It was like throwing a drowning man a life vest. I couldn't believe it."

"You're related to Vivian Gales?" asked Emily, stunned by this surprising fact.

"She's my aunt and Gene Levitt was my father. "

Neither one spoke for several minutes.

"Start from the beginning and tell me everything," Emily managed to say.

Smith laughed and quoted Genesis 1:1 – *In the beginning God created the heavens and earth.*

When Emily didn't react, he shrugged and continued.

"Sorry, I couldn't help myself," he said smiling. "A foster family I lived with for a few months wanted to save my soul. They thought by dragging me to church every time the doors opened would do it. Boy, were they mistaken. My mother, Alice Denise Talbot, was a student at the university. In Alice's second year, she had what was described to me as a nervous breakdown and referred to a psychiatrist. That psychiatrist was Dr. Gene Levitt. The short story is, Alice got better, and she started seeing the doctor socially. When she told him she was pregnant, he denied the baby was his. My mother wasn't a wallflower; she wasn't going to be ignored. Alice filed a complaint with the Tennessee Board of Medical Examiners. That got Levitt's attention, and his entire demeanor toward my mother changed. He proposed to marry her."

"Where in the world did you get this information?" Emily asked.

"Let me finish my story," snapped Smith, his anger boiling to the surface. "I hate it when people interrupt me. It's a sign of disrespect."

"I'm sorry that wasn't my intention," confessed Emily sincerely. "I won't do it again… you have my word on it."

Smith had gone from calm to furious in a split second, and she didn't know why, other than she'd asked a question. This was dangerous ground and she knew it. "What cops do is ask questions, but I should have let you finish," explained Emily softly. "Again, I'm sorry."

The second apology seemed to work, and Smith started talking again.

"It was all a lie. Dr. Levitt and his brother, Emilio, were stalling for time. They came up with a grand scheme to have Alice involuntarily committed to a mental institution."

This time Emily raised her hand to ask a question.

"Okay, what?" asked Smith, seemingly pleased his captive had asked for permission before interrupting him again.

"First, I'm very sorry for what happened to your mother…and to you. This is such a sad story. Did you get this information from Vivian?" Emily ventured guessing.

"Vivian found out what her brothers had done months after it happened and discovered my mother had died at Western State. She confronted Gene and Emilio and threatened to go to the authorities if they didn't tell her what had happened. They confessed to their dastardly deed but continued to lie. They told Vivian that Alice and her baby had died in childbirth"

"So that's why Vivian didn't look for you," Emily stated.

Smith nodded.

Emily raised her hand again, which seemed to amuse Smith.

"Ask your question," he said.

"It's two questions, if you don't mind," Emily said softly.

"Okay, two questions, and then I have some questions for you," said Smith.

"Alice died over thirty years ago. Why did Vivian start looking for you now?"

"Gene had sent Vivian a letter the day before he committed suicide. In it he told her that he had a son, and that he wanted her to find him. Vivian searched for me for almost two years before her detectives tracked me down. What's your second question?" asked Smith.

"Why did you kill Julia Levitt? She had nothing to do with you or your mother," Emily asked.

"After Vivian found me, she approached the judge and demanded I get a share of my father's estate. She even showed the bitch the letter from her husband. The judge laughed and told Vivian the letter would never stand up in court. That's when Vivian came up with the scheme to kill Julia, blame it on Emilio, and petition the court to recognize me as the rightful heir to the estate. Emilio couldn't inherit if he was convicted of murdering his sister-in-law. Vivian said it's called the Slayer

Rule. I suppose you now want to know why I killed Vivian," added Smith.

Emily nodded.

"I suspected she was going to double-cross me," said Smith. "I'd suspected it from the beginning, but Vivian is such a great liar, and I desperately wanted a family. I accidently found out that she was broke. Vivian received a letter from an attorney in Nashville, and I read it – her house had been sold at auction, and she had two weeks to remove her personal possessions. Vivian had always told me that she was rich, and what she was doing for me was to honor her brother. It was all a lie. After that, it was easy to put two and two together. Get me to kill her sister-in-law, plant evidence so Emilio would be convicted of the judge's murder, get rid of me, and then Vivian would step in and be rich again."

Emily raised her hand again which caused Smith to laugh out loud.

"Just ask your questions," he said smiling. "I'm over being angry with you."

"Were you trying to kill David Barnett?"

"Not initially," Smith said. "But that changed after someone with your investigation told Vivian that Barnett was the main suspect in Levitt's death. Then she told me to kill him. Vivian wanted Emilio charged and convicted of the judge's murder, and Barnett was messing up her plans. I couldn't find the sonofabitch, but I found his girlfriend. I was following her to find him."

"Why did you kill Ana Leigh Styles?"

"I followed her to a run-down shack in the sticks hoping she'd lead me to Barnett," Smith said matter-of-factly. "When I realized he wasn't there, I got out of my car and confronted her. The bitch was high as a kite and attacked me with a knife. I have to admit it; I completely lost it. When I calmed down Ana Leigh was dead. I'd strangled her with my bare hands. I called Vivian and updated her on what had happened, expecting her to lose her shit. Instead she calmly changed everything, like it had been the plan all along. It was odd. Now, instead of me killing Barnett, she wanted me to kill Emilio. I don't know why the change, other than Vivian seemed afraid of Emilio. She once said he could see things others couldn't when he was on his medications. I thought it was weird, but what did I know. I trusted Vivian at this point."

"Were you the mystery man that handed Hammersham a bag of money at Martyr Park?"

"That was me," Smith replied smiling. "I didn't want to use Hammersham, but Vivian insisted. She said we needed to know more about her sister-in-law routines before I killed her. She called it a reconnaissance. I called it stupid, bringing someone else into our scheme. I knew I'd eventually have to kill Hammersham, too."

"So what's next, Smith? This vendetta of yours has to have a stopping point."

"It'll stop when I find Emilio," came Smith's response. "He's the last one alive who had anything to do with sending my mother to an asylum and screwing up my life. When he's dead, it's over and I'll go away."

"And what about me? What did I do to deserve this?"

"You got in my way, detective," said Smith. "Will I kill you, too? I haven't decided yet, but you and I both know the odds aren't good. There's paper and a pen in the table drawer in case you want to leave a note for anyone."

THE FINAL STRETCH

"Where are you?" asked Greyson. "Smith murdered your sister today and we think you're next."

"Why the hell do you think I'm calling?" screamed Emilio. "You've got to catch the bastard! He won't stop until he kills me, too."

"Give me an address and I'll send a car to pick you up. You'll be safe then."

"No, you'll send me back to the hospital. You have to catch the Reaper first, he's planning to kill me."

"It won't happen," coaxed Greyson in a calm voice. "You have my word on it."

"Like I believe you," laughed the psychiatrist in the high, deranged voice like someone who's lost touch with reality. "Catch him or kill him, either one works for me."

"It's not that easy, Emilio," said Greyson patiently. "Smith has kidnapped one of my detectives. There's nothing I want more than to lock him up but it's a big city."

"Did you check the boarding house on Poplar?"

"How did you know about that?" asked the stunned detective. "We just found out about it twenty-four hours ago."

"He's been tracking me, so I've been tracking him," said Levitt with a smirk. "It's easy to do if you know how."

"Emilio, can you help me find Smith?" asked Greyson.

"Maybe, but you have to do something for me first."

"What?" asked Greyson.

"I want Julia's estate, all of it. The house, bank accounts, stock…everything. It should have been mine when Gene died. You know that bitch drove my brother to kill himself."

Greyson had to keep him talking even though he was furious and wanted to beat the hell out of the madman. But the wrong word now could sign Emily's death certificate.

"I'll see what I can do," answered the detective. "I could open an investigation into your brother's suicide. There's no statute of limitation on murder."

"Yes, yes," came an excited reply. "I begged them to reopen their investigation when Gene died, but they laughed at me."

"I can start by changing the cause of death from suicide to undetermined. That would start the ball rolling, but we have to get Smith first."

"No, no," screamed Levitt angrily. "I know what you're doing. You're trying to trick me."

"You have to be reasonable, Emilio. If my detective dies and you could have prevented it, I promise you'll be charged as an accessory. You'll never get your inheritance then. You help me, and I'll help you."

"I don't believe you."

"How about this," proposed the detective. "I ask the medical examiner to change your brother's cause of death to undetermined. That automatically reopens the case."

"You can do that?"

"I've done it before," said Greyson lying.

"How would I know you're telling the truth?"

"The West Tennessee Regional Forensic Center determines cause of death in Shelby County and the surrounding areas. Give me half an hour and call Dr. Henry Richards. He's in charge of the center. If he changes your brother's death from suicide to suspicious or undetermined, it starts the clock on a new investigation."

"I don't know," mused Emilio unconvinced.

"Take my offer. It's the only chance you have of getting your brother's estate," stated Greyson trying to keep stay calm. "If you refuse, I won't lift a finger to save you from Smith."

"You can't do that!" wailed Levitt screaming.

"Sue me," came the harden response from the detective.

***

Doc Richards was in a staff meeting when his assistant cracked the door and waved to get his attention.

"Everyone take a ten-minute break," announced the crusty old medical examiner. "What is it, Patty?"

He was speechless after hearing what Greyson wanted him to do.

"He thinks this will work?" Richards asked his assistant.

"He says it's their only chance to save Emily Morgan's life. They have no idea where Smith has taken her."

"Call Greyson and tell him I'll do it. I'll prepare a fake death certificate with today's date on it."

Levitt's call came forty-five minutes later, and Richards was ready.

"Dr. Levitt, my name is Henry Richards, and I'm the director for the West Tennessee Regional Forensic Center. I've talked with Detective Greyson, and he's convinced me to reopen your brother's case. My office has changed Gene Levitt's cause of death from suicide to unknown. This new determination will notify the district attorney's office and initiate a new investigation into the death of your brother. If you'd like I can text you a copy of the new death certificate."

"And this is legitimate?" asked Levitt. "Greyson wasn't lying to me?"

"No, he was telling you the truth. I have to admit it doesn't happen often, maybe three or four times during my career, but it has happened before."

***

Greyson was sweating bullets waiting for his phone to ring, but it was worth the time. His gamble paid off, and Emilio delivered the goods.

"Okay, talk," stated Greyson. "Do you know where Smith took my detective?"

"Not the exact location, but I can get you close."

"How?" asked Greyson impatiently.

"I put air tags on the Reaper's Ducati and under the bumper of his car. He drives an old Mercury Grand Marquis."

"How the hell did you accomplish that?"

"When I walked out of the hospital, I knew the police would be searching for me and the first place they'd look was my house. I grabbed a few things and took off on my old Honda. I decided to hide in a place where no one would check. Julia's house. I hid my bike in the work shed out back and broke into the basement. That's where I was living when Vivian saw me in the backyard and tried to convince me to come inside. By then I knew what my sister and the Reaper were up to."

"Levitt, you're not making sense," commented the detective.

"You're not listening," came a quick reply from Emilio. "My sister and the Reaper were working together and would meet in Julia's house. I overheard almost everything they said. They were going to blame Julia's murder on me."

"Why?"

"Vivian wanted Julia's estate. When I escaped from the sanitarium, my sister realized I could be a threat and sent the Reaper to kill me. I needed a way to track him, so I put air tags on his motorcycle and his car."

"I need your phone, and I need it now," said the detective anxiously. "Tell me where you are, and I'll come get you."

"No way," replied Levitt. "I'll leave it at the Information Desk in the Concourse under your name. The phone's passcode is 1960, the year I was born."

"I'm on my way," declared Greyson on the move and headed for his car. I'll be there in twenty minutes."

The last thing he heard Levitt say was, "Remember our deal."

***

The phone was there waiting and in minutes Greyson, Marcy and a SWAT team were on their way toward Red Banks, Mississippi screaming down I-269. They were meeting Jason Christian, a Mississippi state trooper who had grown up in Holly Springs and knew the area well. The mood was serious but hopeful as members of the special operations team checked their equipment and pulled up aerial maps of the rural countryside. The plan was to check out potential targets using a drone. As they approached exit 21, Greyson could see a police cruiser waiting on the side of the road it's grill lights flashing. Little pleasantries were exchanged between Christian and Greyson when they met.

"I've made some calls," said the Mississippi state trooper. "I believe I know where your man is hiding."

"How far from here?"

"No more than eight miles. If I'm right, Smith is in an old hunting cabin that was built in the 1950s before the area was more populated. A friend told me the drive leading into the place has been cleared. Somebody's been there recently."

"Can we use a drone?"

"It would be tricky," said Christian, shaking his head. "It's set back from the road in a stand of pine and sweetgum trees. I'd suggest we go in on foot."

"Okay, lead the way. No lights or sirens. If Smith sees us, Emily is dead."

Twenty minutes later, the group converged in front of a small farm house on Moore Road. Marcy and Jason Christian walking toward a woman who'd come out on her front porch.

"Ma'am, my name is Marcy Thomas and I'm a homicide detective with the Memphis Police Department. Do you know anything about the hunting cabin down the road?" she said pointing in the general direction.

"Why yes, it belongs to my husband and me. We leased it out to a nice young man from Memphis. He's writing a book. What's he done?"

Not responding to the question, Marcy asked, "What's his name and when did you see him last?"

"His name is James Wesley Talbot, and it's been a while since I've seen James. He mainly deals with my husband. You might ask him."

"Where is your husband?"

"He's probably on the square in Holly Springs. Hap doesn't farm much anymore; he just leases out the land. Most days he goes to the square to drink coffee and gossip with his friends."

"I'll get someone to look for him," said Christian running back to his car.

"What's this about?" demanded the woman.

"We think James Wesley Talbot killed at least two people and kidnapped one of our detectives. Is there a way to the cabin where we wouldn't be seen?"

"You could go around the pond," she said pointing, "and walk down to the end of the soybean field. There's an old animal trail that leads to the back of the place."

"Does your husband have an ATV or side-by-side?" asked Marcy.

"There's two ATVs in the barn. One belongs to our son who's away at college."

"Can we borrow them? It's important."

"Sure," came the reply. "I don't want a murderer around here. My skin's crawling just thinking about it."

Marcy rejoined the group who was busy checking their weapons and putting on their tactical gear.

"Two ATVs are in the barn, and there's a way in. We need to circle the pond," said Marcy. "The question is who goes where?"

"Marcy, you and three others use the ATVs and go around back," ordered Greyson. "The rest of us will take the front. Everyone mute your radios. I want no screw ups today."

It was slow going. The brush was thick with thorns and briars. After everyone was in place, a thermal imaging camera located Smith and Emily inside the cabin. When the signal was given, two cops with a battering ram hit the front door shattering it in pieces and knocking it off its hinges.

Smith was caught off-guard momentarily but reacted fast enough to grab Emily by the hair his knife out ready to drive it into her throat. A shot from the window dropped him where he stood, the round having entered his right eye and exploding out the back of his head. Smith, or whatever he wanted to call himself, would never kill again. The team rushed in, but their work had been done.

"Get this fucking thing off me!" screamed Emily, tugging on the chain. She was covered in blood but didn't seem to notice.

When the collar was cut loose, Greyson had to catch her.

"I thought I was dead," she whispered in a ragged breath. "Thank you, John."

"Don't thank me," he whispered back. "Marcy is the one who saved you. I guess you two are even now."

His comment made her smile just as the tears began to stream down her face.

WRAP-UP

The public was outraged when the story of a young, pregnant woman involuntarily committed to a mental institution hit the news, its salacious details holding everyone's attention - at least until the next gory story took its place. Even the state legislature made noise about an investigation, but they, too, eventually lost interest. In a few weeks, Alice Denise Talbot was all but forgotten; that is, except for the few people who had investigated the murder of a criminal court judge. Greyson made reservations at Fred Gang's to celebrate closing the case and everyone showed up. Even Horace flew in for the occasion. When the retired detective arrived at the restaurant, Greyson was already there drink in hand.

"I heard the Director was going to be here and hand out commendations," Horace said, hugging his old friend.

"That's right, and there's even rumors he's got something for you."

"Like what?"

"He got the contact with your company approved; I'm the point person for MPD."

"That's great news, John. You're going to love what we've developed. I promise it'll double your closure rate."

"I arranged for an open bar tonight," said Greyson, slapping his friend on the back, "and they have Fighting Cock Bourbon."

"You are a prince," remarked the ex-homicide detective, grinning from ear-to-ear.

Marcy was the next person to arrive. With her was Mackinzie

Owens. After introducing the owner of Danny's Showtime to Greyson, they made their way arm-in-arm to the bar. Emily and her date were the last to straggle in, and she seemed genuinely infatuated with her New Orleans harbor cop, and he her.

"Where's your firefighter?" whispered Greyson making sure Avery couldn't hear him.

"Todd was a fling; Avery is the real deal. I'm trying to convince him to move to Memphis. We could use more good cops."

"If he's interested, have him give me a call," came the reply from her boss.

The police director appeared as appetizers were being served, mingled for an hour, and handed out commendations. Marcy received a special citation for saving the life of one of their own. Before dinner was served, Greyson spoke to the group.

"This case started with the murder of my friend, Julia Levitt, but it quickly turned into something more deadly and insidious than we ever imagined: the criminal incarceration of a pregnant woman by people who should have been there to protect her; the callous abandonment of an infant that resulted in a never-ending series of foster parents more interested in a state check than the welfare of a child; and an older sister who recruited and incentivized an angry man to kill for her. All of this spanning decades in the making. I'm so proud of each and every one of you. Enjoy the evening and thank you from the bottom of my heart."

***

Horace followed Greyson home; he was going to stay the weekend before flying back to St Petersburg on Monday. They found themselves sitting on Greyson's front porch sipping a good bourbon at midnight. Blue had put himself to bed hours ago.

"John, when did you figure out Vivian Gales was behind Julia's murder?"

"I think it was after Marcy talked to Vivian's ex-husband. Mark Gales said his wife hated Julia, yet she appeared out of nowhere pretending to be a caring and protective sister-in-law. That seemed odd, but I was initially more focused on Barnett and Emilio. I let my emotions lead the investigation, and I feel bad about that. Everything changed when I found out Vivian was secretly broke. That gave her motive, and it moved her to the top of my suspect list."

"Do you think Gene committed suicide because of how he'd treated Alice?"

"That's what Emilio told us, and he paid for her funeral and headstone. That shows some level of contrition."

"What about the blank card in Julia's car, the one from the Society of Kamadeva?"

"I think Smith left it hoping to throw off the investigation. That's just a guess."

"Julia had nothing to do with Alice being put in an institution. If Smith wanted to avenge his mother, why kill her?"

"It was all part of Vivian's plan. She was broke and saw killing Julia and blaming Emilio as a way to return her family's money where it belonged. To recruit Smith, she promised him his inheritance from his father, Gene. She convinced him that Julia was the only thing standing in his way from getting what was rightfully his. That's what Smith told Emily when he had her captive in Mississippi."

"Did Vivian have anything to do with sending Alice to Western State?"

"She signed the commitment papers, and Emilio told us it was her idea. The district attorney finally got Alice's medical records from Western State. They didn't want to give them up, and for good reason."

"So what's next?" asked Horace.

"Tomorrow you and I are going to deliver a bicycle. My friend Bert at Barksdale's had his custom bike stolen a few months ago. A cop in properties found it and put it in my storage shed yesterday. We're going to deliver it in the morning."

"And enjoy the best country ham and eggs in the world?"

"That, too," laughed Greyson. "Drink up, it's almost time for bed. Blue gave up the ghost a long time ago."

The End

www.ingramcontent.com/pod-product-compliance
Lightning Source LLC
Chambersburg PA
CBHW071456140726
47997CB00005B/1744